I0675066

TO FACE A SAVAGE TRAIL

ALSO BY JOHN LEGG

TO FACE A SAVAGE TRAIL

SAVAGE LAND
BOOK 5

JOHN LEGG

WOLFPACK
PUBLISHING
— EST 2013 —

To Face a Savage Trail
Paperback Edition
Copyright © 2024 John Legg

Wolfpack Publishing
1707 E. Diana Street
Tampa, FL 33609

wolfpackpublishing.com

This book is a work of fiction. Any references to historical events, real people or real places are used fictitiously. Other names, characters, places and events are products of the author's imagination, and any resemblance to actual events, places or persons, living or dead, is entirely coincidental.

All rights reserved. No part of this publication may be reproduced in whole or in part, or stored in a retrieval system, transmitted in any form by any means, electronic, mechanical, photocopying, recording, or otherwise, or used to train generative artificial intelligence (AI) technologies, without the express written permission of the Publisher and the Author, other than for brief quotes and reviews.

Paperback ISBN 978-1-63977-658-0
eBook ISBN 978-1-63977-657-3
LCCN 2024945513

TO FACE A SAVAGE TRAIL

ONE

"YOU SEEM TROUBLED, *MON AMI*," Two-Faces Beaubien said as he expertly skinned the beaver Hawley Cooper had just tossed to him.

"What makes you say that?" Cooper said as he began resetting his trap.

"You 'ave not been yourself lately. You are not the 'Awley Cooper I know. 'E was a man full of life and vigor. Now," the half-breed said with a shake of the head, "you are melancholy much of the time. Even Goes Far is concerned."

Cooper's head snapped around as he turned angry eyes on Beaubien. "You been talkin' to my woman? You've told me many a time that a man does not interfere in the relationship between another man and his woman."

"*Mais non, mon ami.* I do not talk to 'er. But the women, you know, they talk among themselves." He shrugged. "Usually, when they do, they say not'ing to us 'ommes, but sometimes..." He shrugged again. "Dancing Water tells me your woman is worried about you. And because I am a friend and I see signs of darkness in you, I'm concerned too."

"You just keep your nose out of my affairs, Two-Faces. If anything is plaguin' me—and I ain't sayin' there is—it's not of your concern." He turned, scrambled up the bank, and headed downstream toward his next trap.

Beaubien swiftly tucked the bloody pelt under a rope around a mule holding the others they had taken. He mounted his horse, took the reins to Cooper's horse and the mule, and moved on, slowly following the swift-walking Cooper. Worry was written across his bronze, weathered face. He and Cooper had trapped together for a long time, and as rough as the half-breed was, he cared for his fellow mountain man. Hawley Cooper had always been a hardy, venturesome soul with a sense of humor, but lately, he had been glum off and on, and recently more on than off. He shook his head and sighed. As much as he would like to help his friend, there was nothing he could think of to do. *Best leave 'im alone, M'sieur Beaubien*, he thought.

"YOU'VE BEEN FLAPPIN' your gums too much, woman," Cooper said harshly as he slumped to a seat in the crude lean-to he shared with Goes Far. "That don't shine with me."

The Nez Percé woman's stomach dropped. "What makes you say that?" she asked in a voice little more than a whisper.

"Two-Faces told me Dancin' Water told him you've been talkin' about me in a way that does not shine with me either."

"I didn't."

"Don't lie to me, dammit," he hissed.

Before Goes Far could respond, their infant, Strong Bow, squawked, and the woman quickly picked him up and let the year-old boy suckle.

Goes Far raised her head and looked square at Cooper. "I am worried about you, husband. You are not yourself. You are, how your people say, moody, and distant, far from me, many times."

"I haven't..."

"Don't *you* lie to *me*, dammit," she snapped. Her English had improved, but with it came some profanity learned by being around a bunch of hard, profane trappers. "I have seen for some moons now that something was bothering you, Hawley. I should have said something before, but I was afraid to pry too much."

"That never stopped you before."

"I don't know why I didn't, but you seemed far away, more than I ever saw. I was afraid to upset you."

"You've never been afraid of upsettin' me before either."

Goes Far nodded. "I don't know why about that either. You've never treated me poorly, but I worried that you were becomin' like Elson, and that made me hold my tongue maybe. I thought if I didn't say anything, you'd become your old self again."

"I ain't becomin' like El," Cooper said defensively.

"Maybe. But your spirits have turned dark much of the time. And they got worse in the past moon. So I talk with Dancin' Moon and the other women. I not expect her to talk to Two-Faces about this."

"Well, she did, and now he's stuck his nose in my business, and that's something I can't abide."

"I sorry." She seemed more worried than apologetic.

Cooper nodded. "Well, there's no need to fret. I'm just thinkin' about finishin' up trappin' for the season. Beaver ain't as plentiful as in past years."

"I don't think you tell me the truth."

Cooper shrugged. "Doesn't much matter what your thinkin' is, Sally," he said brusquely to his Nez Percé wife, whom he often addressed as Sally, preferring the English word to her language. "I told you what was on my mind. That's all you need to know."

Goes Far bit back a retort. The two had been together for more than six years now and over that time had become comfortable, loving, and caring with each other after an odd beginning to their relationship. And even after the ordeal she had been through two winters ago, an ordeal that would have driven most any man away from her. But he had kept close. He had always been willing to listen to her, reluctantly it was true, but he did so. He treasured her, she knew. But he had changed over the past half year or so, since not long before the birth of Strong Bow. She did not think the boy's arrival had anything to do with his moroseness, but she wondered if she might be wrong. She sighed and rose to place the now sleeping child in his cradleboard.

As she returned to the fire in their lean-to in the temporary trapping camp, she watched her husband, wishing she knew what was bothering him and how she could help.

Cooper glanced surreptitiously at his woman, a feeling of sourness sitting in his stomach at the way he was treating her. It was not his way; he had rarely treated her callously, though in those few times he did, it was because, like now, something was tormenting him, something he could not solve or make better. But life over the past two years had brought significant changes to his life, and many if not most were troubling. And, while like most of the men he knew, he was reluctant to discuss such things with his wife, he had always ended up talking to her, which usually resulted in the lessening of his troubles. But he was not so sure this time. The changes that occasionally flitted through his mind were major and likely would end the life he had known for more than a decade...and might cost him his wife and son.

There was still plenty of daylight left, so Cooper saddled his mare and rode out. He ignored Bill White's question as to whether he was going hunting. He saw no reason to answer. He figured that if he jumped some game, he would take it and haul back just a small amount since he was without a pack mule or extra horse. He eventually spotted a deer within range of his rifle, took aim, then lowered the rifle. He could see no reason for bringing down the animal. They had plenty of meat from an elk he had shot two days ago, which was kept fresh enough in the deep chill of the late fall.

Goes Far was not in the lean-to when he returned and tended to the horse. It bothered him a bit until he realized she was likely with the other women sharing some chores. And talking. That gave him a bit of pause, but he shrugged. If she was talking about him, there was nothing he could do about it. He sat and ate some of the elk that had been hanging near the fire already cooked but being kept warm. Then he crawled into the robes. He pretended to be asleep when Goes Far returned and slid into their bed. She tried to relax beside him, but it was difficult; she knew he was not asleep, and she was saddened and worried by his distance.

"I THINK it's time I moved on, Two-Faces," Cooper said.

"But why?" Beaubien responded in surprise. When no answer was forthcoming, he asked, "Does this 'ave somet'ing to do with whatever is troubling you?"

"Might be but I still don't want to be questioned about it."

Beaubien stood there a few moments his tongue exploring the insides of his cheeks as he thought, then said, "I say to you before, *mon ami*, that you are a friend for many years. We 'ave trapped together, got drunk together, fought the Blackfeet together. That don't mean you owe ne anyt'ing. *Mais non.* But as a friend, you maybe should tell me why you are leaving, eh."

"Sorry, Two-Faces. It just ain't in me to be speakin' of anything—if there is anything—that might be troublin' me. It just ain't my way. I've never done so before, have I?"

"Not that I can t'ink of." He paused. "But maybe..." He stopped. "No, it is not for me to say you should not go. If that is where your stick floats, so be it. You 'ave enough supplies to last ze wintair?"

"Mostly. Be shy of meat, I reckon."

"You shall 'ave some. You did the 'unting for us to make meat. You deserve a share. A big share."

"I'm obliged for your generosity."

"Wintair is coming."

"I know. I reckon I can find a decent place to winter up."

"You are welcome to wintair with us, *mon ami*, even if you ride off now."

"I appreciate the offer. Doubt I'll take you up on it, but you never know."

After a moment, Beaubien asked harshly, "What about ze Blackfeet?"

"What about 'em?"

"You 'ave fought zem many times, eh. Ze few who 'ave escaped your wrath know who you are, I t'ink. You will be in much danger if zey find out you are in their land."

"We're in their land now."

"*Oui.* But do you want to risk mam'selle being taken by ze demons?" He cocked his head. "You are taking mam'selle, eh?"

"If she wants to go, which I reckon she will. She don't, I'll entrust her to you. I know you'll make sure she and the boy get back to her people."

"Zat maybe is a lot to ask."

"Reckon it is, but you're an honorable man and will do as I ask."

Beaubien smiled crookedly, then grew solemn again. "And if you take 'er, then what about ze Blackfeet?"

"I can take care of her no matter how many Blackfeet come against us," Cooper said defiantly.

"You are a brave man, *mon ami*, and you 'ave

come through many dangers alive, but you 'ave 'ad 'elp."

"Not always."

"Well, m'sieur, I cannot argue with you more if you 'ave made up your mind."

"I have."

Beaubien nodded. "You will be missed. When will you leave?"

"Day after tomorrow, I reckon. I'll run my traps tomorrow, then see to packin' what's mine and what I need."

"Does mam'selle know?"

"Ain't your concern."

The half-breed nodded again. "*Bien*. Take what you need of ze meat. Anyt'ing you need but don't 'ave, see me, maybe I can 'elp."

"Obliged, Two-Faces." He turned to walk away, then turned back. "It ain't your business, like I said, to know what if anything is troublin' me, but I want you to know it ain't you or any of the other boys drivin' me away. It ain't like the times when you and the others tried to force me into takin' command of this ragtag band of mountaineers."

"Zat is good to hear, *mon ami*." He paused. "We will run ze traps together one more time?"

"Reckon that shines with me."

TWO

"I'M LEAVIN' day after tomorrow, Sally," Cooper said that night as he was having another cup of coffee after having eaten.

The woman looked up in surprise and a little fear. "I go too?"

"I'd be pleased if you did. You don't want to, Two-Faces and Dancin' Water will take care of you 'til rendezvous and you can rejoin your people."

"I go with you," Goes Far said firmly.

"I'm glad."

"Where we go?"

"Ain't certain."

"You will feel better?" she asked tentatively.

Cooper's jaw tightened, but then he tried to relax. "What makes you think I'll get better? What's ailin' me?"

"I don't know. You not talk about it."

"There's nothin'..."

"Yes, there is. You know. I know. All the others know there is something wrong."

"You're tryin' my patience, woman."

"Like many times."

Cooper almost grinned. "Well, that's a fact. But I don't want to hear any more about it. Understand?" When she hesitated, he said more sharply, "Understand?"

"Maybe."

His eyebrows raised in surprise. "Maybe?"

"Maybe I stop for a while. But if you still act not like yourself, I change mind and pester you."

Cooper thought that over for a few seconds, then said, "Maybe you oughtn't to go with me then."

"You want that?"

"No.

"Then I go." She sighed. "You always liked me bein' feisty, as you say. And pesterin' you. I can't change that. I try to get you to talk about things botherin' you because you are my man and I love you. I want to help."

"I don't need your help, dammit all."

"Yes, you do," Goes Far said matter-of-factly. "Maybe you not think so now, but you will know. Unless," she added with a small shudder, "the bad spirits take over your head, like Elson."

"That ain't gonna happen. And if something's goin' on in my head, it ain't your concern."

Tears of frustration welled up in the woman's

eyes, but she fought them back. "What worries you worries me. I help. If you don't want..."

"Don't say it, dammit. You've mentioned too many times that if I don't want you, I should go away. Well, as I've told you every time, I do want you. If I didn't now, I would've just left camp here and let Two-Faces care for you, I wouldn't be sittin' here askin' you to come with me."

"I worry."

"And I worry about you. You're precious to me. So's Strong Bow. You two are the most important things in my life now, but whatever might be botherin' me ain't your concern."

"Yes, but..."

"There ain't any buts about it, Goes Far. It's like when you were birthin' our boy, I..."

"You weren't there."

Cooper nodded. "Reckon that's so. But even if I had been, I would've had no part in it. That's women's business. Well, there are some things on my mind, I reckon, but they ain't a woman's concerns."

"Then I try not to bother you." She grinned ruefully. "It'll be hard. And I can't ignore for too long."

"Dammit, you're a tryin' woman. I've said that many a time. Maybe I should just part from you."

"You do if you want."

"Ah, hell, you know I don't want that. I just told you that. Now go take care of Strong Bow." The child had begun fussing again.

BOTH COOPER and Two-Faces Beaubien were quiet as they ran their trap lines the next day. And after that was done, the former went about seeing to his supplies—what he had enough of and what he didn't.

The other men kept their distance too, until just before dusk, when Bill White strolled up to where Cooper was checking on his store of powder and ball. "Y'all're bein' a fool goin' off on your own, Hawley," he said. "A damn fool." Before Cooper could respond, he grinned. "But we all are fools sometimes. You've done some mighty damn foolish things—like chasin' after a woman you barely knew in the dead of winter."

Cooper stopped and turned to face the half-Black fellow mountain man. "Worked out, though, didn't it?"

"Seems certain it has. I've done some fool things too. But headin' deeper into Blackfoot country, if that's what y'all're plannin', is maybe the damn fool-ishest thing you've ever done."

"Maybe, but I'll take my chances."

"Even with a woman you care about and your new son?"

"I told her that she and the boy can stay behind. Two-Faces and Dancin' Water'll take care of her."

"So will I, but that ain't the point, hoss. She's your woman and she wants to be with you. Draggin'

her into some horrid fate might not be the best thing
y'all can do. Not when you have a heap of friends
here, men who've stood beside you through all kinds
of hard times—and good ones."

"That's a fact. And to tell true, I'll miss you boys.
But this here's somethin' I got to do."

White wriggled his mustache as he stared at
Cooper's face. Then he shook his head and nodded.
"Well, if that's where your stick floats..." He paused.
"Two-Faces says he told you you're always welcome
back here. I say the same. Be an honor to have you
back among us for winterin'."

"I'll keep that in mind. Like I told Two-Faces, it
ain't likely I will join you boys again, at least this year.
Maybe at rendezvous."

White nodded again and headed off.

Not long after, Beaubien strolled up. "Come sit at
ze fire with the rest of ze 'ommes."

"Goes Far'll have something ready for me."

"She and Dancin' Water, Little Fox, and Bloody
'Air 'ave made supper for us all. If you want to eat,
mon ami, you will come to ze fire with ze rest of the
boys."

Cooper was about to protest, then nodded. "Be
there directly. Soon's I finish checkin' these few trade
goods I got."

THE MEN WERE solemn as they gathered around the fire. Slabs of buffalo ribs and hunks of hump meat, rare those days with most of the beasts having moved on from the area, were roasting over a large fire, juices sizzling and dripping into the flames, making them dance.

The women and children had their own fire with plenty of fresh meat, glad to have some relief of caring for the men.

Soon the men were shoving hunks of meat in their mouths and sipping coffee. After a short while, Beaubien disappeared into his lean-to and turned to the fire with a jug.

"'Aving a real celebration to see M'sieur Coopair on 'is way, means we must make toasts, eh?" We 'ave zis one jug, and zat is all we will 'ave, but there should be enough to enjoy." He hauled the jug up onto the crook of his arm. "We say *adieu, mon ami.* May your journey be safe and free of Blackfeet. He swigged deeply from the jug. "Finest Lightning I ever 'ad," he said as he wiped his mouth on a dirty calico sleeve. He handed the jug to Cooper. "You are ze guest of honor, *mon ami.* You get the next taste."

"Obliged," Cooper said as he took the jug and jolted down a large portion before handing the jug to White.

The revelry was mild compared with the frivolity of rendezvous, but the men were a bit tipsy and joyously boisterous as the celebration broke up, with each man shaking Cooper's hand and wishing him well. Even Cooper himself was almost cheerful.

COOPER WOKE BEFORE DAWN. The tinge of a hangover soured his disposition, and gloominess again overrode the light feelings of the night before. Goes Far kept her silence around him as the two loaded three mules with the plews Cooper had taken, plus food, some trade goods, extra powder and lead, and anything else the mountain man thought he would need. They were done by daybreak.

The other men, some suffering a bit more than others, waved farewell to Cooper as they sat to break their fast at their fires. Cooper nodded and mounted his mare. Looking at Goes Far, who had also mounted her horse with Strong Bow in his cradleboard on her back, and asked, "Ready?"

"Yep," she said with a nod and a small smile.

Cooper just grunted and kicked his horse into motion.

Goes Far followed, holding the rope to the three mules.

Cooper had no idea where he wanted to go, only that he needed to be away from the others. With a shrug, he turned northwest toward the Judith River. It was almost as if he were tempting the Blackfeet to come after him.

He could see the worry on Goes Far's face the

next morning and was beginning to regret having brought her. Even worse, he thought it had been foolish to bring their child. But it was too late now; he would not turn back.

Despite his glumness, he could see the strain growing on Goes Far's face over the days of slow travel. It bothered him, adding to his testiness, but the only solution he could see was to take her back to the camp with the others, and that he was reluctant—no, dead set against—to do.

But ten days out, Goes Far offered another solution.

"I want to go back to my village," she said in little more than a whisper, her voice trembling.

He cursed himself silently for not having thought of this. He had not, he realized, because he didn't want to do so. He wanted her by his side. "Now it's my turn to ask, don't you want me anymore?" He almost choked on the words.

"I do want you." She raised her head to look into his eyes. "I love you, Hawley Cooper. I have for long time. Since soon after you took me as your woman."

"So why do you want to go back to the village?"

"I'm afraid."

"Of the Blackfeet? Hell, I can handle as many as they send against me."

"A little when I remember what you said about how your other woman..."

"Black Moon?"

Goes Far nodded.

Cooper looked as if he had been slapped, and his face darkened with anger. "Don't you dare bring her up to me, woman. She was a damn good woman."

Another nod. "Better than me, maybe," she said rather sadly.

"Damn right she was," he snapped, then sucked in a breath and shook his head. "No, she wasn't. You're ever' bit as good a woman as she was."

"She was killed by the Crows."

"They're not Blackfeet, which makes a difference."

"Almost as bad, I hear you say. But Crows not here. We're in Blackfoot country. Worse."

Cooper's anger rose a little more. "You sayin' I can't protect you?"

"You are brave. A great warrior. But she was...the Crows took..."

Cooper's eyes burned with rage. He pushed himself up and stalked away, teeth clenched.

Goes Far spent the night alone, well, without Cooper. She still had Strong Bow with her, and she clutched the child tighter than usual.

The mountain man showed up in the morning, and ate the boiled elk Goes Far had prepared, hoping for his return.

"I'm also afraid for Strong Bow," she said quietly. "Maybe Blackfeet kill you, take me and child. I can live maybe with what they do to me, but do you want your son to be raised by the Blackfeet? Or killed by them?"

"I don't…"

"You have son to care for now."

Cooper sat quietly, meal forgotten. He had been so melancholy of late that he could not see things that should be so plain to him. "Reckon I didn't consider that. Let me think on it. Might be better if we went back to Two-Faces and the others, though they likely would think I was less manly than before, that I had lost my courage and come slinkin' back."

"They not think that." She hesitated a while, then said timidly, "There is something else I'm afraid of."

"What's that?"

"You."

THREE

COOPER SAT IN WIDE-EYED SHOCK, unable to speak for the moment. Finally he gained his voice. "Me? You're afraid of me? Why? I ain't ever treated you poorly, at least not that I know of."

"No, you treat me good all the time."

"Then why?" Anger was beginning to push the shock away.

Goes Far started off tentatively but gained firmness as she went along. "I say before, I afraid you're becoming like your old friend Elson. Maybe have bad spirits go into your head. Make you act bad, do things you not do before."

"I ain't like that," Cooper snapped. "I ain't gonna get like that."

"El went from good man to crazy man. He was all right, then he began losing reason, became strange, accuse friends of things they not do."

"So?"

"So, you are doing the same. Were good not long ago but you've been acting not like self for several moons. And you're getting worse. Sometimes, you're all right, same ol' Hawley, but more often you're not. New Hawley is not so good a man."

"You're the one who's crazy, woman. I'm the same man I was before. I just got some things on my mind is all. I'll figure 'em out soon."

"Maybe, maybe not."

Cooper sat there fuming. "We'll head toward your village soon's we get packed today. I'll get you there fast as I can. Might mean some long days in the saddle. Tell true, the way you been actin', I'll be damned glad to be shed of you." He stood and stormed away and began packing the mules.

Goes Far sat at the fire a little longer, tears in her eyes. She loved her man, but of late, he had not been like her man, the brave, considerate mountain man, Hawley Cooper. She rose sadly and cared for Strong Bow before helping with the packing.

———

THE NEXT TEN days were tedious and marked by tension and, from Goes Far, frequent tears. She always kept Strong Bow close to her, partly in fear of him doing something to the baby, though she did not really think that would happen. The other reason was that the child's presence comforted her, making the tenseness bearable, though barely.

Cooper made sure they always had meat, and he would build a lean-to whenever the weather looked dicey. Otherwise, he mostly ignored his wife and son. And he rolled out a buffalo robe for sleeping by himself every night.

The second night out, Goes Far slid into Cooper's bed but he shunned her. Heartbroken, she returned to her own robes and cuddled her son, hoping the child would comfort her. But it was not to be. Her anguish was too deep.

Three nights later, she fed him, then went off to care for the child. It was not unusual, and Cooper did not think about it. But two days later, he realized she had not eaten since that night. "You best fill your meatbag, woman," he snapped.

"Not need."

"You don't want to eat, that's fine, but you need to, so you have enough milk for the baby."

"Maybe both of us die, then you be shed of us, like you said. You not care, so I not care."

Cooper was about to offer a harsh retort as anger roared through him. But he did not let it out. Instead, he kept his mouth shut and stared at her. Then he glanced at Strong Bow, who rested in his cradleboard leaning against a nearby tree. His thoughts were jumbled. In the child's first few months or so he had been a father to the boy, holding the infant with pleasure, but the joy had faded as his mind clouded with the darkness that had arisen in him.

He didn't know what had brought on these

melancholy thoughts or his gloom. He had gone crazy once before, but it had lasted only minutes before it passed. Like that time though, Cooper didn't know what caused it, so he had waited, fighting off the darkness that had arrived, figuring it would go away soon. But it had not, at least not for more than a day or two. On those days, he would feel relief and figured the worst was over. But before long, the gloominess closed in on him again. He did not understand it. He had a loving woman, a new child, and a heap of friends. Trapping had been good, and encounters with Blackfeet were fewer than at any time since he had been in the mountains.

It was the same with Goes Far. He had loved her more than seven years now, but over the past few months, he had grown away from her. He hadn't meant to, but he could not seem to fight the blackness that had engulfed him. Something had clouded his mind. He knew what it was in general, but it was amorphous, not quite solidifying in his mind. But he had begun to be worried, as Goes Far was, that bad spirits had dug into his brain and were turning him into a devilish man like Elson Brooks had become.

Besides what else was plaguing him, that thought was always with him, and he did not want to bring harm to his woman or their child. He had not fully realized that until Goes Far had decided to have him take her back to her people. He had decided after a few days that it would be best for her and Strong Bow. Not that he wanted to be shed of them as he had said but more to protect her in case the desolation was to become too much. He thought that if he was able to come to terms with what had originally began to sour him the thought of danger to Goes Far and Strong Bow would go away.

He shook his head. "It ain't true what I said. But as I think on it, it's best that you do return to your people, at least 'til I can get a fix on what's eatin' at me."

"You will come back?" Worry was strong in Goes Far's voice.

"Yep. As soon as I figure out what's been turnin' me into a devilish critter. And if my mind gets clear of the evil spirits that seem to be tryin' to take hold of me." He paused. "And if the Blackfeet don't get me."

"No Blackfoot can't kill you," Goes Far said firmly—and proudly.

FOUR

COOPER HAD NOT LINGERED at the village. He simply left Goes Far, their child, and the two pack-laden mules with her mother, paid his respects to Pale Thunder and rode back out before noon.. He was sad, angry, and miserable all at once as he rode, and a part of him was glad that he had not remained there. There was no telling what might have happened .

The next day, he had the feeling that he was being followed, and he made sure his rifle and pistols were ready. Not long after, he was sure he was being followed. And not long after that, he smiled a little. He finally pulled to a stop and began gathering firewood. "I hope you brought some meat, Sits Down," he said as he knelt to build a fire.

"Much," the big Nez Percé said. He dismounted and hauled a large hide stuffed with buffalo meat.

"Mostly for me though," he added with a great rumbling laugh.

"I wouldn't expect differently," Cooper said flatly. Whatever small joy he had had when he first realized that his large warrior friend was on his trail had quickly faded as his ill-humor returned. He did not see the look of concerned surprise on Sits Down's face.

The warrior dropped the bundle of meat next to Cooper, then went to tend to his horse.

Cooper soon had a fire going and meat cooking. He placed a pot of coffee near the flames, then went to tend his mare and the mule.

Before long the two men were wolfing down hunks of buffalo ribs and gulping down coffee for which Cooper provided sugar. They were silent except for the smacking of lips and the slurping of coffee. Cooper finally leaned back against a log with another cup of the thick liquid. Sits Down still ate. Cooper, like most mountain men, could eat prodigious amounts of meat when it was available, but Sits Down could easily outdo all of them.

The silence dragged on as if a thick fog had drifted over the camp.

Darkness was settling over the land when Sits Down said, "Something is troubling you, my friend."

"Reckon there might be," Cooper admitted. "But it's of no concern of yours."

"Maybe it is. I'm your friend. Friends help. I've seen it among my people and yours."

Cooper shrugged. "Friends don't matter much, Sits Down. So leave me be."

"As you mountain men say, 'If that's where your stick floats.' I won't bother you about it anymore. But you foolish, I say. Friends help, and I'm your friend."

Cooper just grunted, gazing into the fire.

Sits Down stared at him for a minute or two, then shook his head and rolled into his robes. Sleep did not come easy, though, which was unusual for him. But he was worried about his friend.

Cooper finally tossed the dregs of his coffee into the fire and with a glance at the Nez Percé, rolled into his own robes, thankful for the thickness and warmth against the late mountain fall.

"WHICH WAY WE GO, HAIRY FACE?" Sits Down asked as the two men sat to breakfast in the morning.

"We?"

"Yes."

"There ain't no 'we,' Sits Down. I don't know where I'm goin' but I'll find out when I get there. I don't need a guide."

The warrior filled his mouth with another hunk of buffalo and chewed slowly. "You won't find that place. You won't find any place to settle your mind, my friend. Bad spirits are not good companions."

"You don't know anything about what I'm thinkin' or feelin'. Now leave me alone and to go my own way. I don't need your company and I sure as hell don't need your advice."

"All men need advice sometimes."

"You don't."

Sits Down smiled. "I did many times. Maybe will again. But some damn white-eye talk to me, get me thinkin'. Maybe I don't change mind, maybe I do, but I look at it different. A big help."

"Well, go find that damn white-eye and talk to him."

"I find here."

Cooper's head snapped up. "What'n hell's that mean?"

"You are the damn white-eye."

"You're crazy, Sits Down."

"No. You learn about me. Talk to me. Treat me with respect even before you really know me. Made me think. Maybe I don't change but your words, they spoke to my heart and my mind. Later I do change because of your words, because you trust me." He paused. "You are good man, Hairy Face. Strong, brave, have good sense."

"Not all the time," Cooper said sourly.

"About last part, maybe is true. Like now. You let bad thoughts come over you, make world seem dark, forget you have friends and family, people who care about you."

"That's enough, Sits Down," Cooper snapped. He pushed himself up. "I ain't about to listen to more of your nonsense." He headed off to load the mule.

The Nez Percé sat for a bit, watching Cooper's back. He was sad that he could not help his friend. But he would not go away. He too, rose and began picking up the eating and drinking utensils, gave them a quick wipe down with an old piece of muslin, walked over, and silently handed them to the mountain man.

Cooper just nodded.

Fifteen minutes later, Cooper pulled out, loping away trying to put some distance between himself and Sits Down. But it soon became apparent that the Nez Percé was following him. He stopped and turned. "Go back to the village, Sits Down."

But the warrior kept riding toward the mountain man.

"Dammit, go back, I said," Cooper shouted. When the warrior did not stop, Cooper pulled his rifle, brought it to his shoulder and fired. As he had planned, the bullet flew harmlessly by Sits Down.

"Dammit." Cooper turned and kicked his mare into a gallop, towing an unhappy mule behind him. Several miles later, he slowed, then stopped. He dismounted, loosened the saddle's cinch, and let the two animals drink from the rivulet of water that trickled nearby.

While he waited, he chewed on a strip of jerky. He soon began to tighten the cinch. As he did, he glanced along his backtrail across the meadow to the hill beyond. "Dammit," he muttered with a shake of the head when he saw the big Nez Percé loping toward him.

He finished tightening the cinch, mounted the horse, and rode off at a leisurely pace. He figured that if Sits Down was going to follow him, it would be fruitless to try to lose the warrior; Sits Down would continue to follow. He would have to think of another way to lose his shadow.

Just past the noon hour, Cooper spotted a lone buffalo lazily grazing. It was an old bull, but it would provide some fresh meat, even if it was stringy. He got within fifty yards before he brought his rifle up and fired. The bull dropped, and minutes later, Cooper had ground-staked the mare and mule and was butchering the animal. He was joined shortly afterward by Sits Down. The two worked together silently.

Having cut out a fair amount, they loaded it on Cooper's mule, mounted and rode out, both still silent.

As they ate the stringy meat that night, an angry Cooper said quietly, "I'd be obliged if you'd leave off bein' my companion, Sits Down. An unwelcome companion. It doesn't shine with me to have you ridin' my tail every mile I ride."

"I protect you."

"I don't need no protectin'. I can take care of myself as you damn well know."

"You not think straight now. I watch. Make sure no bad comes to you."

"Leave me be, Sits Down. I don't need you protection, and I sure don't want it."

The Nez Percé shrugged, unperturbed.

"You keep botherin' me, and I'll have to wallop you good."

Sits Down laughed. "You can't do that."

"Reckon you're right," Cooper said, anger and frustration fighting for control of his voice and demeanor. "But I can put a lead pill into that fat carcass of yours."

"You won't do that."

Cooper sighed in impotence. There seemed to be nothing he could do to discourage the large Nez Percé. "Your people need your protection more than I do. And winter's almost here, so Goes Far needs food, so does your sister, and maybe others too."

"Pale Thunder gives food to your woman. And Morning Sun has married a warrior, so he will feed her and the children. As for the others? Well, most women and children have husbands and fathers who take care of them. Those who don't, others like Pale Thunder will help them. Not need me."

"You are an exasperatin', ol' hoss." Despite his conflicting emotions, he managed a small rueful grin. "Reminds me of Goes Far."

"She is good woman," Sits Down said seriously.

"That's for certain."

"Then why you leave her with the People? She should be with you. She is proud to be your woman."

"I know. I love her too, but..." He shook his head. "But I ain't myself lately, and I know it. I ain't sure for certain what's eatin' at me, but I don't need to be mistreatin' her while I try to figure it out."

"Maybe talk help you do."

"No," Cooper said with a shake of his head. "I'm a proud man, and proud men don't do such things."

Sits Down said nothing, his face blank.

———

IT WAS LATE FALL, and the weather began to announce its imminent arrival as snow began falling. It was light at first, just a flurry of soft flakes. But it soon began to increase in quantity and the wind picked up, whipping the snow around. As the storm began to grow, Cooper dismounted and hurriedly donned his heavy capote. He was soon glad he did. Before long, the snow had gone from heavy flurries to an outright storm, pushed by a howling, screeching wind. The temperature dropped steadily for a while.

The mountain man looked at Sits Down, who was riding next to him. "You know any place where we might find some shelter from this damn storm?" he asked.

"No place near. Must ride up and down four

more hills before there is place to find some shelter. Some cottonwoods along small stream. Good feed for the horses."

"Well, then, let's push on as fast as we can. The less time we sit out in this devilish weather the better I'll feel. I'm already tired of winter, though it's just really startin'."

"You seen snow many times, like when that wretched reprobate as I hear you call him, left you alone and with nothing in winter.o And you and your woman get caught in bad storms, have to stay in bad place in mountains for whole time. Travel through this kind of weather to chase Crows who took your woman. You travel through another winter to get a woman you didn't know. You and me, we fight the damn Blackfeet in winter. You take Brooks's woman to safety of village in winter. Then when Duncan went under, you took his woman back to village." He grinned looking at Cooper. "I think maybe you like winter."

"You're even crazier than I thought you were, Sits Down. I got no likin' for winter and snow and everything else that comes with it."

"Then you should stay in one place for winter," Sits Down said. "You can go back to stay with Two-Faces and the others."

"Had my fill of dealin' with them too. Two-Faces and Bill are right fine fellers, but the others..." He shrugged. "I reckon I spent more'n my share of time with those boys."

"You sound maybe like you're tired of mountains. Maybe you should go away, back to what you call civilization."

Cooper just grunted.

The wind grew stronger as they crested another hill and started down into the valley beyond. They rode in silence, having trouble hearing each other in the screeching of the wind that tore at the hem and fringes of Cooper's capote and the ends of the heavy buffalo robe Sits Down had wrapped around himself. Hours later, exhausted and irritated, the two men finally reached the sparse stretch of trees. The Nez Percé gathered firewood, started a good-sized blaze near a few large rocks that would help it from being blown or snowed out, and put meat and coffee on, then went to tend his pony. Meanwhile, the mountain man unloaded his mule and tended both it and the mare. At long last, they sat to their simple repast, trying to ignore the storm that thundered around them.

FIVE

"IF YOU LEAVE MOUNTAINS," Sits Down said around a mouthful of antelope, "maybe I go with you."

Cooper gave him a sharp look.

"Maybe we find someplace where there is no winter. Maybe there is no place like that. If there is, maybe it'll be nice. I'd like to spend time there if there is."

"You're crazier than a bedbug, Sits Down."

The Nez Percé shrugged. "Maybe so, maybe not so."

"I've heard there are such places, but if there is, I don't reckon that people will cotton to an overgrowed Indian livin' amongst 'em."

"White men there not friendly with Nez Percé?" Sits Down asked, his face and voice betraying his surprise.

"No, Sits Down, they are not. They don't like any redman, nor black ones, or brown ones either."

"But you and the others..."

"Most of the traders don't mind the color of a man's skin if that feller will trade with them. Most trappers don't mind either, long's the feller carries his own weight. At least I think so. That's the way it is— or was—with El. Still holds true, I think, with Two-Faces and the others. "Maybe others out here don't feel the same. But we're a bunch of fellers that don't fit anywhere else," Cooper added with a shrug.

"Then you will change when you go back to White men's towns?"

"Can't say I won't, but I don't think so. I've found that out here, it's a man's mettle that counts, not his skin color. I might think differently if I go down there. I ain't plannin' to do so anytime soon."

"But you think maybe you should."

"What gives you that notion?" Cooper asked sourly.

"Maybe bad spirits don't want to live in places like that and will leave you if you leave mountains."

Cooper cast a baleful glance at him.

"You're not sure it's right. Maybe means you leave Goes Far and Strong Bow here because of the way whites in those places treat red men."

"I have thought of leavin' 'em here, certain. Sometimes I don't think it'll be too bad. Frontier towns are a heap more tolerant about such things than places farther east, places that are more settled, places where they drove the Indians out a long time ago. But a frontier town might not provide a way for me to make my way in the world."

"I hear talk at rendezvous about a place called Mexico, far to the south. Maybe it's better there?"

"Likely not. From what I hear, many Mexicans don't cotton to Americans any more than the Blackfeet. They just ain't as bloodthirsty. Reckon it's because White men are tryin' to take their land too." Cooper shrugged. "I never did understand why so many men want to take other men's land. Hell, there's enough land for everybody." He shrugged again. "Maybe I'm wrong though. I ain't privvy to the thinkin' of politicians—White chiefs who run things, kind of like your council of warriors, though with more power and an arrogant manner. Nor do I understand the thinkin' of regular men who think they need someone else's land. I don't know. It's all nonsense to me."

"Maybe this is why you aren't the real Hairy Face the last few moons."

"Reckon that's part of it. But I don't really want to leave the mountains."

"Maybe you become Nez Percé. You have *Nimipu* wife and son, maybe..."

Cooper glared at the warrior, his face suddenly a mask of anger and sorrow. Without a word, he rose and walked through the wind-driven snow, both of which had lessened a little as the men had eaten, and threw together a rough lean-to. He spread out his robe and crawled into it, though sleep would not come for some hours. Shortly before he nodded off, he thought he heard Sits Down rustling around the camp, but he decided it was his imagination.

When he awoke, he realized that the noise he had heard in the night was Sits Down leaving. He was no less enraged and sad as he squatted next to the fire. He was thankful that the snow had stopped, and the wind had faded to almost nothing. He wasn't sure whether the Nez Percé had left or was just off hunting. As he poured coffee, he saw a large slab of buffalo meat resting on a hide on the other side of the fire. He grabbed a piece of the meat and chewed angrily.

"About time you left," he muttered as he continued eating. But as he sat, he began to think, and he began to catch a glimpse of what might be plaguing him.

Yes, he had a Nez Percé family in Goes Far and Strong Bow and even pseudo-father and brother in Pale Thunder and Sits Down. But they were not his Shoshoni family, the ones who had saved him, made a man out of him, and gave him his first wife. While Goes Far had more than adequately replaced the late Black Moon and had given him a son, it was somehow not the same. He was not sure why he didn't consider the Nez Percé his family.

As he remained seated at the fire, staring into the flames, realization began to creep up on him. It wasn't so much that he didn't consider the Nez Percé his family. No, it was the way he had been cast out by the Shoshonis, without even giving him a real chance to offer an explanation. That hurt the most, that they had just taken the word of others instead of listening to him. It ate at him. He could understand their anger after his treatment of Slow Bull, but none of the people in that village had died except for the girl whose slaying precipitated the entire affair. He could easily have killed Slow Bull, but he had not, and the warrior had not been too offended by Cooper's action. That the Shoshonis had so perfunctorily shunned him cut him deeply, more so than anything in his life except Black Moon's death.

Still, it was a mystery why it had begun to burrow its way into his heart and brain months after it had come to pass. Nothing that he could fathom had triggered it. But it had happened and now he had to deal with it. Trouble was, he didn't know how or at times even if he wanted to.

Cooper poured himself more coffee and sipped slowly. He felt no pressure to leave because he did not know where he was going and was in no rush to get there except to take up his hunt for beaver before winter closed in. But he decided he could do that as he traveled.

He loved Goes Far as much as he had loved Black Moon, maybe even more, as they had been together for more than six years now. And he was proud that he was a father. But Pale Thunder was no replacement for Cheyenne Killer nor was Sits Down a replacement for Cuts Throat. Then there was Pony Woman, his sister. No one in the Nez Percé village could replace her, not even Goes Far's friend Morning Song, the widow of Zeke Potts, his best friend among the trappers.

Cooper sighed and tossed the dregs of his coffee into the edge of the fire, where they sizzled for the briefest of moments. He rose and headed toward his animals. As he walked, he realized how cold it was now that he was away from the fire. He looked up and saw that the leaden sky promised more snow.

"Damn," he muttered. He abandoned his plan to load the mule and move out. Instead, he gathered up a bigger supply of firewood and bolstered his lean-to. There was a little beaver sign, so he decided to set his traps. He had to break through a thin rime of ice on the stream half a mile from his camp, another harbinger of the winter that was rapidly approaching. As he was doing so, snow began falling again. He stood there up to his knees in the frigid water and shook his head.

"Another goddamn winter with me out in the open, instead of winterin' with the others," he muttered. He finished and trudged back to his camp. He sat and stretched his legs out toward the fire, wishing Goes Far was with him now. She would tend to him, warming his legs, stroking the cold out with warm, work-hardened though gentle hands.

"You are a goddamn fool, Hawley Cooper," he said to the trees and sky, which once more was spitting out snow. "Never should've left Goes Far. She ought to be with me." Then he realized that he had done right to leave her at the village. In his frame of mind there was a danger that he would hurt her, though he doubted that. Still, he knew he would not be a pleasant man to be around these days.

HE SPENT two more days there, pulling in a paltry three pelts, which was about what he had expected though he had hoped for more. His meat supply was running low, so he kept the beaver tails. As he worked or loitered about the camp, he tried to keep his mind off the bad spirits rummaging around inside him. Sometimes he succeeded for a while, at other times, he sat at the fire and stared blankly into the flames as his mind fought with itself trying to wrestle the demons into submission.

Finally he decided it was time to be on his way. He headed northeast, letting the mare choose her own path since he had no destination in mind. As he rode over the next few days, he began to reconsider not wintering with his old companions. He was sure he would be able to find them, and it might be good to be around friendly faces, men he was comfortable with, men with whom he had fought alongside and had suffered and celebrated.

Then another seed of realization sprang to life inside him. Joining his former companions, he came to realize, would be foolish. This, it dawned on him, was another reason why he was so out of sorts. He liked Two-Faces Beaubien and Bill White and a couple of the others. But being around them would be difficult. Too many of his friends had gone under; his great friend Zeke Potts, Elson Brooks who died at Cooper's hand, Duncan MacTavish, Sam Bacon, George Miles, even Jacques Dubois, the crotchety and often unpleasant old French Canadian, Grady Mulligan, a less-than-alert slothful man; and even Luis Gamez, who he had never cared for. Too many companions dead; too much blood spilled by good men.

He spit out his anger and sense of loss more than once as he rode through the days. The bleak thoughts crowded his mind more often than not.

He was tired of seeing friends go under. And he was tired of fighting Blackfeet, of snow and freezing temperatures, tired of risking his neck crossing roaring rivers, tired of being hungry too often, tired of...well, just about everything he faced over his years in the mountains.

"Maybe you *should* go back to the Settlements, Hawley," he said to himself one night sitting at his fire, lazily chowing down some badger meat, something he detested but was all he had.

But he shook his head at the notion. As he had always thought when he considered such a thing, he wondered what he would do. He was not equipped for anything other than trapping beaver and fighting

Indians, and there was not much call for either in the States. And he was not cut out to be a store clerk or a farmer or to do any other civilized job.

Even more though now, he worried over what to do with Goes Far and Strong Bow. As he had told Sits Down, they might be all right for a while in some of the towns on the edge of the frontier, but how long that would last, he did not know. And when Strong Bow began to grow a little, Cooper would want the boy to have some education, and he didn't know how civilization would take to educating a half-breed. He supposed other mountain men had or would send their half-breed children to schools in the towns back in the Settlements, but he couldn't be sure of that. Being a new father, he had never discussed such a thing with others.

There was too much to consider and work through, and he was tired of that too. He picked up a stone and threw it hard against a tree, showing his displeasure at himself. It did not help.

SIX

IT WAS NOT like Cooper to be so lax in awareness of his surroundings, but he was paying little attention with his mind roiling with darkness and insecurity. And it almost cost him his life. Only by dint of looking back on the suddenly recalcitrant mule did the Blackfoot arrow miss him.

"Dammit all," he muttered as he jumped off the mare, hauling his rifle with him as he did. He scooted behind a thick hackberry bush and watched as two warriors drove off the horse and the fur-and-supply-laden mule.

"Not so fast, you red devils," he muttered as he drew a bead on one of the warriors. Moments later, the Blackfoot was dead on the ground.

Cooper hurriedly reloaded, but by the time he did, the other warrior, with Cooper's mare and mule was out of range.

"Dammit all to hell and back again twice!" he roared, kicking at any bush that was near him.

In minutes, the rage faded to a simmer, replaced mostly with a sense of frustration and disgust at himself. "Well, Hawley," he said, breath clouding before him, "if you ain't in a damn pickle again. Afoot with no supplies, and all your plews gone with winter knocking on the door." He sighed. It could be worse, he thought. He still had his pistols and rifle, tomahawk and knife, enough powder and lead to last him a while, some jerky and fire makings in the possibles sack hanging at his side. And he was wearing his capote. He should be warm enough.

"Well, you ain't gonna get your plunder back standin' here. Best move on."

He slung his rifle over his shoulder, jammed his gloveless hands into his pockets, and strode off. He passed the body of the warrior he had shot and got a few yards before turning back. The Blackfoot was clinging to life, though barely.

"You ain't gettin' to join the Great Spirit, boy," Cooper muttered. Without hesitation, he sliced off the warrior's scalp and tossed it in the bushes, then moved off again.

He cursed when the sky began to darken again and the temperature dipped, and once more when the snow started falling.

Lordy, will I never get through a winter without some goddamn misfortune befallin' me?" he muttered as he strode along, the hood of his capote covering his head keeping the light snowfall off him. He was glad that there had been only two warriors and they had been on a horse-stealing raid. As inattentive as he had been, had the warriors been interested in scalps, his would be hanging now from one of the warrior's saddles.

Minutes later, he stopped, pulled off his capote, then slung the rifle back over his shoulder, muzzle facing down. Then he put on his coat again. It was a little tight fit with the weapon taking up some room, but it was not too bothersome.

He hated walking. Had ever since Josiah Weeks had left him alone, unconscious in the heart of a howling winter with nothing to help him survive other than his wits. While this was not as bad, it was stressful in another way—he could not keep his mind on the task ahead. No, his mind kept drifting off wrestling with whatever was plaguing him.

After three days of walking, he saw signs of an Indian village. He stopped and moved off a little way until he was behind a screen of tall, leafless brush, where he pondered what to do. He certainly could not take on a whole village of Blackfeet, even if it might be a small one. But he figured his plews were there as well as his horse. Without either, he would be in dire straits.

With a shrug, he started creeping closer to the village, staying behind trees or bushes as much as possible. He soon was in sight of the village and hunkered down behind a cluster of snowberry and black elderberry bushes growing among the hemlock and aspens. The land here was flat and scrubby, leaving him little view of the village. He counted six lodges that he could see, which meant, he estimated, ten to twelve warriors. Not good odds. He did, however, know where the horse and mule would be—mingled in with the Blackfeet ponies—but he had no idea where his plews were being kept if they still were. He realized they might have already been sold to some trader.

He continued to watch over the village and after quite some time, he realized that while few people were out and about in the cold and off and on snow, none had gone into or come out of one of the lodges. *Maybe they're keeping my plews and many others in there*, he thought.

It would soon be dusk, and he would have to decide what he could do, if anything. As he stood watching the village, he realized that he had no options. He couldn't just waltz into the village, demand his plunder back, and kill every Blackfoot he could find if they refused. No, he would not get within twenty-five yards of the nearest lodge before he was riddled with arrows. And there was no way he could sneak in, carry a ninety-pound pack of beaver plews plus his supplies, find his horse and mule, saddle the mare, if he could even locate his saddle, and pack the mule.

The darkness inside him rose again. Despair began to settle in him. *You got a rifle and two pistols,*

Hawley Cooper, he told himself. *You can sneak in there, kill three of the red devils, and then gain the release of death under the arrows, lances, and knives. But they'd take my hair, leaving my spirit to roam without the peace of the Afterlife.* He sighed. *Hell, Hawley, you ain't gettin' into the Happy Huntin' Grounds nor Heaven neither no matter how you go under.*

His mind was still wandering when he heard a twig snap behind him. He started to whirl, reaching for one of his pistols when a round, wooden-headed war club caught him on the side of his forehead. He went down without a sound. Or a thought.

COOPER CAME to and groggily looked around. Something seemed wrong. The lodges were all upright. They should be sideways with him lying on the ground after having been clobbered. Then he realized he was standing, which he thought was impossible. Until he discovered that he was tied to a pole among the tipis.

Damn, he thought. Despite his foggy brain, he knew he was not long for this world. There was no way out of this, and he dreaded what would lead up to his bloody and painful end. He sighed and drew in a deep breath, then eased it out. It seemed to calm him just a little and to settle his head a bit. "Well, damn you all, you bloody damn savages," he muttered, steeling himself for what was to come, though none of the Blackfeet were paying any attention to him.

As the fog in his brain lifted a bit more, he felt the cold seeping into him and realized he was without his capote and the temperature must be hovering around freezing as dusk was approaching fast. "Well, you sons a bitches," Cooper muttered, "come and start your devilish work."

But it was not to be. Darkness fell, leaving Cooper shivering. He tested his bonds, but he did not think he could break them. Dispirited, he leaned his head back against the pole and hoped his aching skull would go away. There was little else he could do. Any feelings of resisting fell as did nightfall. Despite it all, he nodded off a few times, then jerked awake as he sagged against the horsehair ropes.

It was around midnight, he figured, when he heard a noise behind him. He jerked fully awake and tensed, expecting a knife to the back or a tomahawk to the side of his neck. Instead, he felt someone sawing at the bindings.

"Don't be afraid, hoss," a White man's voice said in a whisper. "I'm gonna set you free."

"Who are you?" Cooper asked in like manner.

"Tom Douglas."

"You a mountaineer?"

"Used to be." The voice was filled with sadness and rage. "There, you're free."

Rubbing his wrists, Cooper turned. "What do you mean 'used to be'?"

"None of your concern, friend. Now go before it's too late."

"Not yet. Are you here because you want to be?"

"You should know better than to ask a damn fool question like that," Douglas snapped.

"Then why?"

"Like I said, none of your concern." He turned to walk away but Cooper grabbed his arm and spun him back.

"If you ain't here of your own accord, then we'll get out of here together."

"Ain't likely, hoss."

"Why not?"

"I'll only be a hindrance."

"Why's that?"

Douglas sighed. "Bug's Boys raided our camp three, four years ago, I lost count. Killed all the boys—six of 'em there was—except me and Dan. They drug us back here. They tortured ol' Dan something awful. Skinned him in places, cut off bits of him here and there. And they did it all while makin' me sit and watch. I was scared down to my mocs, I can tell you." His voice filled with rage overriding the embarrassment at having to admit such a thing.

"But they left you alone?"

"Mostly. Nothin' like they did to Dan. Cut off a couple of my fingers, left me out in the cold with no blanket, starved me." He paused. "And they cut the tendon at the back of one ankle. Now I can't hardly walk on that leg. It's about useless. Which is why I'd hinder you tryin' to escape."

"We'll think of somethin'. We got some time before daylight. We should be able to get us a couple of horses and haul ourselves down the trail aways."

"No, I'd just endanger you."

"Then why'd you set me free if you didn't want help escapin' the clutches of these bastards?"

"I weren't about to let another mountaineer go through what Dan did, or even I did, if I could help it. No, sir, I purely could not do that."

"If they figure you helped me, you're wolf bait."

"Be a blessin' for me to go under here." He paused again. "Can't say as I look forward to the way I'd be goin'." He turned to leave again but once more Cooper pulled him back.

"Stay a bit. I need some information before I skedaddle out of here."

"Like what?"

"Where's all my plunder?"

"You're crazier'n a bedbug if you think you're gonna get out of here with all your possibles."

"Maybe, but if I can figure out a way to do it, I sure as hell will. I don't reckon I can get my plews and most of my supplies, but I damn sure would like to get my rifle, pistols, powder, and ball. And my capote so I don't freeze to death."

"In one of the lodges."

"Really? Never would have thought of it,"

Cooper said, sarcasm missing its mark. "Which one?" When Douglas didn't respond, Cooper asked, "That small, plain one a few dozen yards northwest of here?"

Douglas nodded.

"Figured so." After a few moments' thought, he asked, "Why didn't you put yourself under 'stead of livin' like this?"

"Ain't sure," Douglas said with a shrug. "Reckon I was thinkin' maybe some of the boys'd come by and rescue me. At least at first. Over the years, I just come to accept it, I suppose."

"Well, I'm only one of the boys, but I might be the one to help you do that."

"Like I said, you're crazy."

"Mayhap."

"Think we can manage?"

Cooper shrugged. "What've we got to lose." He grinned grimly. "Except our hair?"

"You won't mind bein' slowed by a cripple?

"Nope. Folks have helped me more than once. Can't say why I shouldn't do the same for some feller who's been ill-treated by these savages."

"Reckon it is time for me to regain some of the self-respect I've lost over the past few years."

SEVEN

"I NEED to get to that lodge," Cooper said.

"I told you that you ain't gonna be able to get your plunder."

"Reckon not the saddles and plews and such. But I need my rifle and pistols."

"They ain't there."

Cooper's head snapped around.

"You don't think these savages are gonna let a mountaineer's fine rifle and pistols sit around, do you? I didn't figure you to be that foolish in your thinkin'."

"You're right. I was plannin' how we can get out of here and so wasn't thinkin'. There anything in there we can use?"

"Doubt it. I think all that's there is your plews and saddle. War chief named Bull Belly has the rifle. Ain't sure who has the pistols."

"Where's his lodge?"

"What are you plannin' to do?" Douglas asked with a deep strain of fear in his voice.

"See if I can sneak in there and get the Dickert."

"Now I know for certain you're crazy. You try that and you'll be tied back on that pole, and I'll be right beside you. You figuring on doin' something so foolish, you're on your own." He turned to leave but Cooper grabbed his arm again.

"Wait." Cooper stood in thought for a minute or two, then asked, "Can you ride bareback?"

"Been doin' so since they took me—when they allow me to ride, which ain't often." There was a deep well of bitterness in his voice. "They think it's funny watchin' me hobblin' along."

"You got another knife?"

"No. They only let me have this one after I'd been here a year or so."

"Horse guards?"

"Might be one. They feel safe in the village here with more than a dozen warriors on hand."

"Well, that might work in our favor. Let's go."

Cooper matched his pace to the staggering, limping, off-center pace that Douglas used. All the while, he forced himself to remain patient. He began to reconsider taking Douglas along with him, but he glanced over and took in the gaunt shell of a man stumbling along. No, he decided, he would be patient.

As they neared the herd, the two men stopped. "Stay here," Cooper ordered. "And give me your knife."

"I thought so, you bastard, you're gonna leave me here and you got me thinkin' I might be free of these devils."

"I ain't thinkin' no such thing. I can be quieter than you while I check to see if there are guards. If so, I'm gonna try to put 'em under and for me to do that, hopefully without them raisin' an alarm, I'll need the knife."

Douglas hesitated, then handed the knife over.

Cooper crept forward trying to be silent, but he figured the shuffling and snorting of the animals would cover any soft sound he made. He stopped behind a scraggly bush in a spot where he could keep a good eye on the herd. He squatted there for a time, eyes searching. He spotted one guard, sitting with his back against a tree maybe fifteen yards to his left. He saw no one on horseback and figured this man was the only guard, and because he was relaxing, he would assume he was safe. Cooper moved slowly and cautiously toward the Blackfoot and right up behind him. The warrior appeared to be sleeping. Cooper's hand darted out and clamped the Blackfoot's mouth closed, and within a second had slit the man's throat. He held onto the body until he stopped jerking and would no longer be able to raise an alarm.

Cooper took the warrior's knife and stuck it in his

sheath, then smiled when he saw the shooting bag and powder horn hanging from the man's shoulders. A glance at the other side of the warrior he saw the fusil. He pushed the man over and managed to get his capote off without much trouble. He put the garment on, then slung the shooting bag and powder horn over his shoulders. Cooper waited another minute or two to make sure there were no other guards around. Fairly certain there wasn't, he headed back to where Douglas waited.

The emaciated mountain man was startled when Cooper suddenly appeared.

"Time to go, Tom," Cooper said, holding out Douglas's knife.

"Don't you need that?"

"Nope. Blackfoot over there offered his to me. The fusil too." When Douglas offered him a quizzical looked, Cooper said, "Well, didn't exactly offer 'em to me, but he didn't really need it after I slit his throat. Now, come on."

They stopped a little short of the first horses. "You know of any animal that'd be easy on you?"

"Chestnut gelding with a white stripe on its face. Smaller than most of the others."

"You see it?"

Douglas's eyes searched the herd, then pointed.

Cooper nodded. "Come on."

Minutes later they were at the horse's side, and Douglas was petting the animal's neck, making sure it did not spook.

"You'll have to use the mane as a rein, you know."

Douglas nodded. "I expected that, of course." He had the smallest note of disdain in his voice.

"Good. Then up you go." He helped Douglas onto the horse's back.

"What about you?"

"I spotted my mare over near the edge of the herd just to the west. Seems like she don't want to mingle with these Blackfoot ponies," he said with a small smile. He started making his way there, moving around the edge of the herd. As he neared her, the mare discovered his scent and walked over to him. "Still can't get away from me, can you, girl?" he said quietly, then leaped on the horse's back. "We'll need to put some distance between Bug's Boys here and us, Tom."

"I can't get away fast enough now that I'm on my way." There was hope in his voice.

They started off slowly but didn't get far before Cooper stopped.

Douglas pulled up alongside him. "What's wrong, Hawley?" he asked nervously. "See more guards around?"

Cooper shook his head. "Nope. Just tryin' to decide whether to stampede the herd. We do that, the Blackfeet will spend some time chasing down their ponies and not be chasin' us. But the stampede will wake the village."

"But if they're chasin' their ponies..."

"That's a good thing but it might not take long for

warriors to catch enough of 'em and get on our tail pretty quick. Most of the men'll have war ponies and buffalo ponies that won't go too far and likely drift back shortly. We just leave now, they won't know we're missin' 'til dawn. We got maybe six hours or so before that so we can be a fair distance from here by then."

"Tough choice."

"Yep." Cooper pondered things for another minute or two, then said, "Let's ride."

They moved off slowly again, not wanting to stampede the herd after deciding that might not be the best. But a quarter mile away, they kicked the animals into a canter.

They rode through the night stopping only a few times to rest the horses.

As dawn was breaking, the two pulled to a stop. "Think you can go on longer, Tom?" Cooper asked.

Douglas nodded.

"You sure? You're lookin' mighty peaked."

"I'm exhausted, yessir. Ain't as spry as I used to be since..." He sighed. "But every mile we get away from these damn red devils, the less I worry about bein' tired or hungry or anything else."

"All right, then. We'll need to rest the horses again, a little longer this time. Let 'em graze some and make sure they get water."

"You'll have to get me down and then back up again," Douglas said in disgust. "Sorry to be such a burden."

"No need to fret, hoss."

"We're far enough away from those critters that you can head off on your own. Make better time to get back to your friends if you leave me behind. I can do all right by myself now."

"Tryin' to get away from me already?" Cooper said as he helped his companion down. "Fellers usually wait a couple weeks before they want to be shed of me."

Dinkins looked at him surprised. "I don't..." Then he saw Cooper's grin. He nodded and smiled himself. It wasn't a big one but it was genuine.

As Douglas took a seat leaning against a rock, Cooper let the animals wander off. With no way to hobble them, he hoped, as he had in their other stops, that they wouldn't go far. He trusted that the mare would stay close and hoped pony would stick near her as it had on their previous stops, though he planned this one to be longer. He squatted, watching the horses, then heard a soft snort behind him. He looked back and saw that Douglas had fallen asleep.

Douglas awoke looking around. He was groggy and couldn't remember where he was, and fear dashed through him. It vanished when he saw Cooper. "How long I been out?"

"Not long."

Douglas cast his eyes to the sky. "About two hours judgin' by the sun."

"About that."

"Sorry. I ain't used to so much activity and it's wearin' on me."

"I ain't concerned, but if you're awake we best be on the move."

"Don't you need some shuteye?"

"Reckon I do, but it can wait. Now, c'mon, let's go."

Near dusk, Cooper stopped and pointed.

"Cave?"

"Yep. Don't know how big it is, but it's better than anything else I've seen. And it looks like we'll be gettin' some snow soon."

"I noticed that. I can travel in snow if you want to keep goin'."

"Nope. I need rest. So do you and the horses."

Douglas nodded and they started up the steep hill. The horses were not happy at the struggle, but they finally made it to the flat in front of the cave. Cooper slid off the mare and went inside. "It's big enough for the horses," he said when he came out. "But barely. And it leaves little room for us."

"As long as it'll keep us out of the snow and maybe have a fire to keep us warm."

"That'd be good. You able to make a fire?"

"Reckon I can if I can find the makin's for a bow."

Cooper nodded. "I'll be back directly." He returned quickly with a seven-inch-long, two-inch wide and deep block that he had whittled from a branch, a stout though slender stick, tinder, and some twigs. He dropped them and pulled a whang off his 'skins.

"That'll do," Douglas said.

"Good. I'm goin' off to see if I can find us something—anything—to fill our meatbags."

"That'd shine with this chil'."

Cooper climbed over the top of the hill, which was not far above the cave and down the other side. He covered the flat ground at the bottom of the hill and walked into the trees. Before long he saw a deer and stopped as the animal looked around, seeking the sound it had heard. It started grazing again, and Cooper edged a little closer until he was only about fifteen yards away. He stopped again as the nervous deer once more searched, then went back to feeding. Cooper raised the rifle and fired. Even through the powder smoke he could see that he missed by a wide margin and the deer bouncing away through the trees.

"Damn fusil," he snapped.

A few minutes later, he also missed a large hare.

He poured some powder into the muzzle and was about to ram a ball down the barrel when he heard chattering. He spotted two squirrels chattering seemingly over an acorn one held. Disgusted with himself, he squatted, grabbed some pebbles and dropped them into the barrel. He tamped them down a small piece of buckskin cut from one of his fringes. He fired, and both squirrels fell. "Great goddamn hunter you are,

Hawley Cooper," he said in repugnance. He picked up the two critters and headed back to the cave.

Cooper dropped the carcasses next to Douglas, who sat at the fire. "This the best you could do, Hawley?" he asked.

Cooper turned flaming angry eyes on him. "Think you can do better with this goddamn thing?" he snarled, holding up the fusil.

"Didn't mean to criticize. I was just hopin' for something more substantial."

"So was I," Cooper said with a sigh. "I'm one of the best damn shots in all the mountains and I missed a deer from fifteen yards, then a rabbit with this damn thing."

Douglas nodded. "They aren't worth a pig's pecker. That's why we sell 'em to the Indians 'stead of the mountaineers."

Cooper just grunted and headed deeper into the cave. Douglas shrugged in resignation, skinned the two squirrels and hung them over the fire on green sticks.

It took far longer to cook them than it did the two hungry men to devour them. Neither man was full nor pleased.

"So what now, Hawley?"

"Ain't sure, Tom. Part of me says ride on at dawn. Another part says to stay here for a day, recruit ourselves, and hope the Blackfeet don't find us. We covered our trail as best we could, and we have a good position here."

"I say we stay. Like you said, we need to rest, as do the horses. We all get some rest, we can ride on the next day movin' a lot faster."

Cooper looked at his companion. The man was even more grayish-looking than he had been. Exhaustion hung on him like a capote. He nodded. "Maybe I can get us some real food tomorrow," he said with a grimace.

EIGHT

THE SNOW, which had never come down hard, had stopped by morning and the sun, while bright, did not provide much heat. Cooper set off, fusil in hand, and headed deeper into the trees at the bottom of the mountain. He found a snowberry bush that, while bereft of leaves, was still full enough with branches that it provided decent cover where he could watch a narrow, animal-made trail.

After a half hour or so, Cooper was getting fidgety. The cold had seeped into his capote, his hands felt like blocks of ice almost as soon as he took them out of his pockets, and his legs were cramping. He decided to give it only a few more minutes before returning to camp and warming himself. He could try again later.

As he was rising to leave, a doe came into view on the trail. Cooper stood stock still and waited for the animal to come closer cautiously. He had been holding the smoothbore's lock inside his coat to make sure it didn't freeze, and he now stuck a hand inside, to thumb back the hammer, hoping the thick wool garment would mask the sound.

The doe must have heard it and stopped, searching around, then moved on again. Cooper was grateful the animal just did not bound off.

Cooper slowly raised the weapon and sighted as best he could with the unreliable firearm. Just as he fired, there came a screech from the other side of the hill. The noise made Cooper jerk a little and the lead ball missed its target. The deer had taken off anyway at the sound.

Cooper rapidly reloaded the fusil, swung it over his back, and charged up the hill, slipping and sliding at times on the patches of loose rock scattered on the steep slope.

He crested the hill just in time to see a Blackfoot peeling off Douglas's scalp as two others watched. The Blackfoot was about to use his knife elsewhere on the still-living Douglas. Before the Indian could do any more damage, Cooper slipped the fusil off his shoulder and fired without aiming. At a distance of maybe ten feet, it was almost impossible to miss, even with the undependable fusil. The ball tore through the side of the knife-wielding warrior's head near the temple and slammed out the back of his head. He fell, dead.

Before the other two warriors could react, Cooper flipped the fusil up and caught it by the barrel. He swung it like a club, smashing the nearest Blackfoot's face. He went down without a sound. Cooper was glad the weapon's stock had not broken.

The third warrior looked at Cooper with wide, frightened eyes, turned, and ran. Cooper dropped the fusil and charged after him, then dove and tackled the Blackfoot. He scrabbled up the warrior's back with his knees and planted one on the man's neck, the other in the center of his back, shoving his face into the dirt. "The world has no place for a shit pile like you, boy. Neither will the Spirit World. He raised his knee a bit, grabbed the Indian's hair, and sliced off his scalp. How do you like that, you festerin', snake humpin' red devil." He jammed the knife blade into the side of the Blackfoot's neck, slicing the jugular.

Cooper wiped the knife off on the Indian's blanket then walked and knelt by Douglas's side. The man's eyes were clouded with pain and his head and chest were covered with blood. "I don't know where the nearest place for help is," Cooper said, "but I'll try to get you there."

"Don't be a damn fool, hoss. I'm gone under for certain. Best you can do is make my end quick. I'll be at peace then. All I ask other than that is to bury me with my hair." He clutched his scalp on his chest.

"I'll do better than that, Tom. I'll bury the hair of three shit piles with you. Then you can lord it over them in the afterlife."

Douglas did not hear him.

"Damn," Cooper said with a sigh. He rose, scalped the two other Blackfeet, and dropped the three scalps on the ground next to Douglas's body. Then he searched for a decent place to bury his companion. But he found none—the hill was too rocky with nowhere to dig more than a couple of inches. He plopped down at the fire again, wishing he had some food and wondering what he should do.

The Blackfoot ponies that had run off when the action started, were drifting back, placidly munching on what browned grass they could find. Cooper eased up to each one and secured the animals to nearby trees. He found a rope on one of the saddles, took that and went to get his mare and the Blackfoot pony Douglas had been using. He tied them too. Then he made his decision.

Cooper tugged the capote off one of the Blackfeet, picked up the three Blackfoot scalps and carried it all into the cave. He laid the capote on the ground, then tossed the Blackfoot scalps on about where Douglas's rear end would be. Then he went and lifted Douglas's frail body with little effort, carried it into the cave and laid it gently down on the capote. Outside again, he tugged off the blanket the third warrior was wearing and placed it over Douglas. Finally he began taking any rocks he could manage to carry and piled them on top of the makeshift grave, until Douglas's corpse was well covered. "It ain't much but it's the best I can do, ol' hoss." He said a prayer over the body.

Weak from the exertion, and the lack of sleep and food, he still managed to drag the three Blackfeet bodies to the bottom of the hill. He checked each one and found fire makings, took another knife from one, a tomahawk from another, and a slouch hat—taken from another mountaineer, he supposed—to replace the one he had lost when captured. There was nothing else he could use on the bodies. He did find more rope on the ponies.

Back at the top of the hill, he checked the Blackfeet ponies. He found nothing usable except for a little hunk of meat. It would hardly make half a small meal for him, but it was better than nothing.

He tossed a bit more wood on the fire, stuck a green twig through the meat and set it over the flames held up some rocks. He slumped down, fighting off the urge to sleep. It was not long before the meat was warmed though, which was enough for Cooper. He wolfed it down, then curled up near the fire and fell asleep moments after he lay down.

HE HEADED down the hill the other way. He hated leaving the horses, but he needed meat. He was lucky this day and dropped a small deer barely ten minutes after he had taken his position behind the bush. He butchered out as much meat as he could carry, wrapped it in a piece of hide, and headed back to the cave. Soon after, he was chowing down chunks of deer, finishing off a good portion. As he ate, he wondered where he should go. Northwest was the Blackfoot village. East, more or less, was where he might find Two-Faces and the others, but he still was uncertain about doing that. Southwest would bring him to Flathead, then Nez Percé, land, but he didn't really want to see Goes Far yet. He still had to figure out what was making him so melancholic and churlish. Southeast was deeper into Blackfoot country, but out here, anywhere was Blackfoot country.

He looked over his shoulder to the small, rocky mound near the back of the cave. As he thought about what Tom Douglas had gone through at the hands of the Blackfeet and the help he had given Cooper to escape, he knew he had to do something to avenge the broken mountain man. He wasn't sure what just now, but he knew he had to do something.

He finished the meat and thought about another helping but decided against it. He felt an urge to be on the move. He got one of the basic saddles from a Blackfoot pony and put the unfamiliar tack on the mare, who seemed unhappy with it. "Don't worry, girl, we'll find you a proper saddle soon," he said, patting the animal's neck.

He tied the four Blackfoot ponies together, then mounted the mare and rode down the hill toward where he had shot the deer, towing the other horses behind him. When hunting, he thought he had heard some water that way but not had time to investigate until now. He hoped it was true as he and the animals needed water.

It did not take him long to find the source—a rivulet coming out of the rocks near head height, spilling over other rocks in a miniature waterfall, and draining down into a puddle about three feet around. The pool was frozen over, but Cooper hacked through it with the hatchet, scooped a few handfuls of icy water into his mouth, then let the animals drink.

Mounted again, he followed the mountain through the trees at the bottom on the same side of the hill, wanting to avoid climbing it again. By midday, he had found a small saddle between two hills and took that to get to the trail—formed by thousands of warriors traveling there over the years. Snow started again soon after, though it was not heavy.

He traveled leisurely, being in no hurry, through off and on snowflakes, still ruminating on what he would—or could—do to exact some revenge, not only for Douglas but for himself. The theft of his horse, plews, and other possibles called for retaliation too.

Still ravenous, he finished up his supply of meat that night, and in the morning managed to bring down a fat raccoon. It wasn't the best, but it was what he had and so what he would eat.

Several times he had to dart into the trees as he heard or sensed something that made him think Blackfeet were around. Surely the people in the village had missed the three he had killed. Whether

Blackfeet were searching for him, he didn't know, but he thought it likely. And he had no intention of being taken by them again.

As he neared the village three days after leaving the cave, he turned northward. There was a small hill that might give him slightly better vantage point to keep an eye on the village. Trees were scattered along the slight slope, and he tied the Blackfoot ponies to one tree and the mare to another. Then he took a position at still another several feet away. He was still hungry and had some raccoon meat left, so he considered finding a place covered enough to build a small fire. He immediately dismissed the idea. It would be foolish to do anything to draw even the slightest attention to himself.

While he could see more of the village from here, it was too far away to see anything except tiny figures scurrying around in the cold at times. Smoke bloomed from all the tipis except the one where Douglas had said his plunder was. He could see the horse herd to the west. He could not, at this distance, tell if there were any horse guards.

As the day wore on, the temperature began to fall, and he hugged the capote tight around him, his anger grew with every minute he sat staring at the village. About an hour after true dark had fallen, he rose, mounted the mare, took the rope to the Blackfoot ponies, and headed north across the hill and turned west as it reached the prairie floor near the horse herd.

As he neared the animals, he dismounted, figuring that a mounted man would make a silhouette. As it was, he would be lost in the milling animals. On foot, holding the ropes to the ponies and the reins to his horse, he walked near the fringes of the herd, trying to spot any guards that might be around. In an infrequent parting of the clouds to let a little moonlight through, he spotted only one, in almost the same place as he found the other.

He undid the ropes to the ponies and let the animals go mingle with the rest of the herd. He coiled the ropes over a shoulder. Still walking beside his horse, he got as near to the warrior as he thought safe.

Creeping up behind the warrior, Cooper called quietly, "Hey, buffler dung."

NINE

THE BLACKFOOT TURNED and caught the stock of Cooper's fusil square in the throat. The only sound he made as he fell was a strangled, soft gargle.

Cooper finished the job by stabbing him in the heart. He took the scalp, wiped his knife off on the warrior's blanket, and walked to the mare. As he did, he tossed the scalp into the midst of the herd, thinking that in very little time, it would get mashed into the earth by the ponies' hooves, which he thought was a fitting end to it.

He mounted and rode toward his mule. He was a little surprised that the animal hadn't wandered off on its own, but he figured the beast was as comfortable here, feeding on relatively plentiful forage amid horses that were not going to bother him. He shrugged. It didn't matter. He was just glad the animal was there.

Cooper looped a rope around the animal's neck and rode off, towing it behind him. He went back to his space on the small hill and kept watch on the village for a while. Darkness had arrived, and only the thin, weak moonlight filtered through wispy clouds allowed him to see anything in the village. He had noted earlier that two lodges appeared to be empty as there was little or no smoke rising from the smoke hole. In the dim moonlight, it seemed to be the same. He figured those families were probably sharing other lodges because their men had been among those that Cooper had killed or because they were away from the village. He had seen few warriors moving hurriedly about the village in the frigid temperatures. If what Tom Douglas had said about there being twelve warriors in the village, there should be only seven left after Cooper had killed two horse guards and the three who had killed Douglas. He hoped that some of those seven were off looking for him.

He waited a couple of hours to give the villagers time to take to their robes. While he did so, he moved about gathering up some small twigs, a few bigger ones, and two good-sized ones. He tied them in a bundle and set it aside. Finally deciding that all the Blackfeet were asleep, he walked to the mule, patted the animal on the neck, and said, "I warned you once before that I'd make meat of you if you kept giving me a hard time. I hope you remember that because if you betray me tonight, I'll stake your ornery hide down in the village and let the Blackfeet feed on you. Understand?" He smiled at his foolishness. The silence grew when the mule let out the quietest bray it could.

Cooper mounted the mare and rode toward the horse herd again, taking off his capote as he rode. He came out of the trees on the west side and rode fairly close to the animals. Then, with a grim smile, he fired the fusil, howled wildly, and flapped his coat as he trotted closer to the herd, still shouting.

The ponies broke and ran, scattering across the wide meadow to the north and west.

Cooper whirled the mare and darted into the trees, then rode as fast as he dared through the trees to where the mule waited. He hopped off the horse, slipped on his capote, reloaded the smoothbore, grabbed the bundle of firewood, hopped back on the horse, took the rope to the mule, and galloped down the hill, all in less than three minutes.

He stopped behind the lodge where Douglas had said Cooper's plews and maybe his other possibles—except his weapons—were kept. Between the darkness and his position behind the lodge, it would be almost impossible to see him, even if the people chasing the running ponies came back. His only concern was that some women or even a child would come wandering by. But he could not let that worry him because it was highly unlikely. Any of them outside in the cold would be watching for the men to return with the ponies. Still, he figured he didn't have much time.

He dismounted and ripped a long slit through the rear of the tipi, then led both animals inside. It was a close fit, but he managed. He cleared a spot near one edge, got his fire-making kit and some tinder, and snapped flint against steel. Over and over. He was starting to sweat despite the cold with the effort and the knowledge that he might not have much time. "Damn," he finally muttered. He put a sprinkle of gunpowder on the tinder and struck the flint against steel. It took several more tries, but the powder flashed, and the tinder caught. He added small twigs as rapidly as possible, then larger ones, until he had a nice small fire going. He didn't want it too big, lest someone see that the lodge was lit. He tossed one of the larger pieces of wood on with just one end in the flames.

With the light, he could get to work. He ripped the Indian saddle off the mare, hurriedly put on his own. He tossed the packsaddle on the mule and tightened it, then began throwing plews, which he had not packed yet, over that x-framed saddle and quickly tied them down.

He stopped for a few moments to settle his breathing. He could hear the faint sounds of the men still trying to gather their skittish ponies.

He led his two animals outside, then rushed back in and grabbed the larger stick, which by now was burning brightly on one end. Back outside, he torched the lodge in several spots. The buffalo skin cover caught after a moment at each spot.

He went to mount the mare, then stopped. He moved around the lodge to where he could see the other tipis. He stood for a moment, eyeing the lodge of Bull Belly, whom Douglas had said had taken his rifle. "Don't be a fool, Hawley," he told himself firmly.

Then, with the animals, he ran across the village and around to the back of the lodge. He sliced through the buffalo skins, hoping there was no one inside. He would hate to have to kill a woman or a child. He breathed a sigh of relief when he found the lodge empty. He searched around, becoming a bit frantic as the seconds ticked by. He was close to deciding to leave, that the rifle was not here, but then he spotted it on a buffalo robe near the flap entrance. His powder horn and shooting bag were next to it. He made a quick check and found that the small pouch of caps was still there, as were some greased cloth patches. He did not see the two buckskin sacks that had contained his supplies, and he figured everything had been taken right off. He took another quick look around and spotted a parfleche, which he checked. It had some pemmican. He saw nothing else he could use. He slung his rifle on his back next to the fusil, hung his shooting bag and powder horn over his shoulders, and grabbed the parfleche. Then he set that lodge on fire in several spots, too. Heading for the slit to get out, he suddenly stopped. He turned, dropped the burning brand, and grabbed the buffalo robe on which his rifle had been lying. He rolled it up and ran outside with the parfleche and robe. He fastened both to the packsaddle, darted back inside, and grabbed the torch. Dashing back outside, he rode off slowly, stopping by a nearby lodge. He dismounted and leaned the flaming end of the torch against the flap, where it too would soon begin burning.

He looked back at his handiwork. With a grim smile, he said, "Once again, Ol' Tom, it ain't much vengeance for you but it's the best I can do, and there's another Blackfoot you can lord it over when you get to the afterlife." He paused, then grinned for real. "Reckon you're there already. Maybe it's you who's been helpin' me all along here," he added.

He mounted the horse and trotted off, the pack mule following. When he looked back, he saw two women running toward the chief's burning lodge. They were so intent on the flames that they did not see him.

Cooper spurred himself east, up the nearby hill, not along the trail to the south. He weaved his way through the trees, down the other side, across a wide meadow, then through a small saddle to a wide stretch of mostly open, ice-covered ground dotted with trees and sagebrush. The land rose and fell gently. It offered no place to hide should the Blackfeet come after him. He didn't think it likely, but he need not press his incredible run of good fortune by stopping. So he rode on, halting only occasionally when he found some water, and let the animals drink. Twice he was fortunate enough to find a cottonwood from which he peeled some bark and let the animals feed. It wasn't much but it would keep them going.

Near midday, he stopped. He did not plan to stay long, but he needed food as did the animals, as well as water, and rest. The was a small, frozen creek and several cottonwoods that would provide water and forage for the animals, and the former for him. Despite being angry at himself not doing so, he did not unsaddle or unload the beasts. He hobbled the animals, then tore off cottonwood bark and laid it out near the stream, which he had to hack open so they all could drink. Then he gathered a bit of wood and started a fire. He put a flattish rock into the flames and let it heat up, then laid a good portion of pemmican on it to warm. It left him little, but he needed its nourishment now. He would worry about hunger later.

He soon began eating, the fat-rich meat and fruit mixture settling welcomely in his stomach. It warmed him on the inside, as the fire was warming him on the outside.

———

HE AWOKE with a jerk when he fell over onto his side. "Dammit all," he muttered as he sat back up and rubbed the tiredness from his face. The position of the sun told him he had been asleep for about three hours. The sky was clear, but more clouds were moving in, and he figured snow was coming again. He was disgusted. "Damn worthless critter you are, Hawley Cooper," he scolded himself aloud. "You should be ashamed of yourself. Must be gettin' old."

He rose, then stood stock still. *Maybe that's what's plaguin' me*, he thought. *I ain't but twenty-eight or twenty-nine, which ain't so old here or back in the States, but I've been in these mountains a decade now, and the mountains have a way of wearin' on a man. Maybe I just can't stand the hardships anymore.*

Gloom settling over him much like the dark clouds were darkening the sky, he headed to the creek and drank some. He considered finishing off the pemmican but decided against it. "Probably fall asleep again, you lazy bastard," he muttered.

He pulled more strips of cottonwood bark from the trees, bundled them up and tied them to the mule. He thought the mule eyed him with annoyance. "Don't you give me that look, you worthless critter."

The mule gave a great honking bray, as if to say, "I ain't the worthless critter here."

Though he knew it was a ridiculous thought, it still increased his gloominess. "Maybe you're right, ol' feller."

Trying to shake off the glumness and the tiredness, he mounted his horse and pushed on. He did not think the Blackfeet would be after him for some time. It would take them a while, he figured, to round up all their ponies. And then there were the burned lodges they would have to deal with. Still, he could not be sure of that. Besides, this was still Blackfoot country.

He rode on.

TEN

COOPER AWOKE COVERED IN SNOW. He was groggy, and it took some time for his mind to clear a little and realize where he was. A great, blaring noise was coming from somewhere, and it was nearly a minute before he realized it was his mule braying. A light, soft shove on his cheek made him turn his head, which he shook when he saw a large brown...thing inches from his face. His beclouded mind took a few moments to realize it was the mare's face, gently nudging him awake.

He groaned as he pushed himself gingerly to his feet. He was stiff with soreness and the cold that had seeped into his bones and clung there, he learned when he tried to shake off the snow. His hands felt like blocks of ice, and he recalled with some fear a time many years ago when he had been caught in such a situation and had to cut off part of a pinkie that had been frozen. He looked down and saw that while his hands were pasty white, they did not seem to have fallen prey to frostbite. He was surprised when he realized that his face did not feel as cold, and he decided after a few seconds that his horse's breath had given it some warmth.

With a deep breath, he surveyed the world around him. He was in a vast white wilderness, with nothing but emptiness to slow the wind and snow. He painfully stamped his feet and swung his arms, trying to restart his blood circulating. In a few moments, he stopped to pat the horse on the big neck. "Thanks, girl. Saved my hide again."

The mare nickered softly and shook her head.

The mule brayed again as Cooper returned to trying to build up some heat inside him. "I suppose you're tellin' me you're hungry, you wretched beast. That it?"

The mule honked again.

"Well, so am I and so is the mare." He almost smiled though when he saw that the horse had pulled some of the cottonwood bark off the pile tied to the mule's back and had even apparently dropped some for the mule.

He glanced up and saw that there was no break in any direction of the dark clouds that were still heavy with snow. And with the clouds, he could not tell what time it was or how long he had been here.

And that got him trying to remember what happened. But nothing was clear. The last he could remember, he was still riding slowly along, chin drooping on his chest, tiredness overwhelming him. Then...nothing. He supposed he nodded off and fell from the horse.

"Damn, you are a miserable critter, Hawley Cooper," he muttered, watching the words escape on a cloud of almost crystal vapor. He patted the horse's neck again. "Sorry, girl, but we got to go on. Can't stay out here in the open."

The horse bobbed her great head, and the mule blared its annoyance and the need to find food.

Cooper climbed into the saddle, which was a block of ice almost. He was glad he had the capote between his rump and the rock-hard leather seat. He wrapped the reins around the saddle horn, knowing the mare would not do anything unwarranted if he was not holding them, and took the rope to the mule in one hand. He stuck the other hand in his pocket with a sigh of relief. As he rode through the day, he would switch hands.

He tried to stay awake as they plodded along, pushing off the overpowering desire to sleep. He had felt this poorly only a few times in his life, and he was no more appreciative of it now than those times. He did not know what kept him going, really, just some urge to survive, he supposed. Like when Josiah Weeks had left him alone with nothing in the dead of winter so long ago. He kept pushing on then, despite the odds of survival being slim at the very best. It was the same now. As a mile passed, he realized that while he had no reason other than survival itself then, he had a reason, well, actually two, now: Goes Far and Strong Bow, as he had when he and Black Moon Woman had been caught in that dreadful winter high in the mountains, starving, freezing, with little to aid them. Yes, he thought, I must go on, for them, for us.

But as another mile fell behind, he also realized that before he got back to them and the three of them could restart their life together, he had to find out—and more importantly, conquer—whatever had brought him to this place to start with. The anger and despair, unusual for him, that had settled over him months ago and clutched at him, disinclined to leave him no matter how much he willed it to.

The cloudiness and the snow made it hard to determine when night was falling, but soon it was dark. Still, he kept on plodding along, having come across no place to stop for the night. He did halt every couple of miles to let the animals get some water in them by ingesting some snow. He did the same. He also broke off a few small bits of bark from the rapidly diminishing pile to feed to the animals. And he tried to ignore the growling in his belly and the shriveling of his body for want of food.

They crossed several small creeks, frozen over, for which Cooper was thankful. The mule broke through a couple of times, but the water was only a few inches deep. The mule brayed its protest but continued without a struggle.

Cooper did not know what time it was or how long they had been moving when they came across a small stand of trees in the middle of this vast hilly meadow. Nor did he know how such a small batch of trees—aspens mostly—had come to be in such an otherwise desolate spot, but he did not care. It was enough that they were here.

Despite his exhaustion, he unsaddled the horse and unloaded the mule. He had no curry brush so he settled for giving them a tough tending with his apishamore. He hobbled them and let them out to forage on whatever they could find, the last of the cottonwood bark having long been gone.

Stumbling with tiredness and cold, he gathered wood and got a fire going—after several tries and a plethora of cursing. He took the last little piece of pemmican and set it on a rock to heat. It took him barely two minutes to devour the meal. It did little to assuage his hunger. He stared into the fire, welcoming its heat but finding nothing to cheer about in it. It crossed his mind that perhaps this was the time he was not destined to survive. He had lived through many a hard time since he came to the mountains, but maybe his good fortune had run out. Perhaps this was the time the mountains would claim him. Instead of fighting any longer, perhaps he should just lie down and let the cold suck his life away. It would not be a noble death as would dying with a Crow arrow or Blackfoot lance in his heart. But it would be death just the same. And he would not be around to listen to anyone who came along and said it was a poor thing that a mountaineer had given up and let himself go under.

But there was something in his heart—and in the very fiber of his being—that would not allow such a thing. No, he would go down fighting to the end, whether that be with warriors or the cold or savage beasts or starvation.

"I am Hawley Cooper!" he shouted into the wind. "I am a true mountaineer, unafraid of anything, and by God, I ain't goin' into the afterlife without a fight! Waugh!"

He sat a few minutes, then smiled sadly. "That's all well and good, ol' hoss, but you ain't got much fight left in you."

Shaking his head, he looked around. His eyes settled on his pile of plews, and he considered whether he could scrape all the fur off one and eat the bare hide. Then he shook his head. He had neither the energy to do so or the desire to do all the work only to perhaps learn it would be useless. He had never considered eating beaver hide before, though the tail was a delicacy to be enjoyed now and again.

Then he saw the parfleche next to him. He picked it up, pulled his knife, and cut through some of the sinew stitches until he had a hand-sized piece. As he poked a stick through a slit he cut in it and hung it over the fire, he mumbled, "This might not be edible either, but at least it didn't take much work to give it a try."

When it began to sizzle, he pulled it free and with a grimace, tried to tear off a piece with his teeth. The effort was not successful. "Damn," he muttered, wondering if he had broken any teeth. He wished he had a pot. With one, he could have boiled the leather, possibly making it edible. Since he did not, he resorted to basically sucking the grease out of the hardened buckskin and several pieces after, until his jaws were aching. It was not very satisfying, but it added a little—very little—to his stomach. It did revive him the tiniest bit. So he sat, hungry and tired, unable to find any enthusiasm to do anything but continue to sit there.

He glanced over at the small pile of plews again and wondered if he should leave them behind. There were not nearly enough to outfit him for next year. Even if he made the spring hunt, there was no guarantee that there would be enough. Besides, he couldn't cache them, at least in the ground. The land was frozen, and he had no shovel. He wondered if he might find a cave or someplace where he could store them. There was the risk, of course, that another trapper or some animals would discover the furs. And there might not be any likely place. He was still in a land of small, rolling hills, a valley between stark, treeless peaks.

He started to turn back to the fire when his head snapped back around. "You goddamn fool, Hawley," he muttered, angry at himself. He rose and staggered to the pile of furs. He picked one up, cut several pieces, and tied one around each foot, using fringes cut from his pants. He used two more of the very few left to wrap a piece around each hand and managed to tie them down, forming a makeshift form of mitten. He cursed himself again for not having thought of it earlier, but he was so befogged from tiredness and cold that his brain was not working well.

He spread out his stolen buffalo robe near the fire and threw more wood on the flames. Then with a sigh, he stretched out, pulled the last piece of beaver skin over his face to keep the snow off, and fell asleep.

He awoke to a frigid day but at least the sky was clear. Blindingly so. He took that last piece of beaver fur, cut a long strip off it, trimmed the ends down until they were little more than strings, cut eyeholes in it, and tied around his head. It helped, but not nearly as much as he wanted it to.

His stomach rumbled and he looked longingly at the fire, wishing there was some meat there. But there wasn't. He started loading the mule, then spotted a rabbit sitting, wiggling its nose nearby. "Dammit," he snapped when he realized he could not get his rifle ready to shoot because of the mittens. He tore them angrily off and cocked the rifle, but the rabbit was gone.

With a sigh of dejection, he uncocked the weapon, set it down, and began working once more. But again he saw a rabbit, hard to distinguish against the snow, but he was ready this time. He slowly lifted the rifle, cocked it, and stopped as the rabbit searched for the sound. When the animal took a few hops, Cooper jerked the rifle up and fired.

ELEVEN

"HAWLEY COOPER, GREAT HUNTER," Cooper mumbled in disgust as he gutted and skinned the rabbit. "Twice of late you've taken down a few of the west's wildest critters—two squirrels and a snow hare. Goes Far would be proud of you."

He hung the carcass over the fire, then sat eagerly watching it brown nicely. Even eating the whole thing, right down to nibbling off the little scraps of meat clinging to bones, did not fill him, but it stopped his stomach from growling so much and gave him a bit of energy.

A little refreshed, he loaded the mule and saddled the horse. Both animals had scrounged up enough forage to keep them going for a while. He mounted up and, with the fusil across his back and his rifle in its familiar loop near the saddle horn, Cooper rode out, moving slowly, continuing to the east, still undecided where to go and what to do.

He plodded along, considering his predicament. Things were starting to coalesce in his head but would not come out fully formed. It was ever-present in his mind, making it hard for him to concentrate on life at the moment, which also angered him whenever he realized it.

Suddenly an arrow creased the outside of his left calf and drove deep into the side of the mare's chest. The horse stumbled a few steps, caught up with itself, ran on a few strides, then went down on its right side.

Startled by the initial shock, Cooper cursed as his survival mode kicked in. He dropped the rope to the mule and jumped off the horse, rifle in hand, before the mare had collapsed. He landed hard and rolled, grunting with the fall.

The mule galloped off. Cooper scrabbled to where the horse was still struggling vainly to rise. He slid behind the horse's back, away from the hooves, eyes searching the trees across the short meadow. Cooper tried, unsuccessfully, to calm the animal.

Then a warrior burst out of the trees, bow in hand. Cooper rolled to his left as the Blackfoot fired three more arrows in a span of just seconds. One hit the mare in the throat, one in the chest. The third stuck, quivering for a moment, in Cooper's saddle.

"Damn red demon," Cooper shouted. He shoved off his makeshift mittens, brought the rifle up, and fired, just as the Blackfoot sent another arrow, this one in his direction. The arrow dug a divot in the frozen ground a foot to Cooper's left, but the mountain man's rifle ball blew the warrior off his pony. Cooper reloaded, then rose and stuffed his mittens into a pocket. He walked the few steps to the mare, who was still struggling to rise, though her efforts were considerably weaker.

"Damn," he muttered, shaking his head. Several harsher curses flittered through his head. He looked down and knew the horse would never recover. He knelt by the animal's back and patted her a few times. With a deep sense of sadness, he pulled his knife. "Sorry, ol' gal," he said softly as he slit the horse's throat. He stood, stung by the loss. The mare had been a fine companion, a trusty animal, and had endured many a hardship along with Cooper, never deserting him—if she had run off at such times, they always found each other again.

Alert, he strolled to where the Blackfoot lay. The warrior was still alive, though barely, with a large hole in his back where the flattened lead ball had blasted out. With a foot, Cooper rolled the Indian onto his back. His chest was bloody around a small hole in his chest where the ball had punched itself in.

"You killed a fine animal, there, you shit pile. You weren't even good enough to eat that mare's dung, damn you." He knelt at the Blackfoot's side and laid the rifle down next to him. "What's done is done, I reckon, and there ain't much I can do about it but make sure you rot here on the ground instead of spendin' joyful days in the Afterlife with your kin and friends." He spat on the Indian's face, grabbed his hair, and slowly sliced the scalp off.

To his credit, the Blackfoot made no sound, but his terror at what awaited him after death was strong in his eyes.

Cooper stood and looked around, trying to spot the Blackfoot's pony, hoping to catch it to replace the mare. But the animal was nowhere to be found.

As he plodded back to the mare, his dejection arose strongly again. He began to wonder if perhaps he had angered God or the Great Spirit. Or both. Or maybe he had just used up all the luck he had been endowed with when he was born. He had to admit that he had been mighty fortunate in his days in the mountains. Not that he had not faced any adversity, but he had come through it all, having faced savage Indians, savage animals, savage lands, savage mountains, savage winters, and savage times, yet here he was, still on his feet and still with his hair. But maybe his time was coming to an end, maybe he had angered the spirits or maybe his medicine had just turned bad. Whatever it was did not bode well for a good future.

He stopped next to the dead mare and considered what he should do. He figured he should just move on, but he still, to his disgust, had a kernel of hope inside that he would find a horse, and if he did, he wanted his saddle.

It took a lot of effort, but he finally worked the saddle free from the horse's dead weight, leaving him sweating despite the freezing temperature. He hefted the heavy piece of gear to one shoulder, took his rifle in one hand, and walked off. He stopped after a few steps and looked back. With a sigh, he returned and dropped the saddle and set the rifle down. He knelt and pulled a knife. "Sorry again, girl," he said and began carving out some of the meat. He didn't much like horse meat, but at this point any meat was meat. Besides, he told himself, he should get his share before the wolves and coyotes and other scavengers had their fill. He tied the meat in a large piece of hide with one of the very few remaining fringes on his trousers, hung it on the saddle horn, picked up the saddle and rifle, and stepped off again.

Shambling along, he wondered why he was bothering. His sole possessions were his rifle, the fusil, some powder and ball, his capote, and a few pounds of horse meat. He was afoot in Blackfoot country, all his early catch, as small as it was, had disappeared with his mule, as had his traps and his sleeping robe. His wife and new son were hundreds of miles to the west; his trapping partners hundreds of miles east or northeast; more snow was threatening.

"Waugh!" he muttered. "You're in piss poor shape, ol' hoss."

One part of his mind argued that he should just give up and let nature take him. The other part of him, the primitive one, the one that drove his survival instincts, would not listen. He wasn't sure he appreciated that at the moment, but he followed its directive to move on.

Less than an hour later, the snow began to fall lightly, though it grew in strength after a short while but did not become a raging storm, just a steady fall of heavy, wet flakes. With a sigh, he pushed on again, heading for the trees still more than a mile away. As he waded through the snow that was beginning to build up on the foot already on the ground, he cast occasional glances behind him, making sure no more Blackfeet were about.

It did not take long before he reached the meager shelter of the string of pines lining a frozen creek. He found a stately spruce that had little snow under it. He put his burden down and with his rifle, rattled the lowest branches, starting a small cascade of snow that had gathered on the branches. Then he set about gathering firewood. He had hoped to build a fire circle and use some heated rocks to keep him warm as he slept, but he could find no dry ones. Those along the creek were wet, of course, as were all the others in the grove, which were or had been covered with snow. He had experienced using wet rocks for such purposes before, but they had once exploded on him, and he did not want to undergo that experience again. So he cleared away what little snow there was under the pine and built a good-size fire, then hung a hunk of horsemeat over the flames.

Fighting off the exhaustion, he waited just long enough for the meat to thaw and get a bit warm before he dug in. It was no tastier than the other times he had eaten horsemeat, but he could feel a little strength flow back into his limbs as he chewed and swallowed. He ate several pounds of it, threw more wood on the fire, and curled up next to the flames, tugging the capote tightly around him.

He went a little lighter on the horsemeat in the morning. When he finished, he kicked snowy dirt over the fire, hefted the saddle over his shoulder, grabbed his rifle and the hide-bound package of horsemeat, and headed off through the trees. It snowed on and off all day, but the temperature inched above freezing during the later part of the day for which he was grateful. He finished off the horse-meat two days later. It was a saving grace with its rich bounty of protein and despite his not much caring for the taste or texture, he was glad to have had it since he had seen no game in several days.

Despite the nourishment, fatigue still clung to him like a banker clung to his money.

Two days after that, hungry once again, he heard an odd, though familiar, noise. Then he grinned. "It can't be, it just can't," he said when he heard the distinct honking bray of a mule, which sounded as if it were in trouble. Then he thought he heard growl-ing. He dropped the saddle and charged along as best he could. He burst into a small group of widely spaced trees to see four wolves attacking the mule, which was indeed his. Another wolf was off to the side, weaving, blood coating his fur in various places. Still another was lying, probably dead, Cooper supposed. The mule was braying and honking in fright, but it was active in kicking out at the animals besetting him. It tried to run, but the wolves cut off its escape route.

Cooper slammed to a stop, brought up the rifle and after a moment or two to settle on a target that wasn't moving as much as the others, he fired, sending another wolf yelping onto its side where it shuddered in its death throes.

Cooper dropped the rifle and grabbed the fusil he still carried. He ran a little closer, and when one wolf looked at him as if deciding to charge this new prey, Cooper fired. As he had been doing since he had left the cave where Tom Douglas had died, he had filled the fusil's barrel with rocks. The scattering pellets tore into the face of the wolf, sending him whining and scampering away.

One of the remaining wolves had managed to get a grip on the mule's rump and was hanging on for dear life as the pack animal bucked and jumped and kicked. The last wolf was heading for the mule's snout. Cooper swung the fusil around. With the barrel in both hands, he slammed the stock against the side of the wolf at the mule's rear. The canine yelped and let go, then turned its snarling visage on Cooper.

"Come on, damn you, you son of a Blackfoot squaw and Satan himself." He hefted the fusil, the stock of which had shattered. But as the wolf took a step toward Cooper, the mule kicked out with both rear legs. The hooves caught the wolf in the side, shattering bones, the wolf tried limping away but was having trouble doing so. The last wolf fled.

Cooper smiled again as he approached the mule. He was surprised to see that his plews were still tied to the beast's back. *Maybe all my luck ain't run out yet*, he thought.

Still nervous and scared, braying lustily, the mule calmed a little as Cooper neared. It looked at the mountain man as if to say, "It's about time you got here."

Cooper took note of the look. "Well, if you hadn't run off, scaredy thing that you are, this wouldn't have happened." He stroked the calming animal's powerful neck. "Reckon maybe you ain't such a miserable critter as I've thought."

He looked at the fusil. It was useless, so he tossed it away. He picked up his rifle and reloaded it. He grabbed the rope to the mule, wondering how the animal had not gotten tangled up in some brush with it dangling the way it was. They walked back to where Cooper had dropped the saddle. He picked it up and grinned when the mule looked askance at him.

"No, I ain't aimin' to ride you, you ornery, yellow-bellied critter. But you can carry this thing a heap easier than I can."

TWELVE

"HALLO THE CAMP!" Cooper called. "Mountain boy comin' in, if you don't mind."

"You alone?" a voice came out of the shadows.

"Just me and my mule."

"Come on in, then."

Cooper was aware of at least two men with rifles ready behind some trees.

One man stepped forward as Cooper walked into the camp towing the mule. "Name's Jim Thorne, captain of this bunch of the dirtiest, best trappin'est, fightin'est, fartin'est troupe of mountaineers you'll ary come across."

Despite the gloom that had become like a second skin to him, Cooper smiled. "Well, from the looks of the fellers I see, you're right about you boys bein' the dirtiest hosses around. And by the smell, you prove you're the fartin'est bunch too." He held out his hand. "Name's Hawley Cooper."

"Welcome," Thorne said. "How'd you lose your horse?"

"Blackfoot arrows. Powerful loss for me. Not only put me afoot but the mare was a damn good horse. Be hard to find another like her."

"Some horses are like that, certain. Go tend to your animal and then set to the fire with us fellers."

As he was doing the former, Cooper looked around the camp. There were three small tents across from a rickety log cabin. The fire was a roaring blaze—big enough to easily fight off the softly drifting snow—in the open between the tents and the cabin. Three women moved quietly around the tents. Finished, he sat at the fire. Someone handed him a tin mug of coffee, for which he nodded thanks.

Each man introduced himself with a simple name: George, Worley, Hamp, Jed, Zeke..." They stopped at the pained look that crossed Cooper's face. "I say somethin' to get your goat?" the last asked, voice a little hard.

Cooper shook his head. "No, just a hard remembrance. A feller named Zeke and me was best friends and trappin' partners. Blackfeet made wolf bait out of him a couple years ago. I still miss my friend."

"I can understand that," Zeke said. "I'm sorry to hear it."

Cooper shrugged. "Well, thanks, but you didn't know him."

"Don't matter. Any time one of us mountaineers

goes under for any reason—most of all at the hands of damned Bug's Boys—it's a sad thing."

The others murmured their agreement.

The last two identified themselves as Petey and Hugh.

Cooper couldn't help but stare at the hunk of elk hanging over the fire.

Thorne noticed. "Help yourself, friend. Best luck huntin' we've had in a spell, but it ain't right not to share. Looks like've had yourself some starvin' times."

"That I have," Cooper said gratefully as he tore off a hunk of meat and began gobbling it down.

"You look a little familiar," Thorne said. "We ever met before? Down to rendezvous maybe?"

"Come across you a few years back," Cooper said between bites. "Me and a partner..."

"This Zeke feller?"

"Yep. We were lookin' for a place to winter and came across your camp. You were willin' to let us join you, but we decided against it since game was scarce enough to hardly keep you boys fed. So we found us another place." He grinned ruefully. "Wasn't much game there either, but we made it through." He shrugged and took another mouthful.

"Didn't I see you with another group of free trappers at rendezvous?" He paused, thinking. "Elson Brooks was the cap'n?"

"True enough."

"You ain't with him no more?"

"He's gone under. Took a lead pill durin' a fight."

"Blackfeet?" Hamp asked.

Cooper shrugged noncommittally.

"That why you're out here alone?" Hugh asked. "Left the others when he went down?"

Cooper shook his head. "Nah. We was still together. My woman was with child, so I took her back to her people—Nez Percé. Left her there for the birthin' whilst I went out trappin'. Got waylaid by Bug's Boys."

"Reckon you was hard used by 'em," Strong said.

"Not so hard, really." Cooper wiped greasy hands on his buckskins and took a sip of coffee. "Was tied to a pole waitin' on them to start their devilish entertainment on me."

"They couldn't have done too much. You don't look that poorly used."

"Surely wasn't. A fellow mountaineer who had been captured a few years back and was made a broken man by them, cut me loose. Since he helped me, I helped him get away too. He was killed a few days later where we'd made camp. I was off a little ways huntin' when I heard Blackfeet whooping. I hurried back. Blackfeet had just about done him in when and were fixin' to take his scalp when I got there..."

"While he was still alive?" Worley asked, horrified but not surprised at the thought of that happening to one of them.

"Yep. I stopped 'em, killed all three, and scalped 'em. Later took 'em away from the camp a bit so the wolves could have 'em. Tom didn't linger more than a few minutes."

"Where'd ye bury him?"

"The cave where we'd taken refuge. I buried him there, with the Blackfoot scalps under his ass."

There were murmurs of approbation from the others.

"What was his name?" Strong asked.

"Tom Douglas."

"Wasn't he..." Hamp asked.

"Yep," Strong said. "He and a partner, what was his name?"

"Cal Dinkins," Hugh said.

"That's right," Thorne said. "The two of 'em rode with us for a while, then decided to go off on their own. I always wondered what happened to those fellers since we never saw 'em at rendezvous again. Do you know what happened to Cal?"

"Tom said Bug's Boys tortured and killed him right before his eyes. They kept Tom as a slave, cut his leg so he couldn't run. By the time I was in that village, like I said, he was a broken man. Moreso even than Tom Fitzpatrick some years ago. At least Fitzpatrick recovered."

"Damn, if that ain't the shits," Jed said.

Everyone agreed.

"The other fellers in your group still together?"

"Mostly."

"You headin' on back to 'em, then, I reckon."

"Ain't sure to tell true. Ain't had much of a hunt

as you can see by the pitiful pile of plews I got. And don't think I can do much trappin' before the spring hunt with most of the creeks and streams froze up. Ain't got much in the way of supplies either. Hell, I ain't got any supplies. I might wander into one of the tradin' posts, trade in the few plews I have, and see if I can work a bit to bring in some money to outfit myself for next year. Meet my pals at rendezvous."

"What about your woman? Plannin' to leave her?"

"Nope. She'll be at rendezvous with her people."

There was silence for a while as Cooper ate and the others drank coffee or smoked their pipes.

"You can join us, Hawley," Thorne said. "We always have room for another good hand, and from what I've heard, you're a damn good man to have along."

"I'll think about it, Jim. Need to mull it around, see if it'd be good for both of us."

"Makes sense, hoss. You're welcome to stay with us for a spell. While you're here, you can take part in camp chores."

"I'd expect so."

"Got to tell you, though, hoss, that you can't stay long. Week, maybe two weeks at most."

"I'll decide on your offer before long, no more'n a couple, three days, I expect. I won't be a burden while I'm here."

"Didn't figure you'd be or I wouldn't have made the offer. You can stay with me, Sam, Hamp, Zeke, and Petey in the cabin or find yourself a place under a tree."

Cooper nodded. He chose the latter, not wanting to be cooped up with a bunch of men as unwashed, blood and grease-coated, and high-smelling as himself. Nor did he want company.

————————

IN THE MORNING, Cooper joined all the others, except Worley, who had been on guard duty and headed off to the cabin without bothering to fill his meatbag. Cooper ate sparingly. He was still ravenous, but he did not think it right to take anything more than a minimum of food away from his fellow mountain men. They were short enough as were most winter camps. He did have a second cup of coffee though.

Afterward, he went off with Hamp to gather firewood and strip cottonwood bark for the horses. He was glad that Hamp had little to say other than he had been in the mountains for six years, was born in Norway, and was brought to America when he was nine or ten.

Finished by early afternoon, the two men enjoyed themselves a mug of coffee, some of which was kept hot near the fire all the time. As they were appreciating the heat of the drink as well as that of the fire, Thorne strolled up and sat.

"Once you told me your name, Hawley, I remembered hearing some things about ye."

Cooper stopped with the cup halfway to his face, then lowered it. "That troublesome for you?"

"Hell no. Builds up my respect for ye if even half those things are true."

"Like what?" Hamp asked.

"Like ye once held off more'n half the Blackfoot Nation by yourself a couple, three years ago."

Hamp looked at Cooper, who shook his head. "Ain't true," the latter said.

"None of it?" Hamp asked.

"Well, not much."

"Ah, hell, boy, tell true now," Thorne said.

Cooper sighed. "It wasn't half the Blackfoot Nation. Weren't more than a couple, three dozen maybe a little more. And I wasn't alone."

"Five others, I hear."

"Just two others. My good friend Zeke..."

"That the one you mentioned last night?"

"Yep. Took a Blackfoot arrow in the throat."

"Damn," Hamp said.

"Who was the other?" Thorne asked.

"Nez Percé warrior travelin' with us."

"I know him?"

"Reckon not. Feller named Painted Wolf," Cooper lied.

"Nope. Never heard of him. Still, three of ye takin' on all those Bug's Boys and two of ye comin' out with your hair is a tale worth tellin'."

"I'd be much more pleased was people to forget it. Weren't nothin' else any mountaineers'd do if called upon."

"Like hell," Hamp said. "Any three of us here faced that many Blackfeet would be roamin' the earth with no access to the Happy Huntin' Ground without our hair and some other parts missin', too, knowin' those sons a bitches."

"Much as I hate to admit it," Thorne added, "I got to agree with Hamp. Such doin's wouldn't shine with any of us, nor siree."

"It's over and done now. More'n two years ago," Cooper said with a shrug.

Hamp started to say something, but Thorne cut him off with a wave of the hand, then said, "I also heard you're a damn fine hunter. One of the best maybe."

Cooper started to protest, then stopped and said, "The best. Except maybe for Zeke."

Thorne grinned. "'Bout time you admitted somethin' good about yourself, hoss."

Cooper shrugged again.

"How'd you like to try your luck bringin' in some meat for us boys?"

"You said there ain't much game about and gettin' that the elk we've been eatin' was the luckiest huntin' you've done in a spell. You expect me to make magic?"

"Hell, after all you've come through with your

hair still attached to your head, you must have some mighty strong medicine."

"Bah. I only said I was a great shot. Didn't say nothin' about me findin' game, especially where there ain't any."

"I reckon you'll do all right. If you don't find any we're no worse off than we are now."

"I'll need a horse."

Thorne grinned and nodded toward the large remuda of animals. "Reckon we can find ye one."

Cooper nodded.

"Ye got enough powder and ball?"

"Reckon so, unless I run into a large herd of buffler and try to bring 'em all in so you fellers don't have to worry about feedin' for a year or two."

"Shines."

"I could also use a mule. Mine's been worked mighty hard of late."

"Done. You need anything else to get you started? Maybe get you out soon."

"Don't need anything else. And it's too late in the day to start now. Maybe I'll pick out a mount now and head out at first light."

THIRTEEN

"WE CAUGHT that elk a few miles west and south from here," Thorne said as Cooper was saddling his borrowed horse the next morning.

"Any reason to think there might be more that way?"

"Nope. We only saw that one, but I reckon that if one was there—and a healthy one to boot—there's likely to be others about."

"Reckon that's a good a place as any to start lookin'," Cooper said as he tightened the cinch and pulled down the stirrup that he had hung on his saddle horn.

"You want company?"

"Nope."

"Well, then, good huntin', hoss,"

Cooper nodded. The morning was blazingly bright and the temperature hovering around freezing when Cooper rode out on a sturdy mustang provided by Worley and a mule offered by Thorne. He was glad to be back in the saddle after several days of being afoot before he had come across Thorne's group of free trappers.

On the other hand, it also gave him time to think, and that was not as welcome. While he wanted to discover what was plaguing him so he could address it, the considerations were not pleasant, especially as he had been unable to come to any conclusions—or solutions.

Despite the persistence of his mind to get him to think of these things, and his fight to prevent it, he realized after half a day's travel that someone was following him. He did not know how he knew. He just did. And he did not question it. It had some time ago just come to him that he had such an ability and he had accepted it. Of course, just because he knew someone was following him did not mean he knew who was behind him or what he or they might want. He sensed that it was a sole man, which could be a Blackfoot warrior alone looking to steal horses or raise hair. Or it could be a solitary mountain man like himself, but why anyone other than him would be traveling alone through the depths of winter was beyond him.

He picked up his pace a little, wanting to get past the empty meadow and the barren hills surrounding him to find a spot where he could find a safe place to check out his follower.

An hour later, he crossed a saddle between two

small humps of rock and snow-covered sagebrush into another valley. More than halfway across to another hill stood a stunted cedar, twisted grotesquely by the wind and other elements. He stopped next to the tree and looked around. He saw nothing else that looked promising. "Reckon this'll have to do," he said as he dismounted. He tied the two animals to the tree, hoping they could find a little forage under the snow or on the tree. He leaned his rifle against the trunk, then began gnawing at one of the strips of jerky Thorne had given him along with a small buckskin bag of elk meat, a small coffee pot, a cup, and a bit of coffee. Before long, he, too, leaned against the tree. The jerky was gone soon after.

The chilly air was beginning to sneak into his compote and his flesh before Cooper saw s lone rider coming toward him. When the rider was about fifty yards away, Cooper picked up his rifle and cradled it in his left arm, then stepped a little way away from the cedar. "You've come as far as you're going to, hoss," Cooper shouted. "Turn yourself around and head in some other direction."

"That you, Cooper? It's George, George Lynch." His voice sounded surprised, as if he had not expected to be found out.

"Why're you followin' me, George?"

"I ain't followin' you. I'm huntin'. Didn't know you was out this way."

"Huntin', eh? Without a pack animal to tote the meat back to camp?"

"Uh, well, I wasn't sure I was gonna find much. Figured if I did, I could carry some back on my horse here."

"That's the largest load of buffler dung I've heard in a long time, hoss. Now why're you followin' me?"

"I said I ain't. I..."

"Whether you are or you ain't, I don't appreciate you on my trail. Now, like I said, haul yourself around and head off in some other direction."

"Or what?" Lynch asked, voice turning harsh, as he moved a few yards closer.

"Or you'll be feedin' wolves right where you are."

"You think you're that good?"

"Yep. It's why Thorne had me out huntin' instead of you. As close as you are, I could put a lead pill right smack through your nose." After waiting a few moments while Lynch seemed to be trying to decide, Cooper said, "You have one minute by my countin' to leave or I'll drop you where you stand."

Lynch stalled for just a bit, then angrily jerked his horse's head around and trotted off.

Cooper remained where he was for a while, watching until Lynch was just a speck across the meadow. Then he turned untied the animals, mounted the horse, and rode off with the mule behind him. He was certain that Lynch was following him for a reason, though he could not figure out why. He was also certain that Lynch would not just ride off. He would have to be careful. He picked up the pace a bit.

Skirting another scrubby hump of a hill, he crossed another short meadow and into a grove of trees hugging a slope perhaps fifty feet tall made of large rocks and boulders that had tumbled from the mountain face in a jumbled mass. A trickle of water had dribbled down from the rocks to freeze in a small puddle at the bottom. The trickle itself was frozen, too, but with the pond, he and the animals would have water. The trees were mostly cottonwoods and a few willows, barren of leaves now, but the bark was untouched and would feed the animals. The stony wall cut down what little wind there was to almost nothing which meant the temperature felt a bit higher than it really was. The sky was darkening. Allowing a cluster of stars to begin sparkling around the faint shape of the moon.

He tended to the animals, then gathered wood and started a fire. He put some coffee on and hung the small piece of meat over the flames on a stick. The meal was done by the time he had thrown together a small, crude lean-to.

He ate rapidly and added wood to the fire so it was blazing well. After grabbing his rifle and another cup of coffee, he climbed the rocks and took a perch about a quarter of the way up. He sat, drew his coat close around him, hood up, and waited.

In less than an hour, it was fully dark except for the moon and stars.

Cooper had a little trouble staying awake, but he managed. A few hours after he had taken his post, his horse snickered in a way slightly different than normal, and he saw a shadow moving slowly toward where he had laid his buffalo robe over a small log. Cooper watched as the man raised a tomahawk, the blade reflecting a little firelight, and brought it down hard of where Cooper's head would be under the robe.

The shadow jerked backward, his surprise evident in his posture. He carefully pulled back the robe and then swore softly.

Cooper fired, smashing the shadow's hand where it still held the robe.

In shock and surprise, the shadow fell back on its rump, howling.

As Cooper reloaded his rifle, he said, "Next one drills a hole through your brainpan, Lynch."

Cooper was not too surprised when Lynch flopped down and rolled, trying to keep out of the firelight. Cooper did not hesitate, and he fired before Lynch was completely lost in the darkness. As he reloaded, he watched Lynch pulling himself along the snowy ground as if one of his legs was not working. He carefully climbed down from his perch, grabbed a burning branch from the fire, and warily strode to where he figured Lynch would be. As he neared the spot, he heard a gun being cocked. He grinned grimly and stuck the torch about head high in the crook of two branches of the tree. Then he slipped into the darkness and silently made his way toward where he figured Lynch was. It was not long, despite the dim starlight filtering through the bare branches of the cottonwoods, before he spotted the man, back resting against a tree trunk. He stopped and knelt. "Drop the pistol, Lynch."

Instead, Lynch fired at where the torch was stuck in the tree.

As soon as he did, Cooper stalked out of his cover behind a cottonwood, and kicked the pistol that Lynch was frantically trying to reload with little use of the wounded hand out of his grip.

"You mind tellin' me just what in hell you're doin' tryin' to make wolf bait out of me?"

"I ain't tellin' you anything."

"Might be good if you spoke up, hoss. Even in the dimness, I can see you're bad hurt. Looks like you got a broke leg and blood's flowing out pretty well. Maybe you tell me what's got into your craw the good Lord might look a little more favorably on you. I reckon you got a lot to answer for when you get to the pearly gates. Talkin' now just might smooth the way a little, though it's doubtful. Still, might be worth your while."

"You'll take me back to the others where they can tend me?"

"Doubt it'll do you any good, but I'll try."

Lynch thought for a minute, then said, "You killed my nephew, Jake."

"Jake? Who the hell is Jake?"

"Jake Hines. Jacob."

"Never heard of him."

"Don't matter that you don't know his name. It's enough for me that you killed him."

"When and where was I supposed to have killed this feller?"

"A week or so after rendezvous two years ago. Up along Black's Fork."

"Wasn't anywhere near then, hoss, not then nor ever."

"Like hell."

"Were you there?"

"No."

"Then what makes you think I killed him?"

"Good friend told me. Dan Anderson."

Cooper was shocked. "He wasn't there either. He was with me and the rest of Elson Brooks's band of free trappers headin' northwest to Nez Percé land."

"Don't matter what you say. I'll believe Dan afore I'd believe the likes of you." His voice was filled with pain brought on by his wounds.

"Anderson's a duck-humpin' son of a bitch. When did he tell you this?"

"Last rendezvous, maybe the one before."

Cooper thought that over for a bit. If what Lynch said was true, it was possible that Anderson had fabricated the story he told Lynch to avenge Malachi Webster's death at Cooper's hands. He also figured that Anderson did not have the courage to kill Cooper himself. He did wonder though, whether Dave Wheeler, who was even closer to Webster than Anderson, had anything to do with this plot, if true.

"Got nothin' to say?" Lynch asked, trying to sneer.

"Nothin more than I already said—I don't know who your nephew was and I was nowhere near where his killin', if it's even true, happened."

"Oh, it's true all right. I had hoped to catch up to you at rendezvous last summer, but you were hard to find. "Imagine my surprise—and luck—when you walked right into our camp."

"Luck? Sure. But it ain't good luck for you."

Lynch tried laughing but it did not work well. "Damn," he finally muttered. "We'll see about that. My friends'll likely have something to say about it all. So now, get me back to the camp."

"Mornin's soon enough."

"You mean to let me lay here all night? With my leg bleeding and my hand mangled?"

"Yep. If you keep your trap shut, I might even move you over near the fire."

"You damn well better."

"Well, now, I'll just have to reconsider." He set down his rifle, pulled Lynch up by the shirt, and pulled off his shooting bag. As he went to do the same with the powder horn, Lynch reached for his belt knife. Cooper dropped the powder horn's strap and slammed a fist on Lynch's shattered hand. "Behave yourself," Cooper snapped as Lynch gasped in pain.

Cooper removed the powder horn, then Lynch's knife and tomahawk, and even his patch knife. He picked up Lynch's pistol, rose, grabbed his own rifle, and headed off.

"Hey, what about me? You said you'd get me over to the fire."

"I'll be back. Maybe. You get a better chance of me doin' so if you keep your mouth sewn up." He took a few steps, then turned back. "No rifle?"

"With the horse."

"Where?"

Lynch chucked a thumb over his shoulder. "Near the edge of the trees a few dozen yards to the northeast."

Cooper nodded and left. He picked up his torch, placed Lynch's weapons and accoutrements near the fire, then went and fetched Lynch's mount. He unsaddled the animal and briskly tended to it. He finally returned to Lynch. The man was in bad shape. By the light of the torch, Cooper could see the puddle next to Lynch's thigh had grown considerably, and he figured his shot must have nicked the big vein there and the blood was flowing out steadily if not quickly. He grabbed Lynch's shirt, dragged the groaning man, and dropped him near the fire.

FOURTEEN

WHEN COOPER ROSE in the stillness just before dawn, Lynch was dead, having bled out. Cooper felt no remorse. He had defended himself, again. Lynch's death was just another consequence of a life in the pitiless mountains.

Cooper ate what little food he had left and finished up the rest of the coffee. Then he put his saddle on Lynch's horse and Lynch's saddle on the animal Cooper had borrowed from Worley. Dawn was just breaking when he rode out, towing the mule and the horse with Lynch's body draped across the saddle. He went the same way he had been going yesterday, traveling slowly, hoping he would run across an elk or two, or at least a deer.

A few hours later he was beginning to wonder if this wasn't a fool's errand and considered turning back. But he decided to push on a little longer. He was glad he did when he spotted a small herd of elk just after he eased out of the trees into a small meadow. He pulled back into the woods, dismounted, and tied the animals to branches. He grabbed his rifle, cautiously stepped into the meadow and continued walking. A few of the animals looked up, suspicious, and Cooper stopped, waited a few moments, then took several more steps and stopped again. He picked out a good-size doe, dropped to a knee and fired. The doe fell, legs kicking. The other elk charged off, heading into the forest on the north side of the meadow. Cooper reloaded the rifle, mounted his horse and with the two other animals behind him rode to where the elk lay, stopped, and dismounted. He ground-staked the animals, removed his capote, pulled his knife, and began the butchering.

He was sweating by the time he had finished and loaded almost two hundred and fifty pounds of meat on the mule. He had considered riding back to Thorne's camp but decided that it would be almost nightfall when he got there. He also passed up his campsite from the previous night and rode on until he found a decent enough place to spend the night. Though the temperature had fallen again, the sky was clear. He unloaded the mule and unsaddled his horse but left Lynch's body—frozen now in an arc across his saddle—where it was. He fed well on elk that night, but while he was eating had to kill two wolves that came around at separate times, drawn by the smell of the fresh kill. He slept uneasily that night, though nothing untoward happened.

He fed on more elk in the morning, then loaded the mule, saddled his horse, and made his way at a decent rate toward Thorne's winter camp.

"It's Hawley Cooper comin' in," he announced as he arrived.

The men in the camp gathered around as he rode in and stopped. Their looks were curious when they saw Lynch's body. Thorne jerked his head at the corpse. "Blackfeet?"

"Nope. Me."

The men's looks took a decidedly unfriendly cast. "What happened?" Thorne asked, voice rough.

"Son of a bitch was aimin' to raise my hair. I disabused him of that notion."

"Why would George try to kill you?" Jed asked harshly.

"Said I killed a nephew of his a couple years back. Up near Black's Fork."

"Did you?"

Cooper's eyes narrowed in anger. "Nope. Like I told him before he went under, I wasn't near Black's Fork then nor ever."

"Then why..." Hugh asked.

"Told me that one of the men who rode with Brooks's group with me told him I did it."

"Why would he say that if you didn't do it?" Worley asked. His face was tight with anger.

"Feller who told him wasn't happy that I killed a friend of his."

"Did you?"

"Yep."

"You go 'round killin' White men all the time?"

"Only when there ain't no Blackfeet 'round to raise hair on," Cooper said angrily, raising the eyebrows of the other men. "I don't kill White folks lightly, boys. Only done so a few times, and all of 'em deserved it. The one who told Lynch I killed his friend certainly deserved it."

"Says you," Worley said.

"Reckon then you'd be all right with a feller attackin' your woman, causin' her to lose a child she was carryin' in her belly, eh? And later tried to rape her? That the kind of snake humpin' shit pile you'd think was a kindly feller who should live a long and peaceful life?" Cooper's voice had turned into a cold, harsh growl.

There was a buzz around the men before Thorne asked, "Who was this feller you killed?"

"A walkin' dung heap named Malachi Webster."

"Heard of him," Hamp Ullmark said. "Heard he wasn't a shinin' lad at all."

"That he wasn't."

There was silence for a bit before Thorne said, "All right, boys, take George down. We'll bury him this afternoon."

Two men went to take Lynch's body from the

horse but stopped when Worley asked, "What about his horse? The one Cooper's ridin'?"

"I'm keepin' it," Cooper said before Thorne could interject.

"Like hell you are, boy," Worley snapped. "You want that horse or any other, you'll have to pay for it."

"He don't need it."

"Don't matter none. It ain't yours, and it ain't your decision."

"Ain't your horse either, nor is it your decision. I aim to ride out on it, and ain't no one here gonna stop me."

"You sure about that, boy? There's seven, eight of us here. You gonna take us all on?"

"If I have to. I've faced a heap worse odds before. But it don't look like anyone else here's concerned enough to fuss over it."

"We'll just see about that..."

"That's enough, Worley," Thorne said. He looked up at Cooper, who was still mounted. "The horse is yours."

"Thanks," Cooper said only a little sarcastically. "I'm takin' his pistol and the possibles that go with it. You can keep the rifle. I want all his powder and ball, though."

"Certainly." It was Thorne's turn to sound sarcastic. "Anything else?"

"A good blanket if he has one. What all coffee he has, plus any jerky or pemmican and any other supplies might keep me alive for a few weeks."

"Seems like a lot."

"You boys still have all his plews to split."

There were nods all around.

"You plannin' on leavin' then?" Petey Bester asked.

Cooper nodded. "Reckon I've worn out my welcome amongst you fellers, so I best be on my way."

"Zeke, go fetch what Cooper wants of George's things. Hugh, you and Petey take care of George—after you get the elk unloaded and put some on my fire. George can wait a bit. And Jed, take care of my horse, please. Come on down from that horse, Hawley. Hamp will take care of it."

"Is that wise?" Cooper asked, concerned but not afraid.

"It is. Anyone tries to start something with ye, he'll have to answer to me. Your horse needs a rest, I reckon, and you could use some food before ridin' on."

Cooper hesitated only a few seconds, then dismounted and handed the reins to Hamp Ullmark with a nod. He sat at the fire with Thorne outside the latter's tent.

"What happened out there, Hawley?"

"You questionin' my integrity?" Cooper asked harshly.

"Nope. Just would like to know the particulars."

Cooper nodded, temper easing. "I realized someone was followin' me. Didn't know if it was a mountaineer or an Indian. I found a spot to wait for whoever it was. George came along and I warned him off."

"He say why he was there?"

"Not then. Just said he was huntin', which is a pile of buffler dung. He had no mule for one thing. He left in a different direction, but I didn't trust him. So when I made my camp that evening, I was done eatin' and such before dark, then I went up and waited in the rocks. Sure enough, he come along, and stuck a tomahawk into the log where he figured my head should've been. I shot him in the hand. He started to crawl away, but I shot him in the thigh. That's when he told me his story." He shrugged. "He bled out overnight."

"Do you believe he even had a nephew?" Thorne nodded as Hugh brought over a hunk of elk and hung it over the fire.

"Nope. I figured he knew Anderson—one of the men riding with me, and Brooks—who told him I had killed Webster and figured George was man enough to come after me because Anderson was too yellow-livered to do so himself."

"I didn't know Anderson, but I had heard about Webster down at rendezvous. Heard, too, that you had killed him for defilin' your woman, or tryin' to. Can't blame a man for that."

"Thanks."

"Too bad you've got to ride out. I hate to see you

go. I still would've liked for you to join us, but I reckon that ain't such a shinin' idea now."

"Nope. Don't suppose it is. I ain't sure if I would've stayed anyway, but I hate it bein' decided by something like this."

Thorne nodded. "Most of the boys'd be all right with it. Most will believe you. But there's a couple..."

"Includin' Worley?"

"Especially him. And Jed. I'd as soon as ask them to leave, but they've been with us a spell and are good hands even if they are irascible at times."

"Well, I wouldn't have wanted to stay knowin' it might cause dissension among your boys here. Had enough of that with Elson."

"What really happened to El? You never really said."

Cooper glared at Thorne for a bit, cutting off a piece of meat and chewing slowly. He swallowed and decided the man was simply curious. "Ol' El lost his reason. Ain't sure why. Reckon a feller never knows why. I was takin' a woman back to her band of Nez Percé when he and another feller—kin of his—come after us."

"A woman?"

Cooper hesitated, then said quietly, "His woman."

"You took his woman against his wishes? Mountaineers don't do such a thing."

"I know. But he was abusin' her and..."

"Don't make no never mind."

"I know that too. I knew it then, but I had to make a decision, so I made it. Might've been the wrong one—at least in some people's eyes, but I don't reckon so. She was a widow whose man was killed by Blackfeet. El said he'd take care of her but took her to his robes much sooner than he should have. And then started to lose his reason. My woman figured if we got her to her village where she could be safe, maybe he'd regain his reason and could go and fetch her again."

Thorne nodded slowly. "Damn if choices ain't difficult at times."

"That's a fact."

"And if you're tellin' true, which I believe you are," Thorne said around chewing some meat, "ye made the right decision under the circumstance." He paused, then, said, "That when you put him under?"

Cooper nodded sadly. "Like I said, him and kin— a nephew who joined us that summer—come after me." He shrugged.

"Both of 'em?"

"Yep. I didn't mind makin' wolf bait out of the nephew. He wasn't nothin' more than a duck turd, but damn, putting El under was some difficult." He sighed, blowing out a stream of frosty breath. "He regained his sense for a few seconds just before I was gonna send him across the Divide and begged me to kill him before the dark spirits took him over again. Made it even worse, though I had to do so."

"Damn, between that and that fracas a couple

years ago where I heard ye held off most of the Black-feet Nation makes ye a hell of a mountaineer."

Cooper shrugged, embarrassed. "Wasn't that bad. Just did what needed doin'."

"Ain't what I heard."

"And it ain't likely for a mountaineer to embellish the doin's of one another," Cooper said with a wry grin.

"I nary heard such a thing," Thorne said with a laugh. "All the fellers I know out here speak only the truth at all times."

"I'll try to remember that next time somebody like you starts recountin' his bravery against the Blackfeet and Hudson's Bay boys together."

Both laughed as they continued eating.

———

THE TWO WERE STILL EATING when a couple of the men came by and dropped a few armfuls of Lynch's possibles.

Cooper nodded, finished the last piece of elk he had in hand, rose, and said, "Reckon it's time for me to be on my way, Jim."

Thorne nodded as he also rose. "Reckon I can give ye a hand."

"Eager to get rid of me, eh?" Cooper said with a smile.

"That's a fact. As much as ye eat, if ye stay

around another hour there won't be a piece of meat left in the whole camp."

FIFTEEN

BEING on his own was nothing new for Hawley Cooper. He was used to it, had survived many a time that way. But he missed the companionship of the other mountain men, fellows with whom he could share good times and hard ones, men he could laugh with, drink with, fight with and alongside, men with whom he could swap tales. Even more so, he missed the company of Goes Far, as he had missed the company of Black Moon Woman those years ago. And he realized that he missed his Shoshoni family terribly. He had known it all along, but his mind did not want to bring that into the light because it was, he figured, too painful. And perhaps therein, he wondered, if that was the beginning of his recent misery and unsettledness.

His rejection by Cheyenne Killer, Cuts Throat, and Pony Woman had affected him far more than he had cared to admit, and so he had buried it deeply, leaving him troubled. But his mind still worked underneath, drawing in more things, mixing them around, leaving Cooper with jumbled thoughts, confusion, and an intensifying uneasiness.

As he rode along in his solitude, with an unfamiliar horse under him and a mule laden with too few plews behind him, his mind tried to force him to think of his gloominess and what was causing it. But he fought it off. He wanted to know so that he could go about trying to fix whatever it wasm, but he did not want to let it out into the open where he had to face it. Only one thing had ever filled him with fear—not ferocious animals, hair-raising savages, starving times—Mother Nature and her unpredictable vindictiveness. Until now. Opening his mind to face what was lurking there these days was frightening because it was an unknown that he was not sure he had the strength or will to conquer as he had every other hardship he had faced,

"Dammit! Leave me alone!" he bellowed into the frosty air, sending his words fleeing across the hills in a cloud of cold vapor.

The shout had his new mount dancing in agitation, forcing Cooper to work at controlling it. "Calm down, you wretched devil of a beast," he said, trying to keep his voice soothing. "Calm down." It took a few minutes, but the gelding managed to settle into a serene, normal walk.

"Me and you will have to come to an agreement, you fractious beast," Cooper said in an even voice, not wanting to set the animal off again. For the thousandth time in the three days he had been traveling with the horse, he wished he still had his mare, a tried and trusty steed that at times almost seemed to know what Cooper wanted before he asked for it.

After three nights of poor camps, mostly out in the open, he was hoping to find a more sheltered place to spend the night. But it was not to be that night either. He unsaddled and tended the gelding. Then, as he was unloading the mule, the animal appeared to him to look at him as if to say, "I'm hungry, Hawley."

"So am I," Cooper muttered. "And so's the damn horse."

"Don't care about the horse," the mule said without saying.

"Me either mostly." He shook his head. "Damn, maybe I am losing my reason," Cooper muttered. He finished caring for the big-eared gray beast of burden. Then he gathered wood and built a fire. He placed the next-to-last small piece of elk he had taken from Thorne's camp and placed it over the flames on a green stick. He hoped he would find some game the next day as he had only the little hunk of meat left, and that would be his breakfast in the morning. He had husbanded the elk meat since he left Thorne's winter camp, but it still had only lasted these few days. He had faced far more than enough starving times since he had been in the mountains that he did not look forward to another. Not with all the travails he had encountered in the past few months. He sighed, mumbling, "Well that can wait 'til tomorrow." He was glad though, that he still had a fair amount of coffee, which would last at least a couple of weeks if he was careful with it.

He ate without enthusiasm, had two cups of coffee, and turned in. As he tried to drift off to sleep, he thought, *Reckon things ain't so bad. I got my buffler robe and a blanket, a few plews I can sell, I'm mounted again, have my rifle and a pistol and plenty of powder and ball to go with 'em. And it ain't snowed in a few days. Might not be shinin' times, but I've been in worse fixes.*

He finally nodded off but woke sometime later when the horse and mule began fussing, stomping, neighing, honking. Even as tired as he was, the ruckus roused him, and he awoke with senses instantly alert. He reached for his pistol as he continued to lay where he was, waiting to figure out what was making the sound.

The animals' unease increased, so Cooper rolled out of the robes, pistol in hard. There in the dim starlight and the meager glow of the dwindling fire, he saw the shadow of a wolverine brazenly heading for the meat.

"No you don't, you son of a bitch," Cooper snapped.

The critter stopped at the sound, bared its ferocious fangs, and emitted a high-pitched chirping growl.

Cooper cocked the pistol and fired. "Dammit," Cooper snarled when the ball only winged the creature, which had shifted at the sound of the pistol being cocked.

The wolverine darted forward, but Cooper jumped to the side, keeping the fire between him and the animal. He snatched up a burning branch as the critter darted around the fire and raked Cooper's leg with its long, brutal claws.

Cooper managed to dodge the wolverine's fangs a moment later and jammed the branch, which had little flame but did have a red-hot ember on the end, against the side of the animal's neck.

The creature scurried away, its screeching chatter chilling.

Cooper tossed the empty pistol aside, leaped over the smoldering embers of the fire, dove toward his robe, grabbed his rifle, and rolled, coming to a stop and standing.

The shrieking animal dashed toward him, fangs and claws reaching for Cooper's flesh. Sweating despite the freezing temperature, Cooper dropped to a knee and shoved the rifle barrel forward. He thanked his shining medicine when he managed to jam the barrel into the creature's mouth. The animal let out a devilish sound as it bit down on the metal. Cooper pulled the trigger, and the .54-caliber lead ball roared through the critter's insides, tearing out through its side near the tail.

Still, the animal tried to charge forward, shrieking and chattering in its rage.

Cooper stood his ground, holding the animal at bay. The wolverine's shrieks and efforts soon began to fade. Still, Cooper waited until the beast was barely moving before he pulled the rifle out. He swung it up and slammed the butt down on the wolverine's head, smashing its skull.

Cooper looked down at his leg. Blood was dripping down onto his moccasins. He pulled his pant leg up and shook his head at the furrows running several inches up and down the outside of his calf. "Devilish goddamn critter," he snapped. "I've a good mind to make a hat out of your miserable hide, but I ain't got the wherewithal."

He looked down at the now-not-so-ferocious beast. "I've heard makin' meat out of a critter like you don't sit so well in a feller's meatbag," he said. "I might have to see if that's true if I don't find some game in the next day or two." Though thinking about it, he decided he was not brave enough to take the risk. Being hungry was better than dying from bad meat.

He dragged the dead animal away into the trees in case some scavengers appeared, then went to calm the mule and the horse. Finally, he was back in his bed, trying to forget about the pain in his leg. He figured he would have to do something about it in the morning. Right now, he needed to get back to sleep.

It was still hurting but there was little he could do

except slap some snow on it to try to clean the wound out even though it had started to scab over. He cut a piece of beaver skin to use for bandaging and a thin strip of the same plew to tie it on. *Well, ol' hoss,* he thought, *starvation ain't killed you yet, nor have Blackfoot warriors. Reckon this won't either.*

It was still dark when he stoked up the fire and ate the last of the meat, drank the rest of the coffee in the pot, and sat for a while, staring into the flames, once more wondering where he should go. He could turn northeast, looking to connect with Two-Faces Beaubien and the others, but that did not appeal to him. He wanted nothing to do with people these days. And returning to Goes Far and Strong Bow would be too hard. He would not fetch them until his dark mood had passed for good. If it ever did. That worried him at times, which were getting more frequent.

When the sun had risen in a bright, cloudless sky, he decided that he would just keep moving in the direction he had been heading and try to find a place to winter. In the spring he would head for rendezvous, though he was not certain of that. Lethargically, unhurriedly he loaded the mule, saddled the gelding, packed up his few cooking utensils, mounted his horse, and rode out.

TWO NIGHTS of sleeping on an empty stomach and the second of those nights going without coffee had Cooper beginning to consider killing the mule and living off the meat for a while. The only thing that had gone right was the weather—temperatures just over freezing and no snow. But both were changing fast. Freezing air was sweeping over the land, and dark clouds were building just to the west.

Cooper was beyond swearing at such a turn of events and just kept plodding along hoping he could find a place to hole up for a few days. He hoped even more to spot some game. It had started snowing again, making the former the more urgent, but the best he could find were two stunted pines at the bottom of a bare hill. With a sigh, he muttered, "This'll have to do."

As he unloaded the mule, he once again considered killing the animal for the meat to sustain him. He considered the horse too, since he favored its meat a bit more, but it would be better for riding than the mule.

After hobbling the mule and letting it loose to find what forage it might, Cooper started to unsaddle the horse when he saw a snowshoe hare. He wondered for only a moment what the critter was doing outside its burrow, but he did not care. He carefully pulled out his rifle, aimed, and fired. "Ain't much," he mumbled as he reloaded. "But it's better than horse or mule."

He got the hare, then finished unsaddling the

gelding, which he also hobbled and let loose. He gutted and skinned the hare, then built up a fire. Before long, the meat was sizzling over the flames. He forced himself to wait until the meat was at least warm throughout, then grabbed it and started wolfing it down. It was gone in mere minutes.

"Well," he said as he tossed the last bone in the fire, "it didn't fill my meatbag for certain, but at least it'll stop it from rumblin' too much for a spell anyway."

He looked up and shook his head as the snow started again. He once again considered butchering the mule, but decided against it just yet, as he sat out two more hungry, snowy days before he was finally able to pull out, still heading southeast with no plan other than to find a place to winter.

SIXTEEN

COOPER FOUND the small canyon with a combination of luck and an educated guess. He worried a bit as he explored the place, learning that there was no way in or out other than the way he had entered the canyon. The sidewalls were no higher than forty feet at their tallest. They were sharply sloped in most places, but not perpendicular. A frozen creek wove through the cottonwoods, willows, and some aspens on the southwest side. Various brush spread over the open parts of the valley. Unlike outside the canyon, where the snow was still a foot deep in most places, the canyon had but a few inches.

Cooper stopped and scanned the area. There was water, plenty of wood, and sufficient supplies of sweet cottonwood bark for the animals. The only thing missing was meat on the hoof, though he thought he did see a few elk at the far end of the canyon. The light and shadow might be playing tricks on his eyes, but it left him with at least a little hope that he could feed himself as well as the animals. And the weather appeared to be rather benevolent for the time and place, though he had been wrong about such things before.

He nodded. "This'll shine, it will," he said.

Since it was late in the day, he hurriedly tended the animals, gathered firewood, started a fire, and began cooking another rabbit he had shot that day. He grumbled as a chill rain started while he was climbing into his sleeping robe.

In the morning, he set about his two most important chores in making his camp—building a lean-to and cutting up cottonwood bark for the animals. The work was long and tedious, though not very difficult. The off and on rain made it more so, but he persevered, trying to let the drudgery keep his demons at bay for a spell, though often with little success.

But after two days, he had a sizable and rather sturdy lean-to and sufficient forage for the animals to last almost a week if he kept them from getting too much at any one time.

So the next day he rode out, aiming to see if there was a herd of elk in the canyon. But if he had seen them, they were now gone. The only evidence that any elk had been there was the pretty well-worked-over carcass of one that had fed a mountain lion or two or perhaps a small pack of wolves. He dismounted and checked the carcass. It was no more than two or three days old and what was left—very little—had been preserved well enough in the freezing temperatures. Cooper gathered what few scraps he found. They would make a small but welcome meal. He would worry about later days when they arrived. But to help make do in the interim, he set several rabbit traps on his way back to camp. They worked and so Cooper had meat. It wasn't much and didn't nearly fill his stomach, but it was far better than nothing.

So he settled in, not doing much besides caring for the animals, making sure that what little gear he had was in proper working order. And watching the rain and snow when it appeared. The first time that snow showed up worried Cooper. It was coming down hard and fast. But it started, slowed, stopped, started, stopped, and started again. In between were short bouts of rain, which helped wash much of the snow away. After two days, there was less than a half foot of it on the ground, though it was covered with ice.

IT WAS late in the afternoon, a mild one if just below freezing could be called mild, much to Cooper's surprise, and he was sharpening his knife when he heard someone or something crunching slowly through the ice-crusted snow outside the lean-to. He put down the honing stone, slid the knife back into its sheath, grabbed his rifle, and stepped outside. In the dim afternoon sunlight, he saw an old buffalo bull a hundred yards away.

Cooper smiled a little. Poor bull was not the best eating, but it was meat and more filling than rabbit, even if it was tough and stringy. He raised the rifle, took aim, and brought the weapon down, uncocking it as he did. He set the butt in the snow and leaned on the muzzle, watching.

The bull shuffled slowly toward him either not noticing the mountain man or not caring. As the animal neared him, Cooper saw the ravages of a hard life that had worn down the old fellow. The bull carried the marks of that rough existence—a horn missing several inches off the point, scars spread all over him, a decided limp, his head hanging low in the defeat that time had dealt him.

Cooper started to raise the rifle again but stopped before he had it halfway to his shoulder. Instead, he slung it across his back. There was no way he would shoot this old fellow. It would be, he realized, like shooting himself, for he too, bore the scars of a rough life. The only difference was that he was not willing to give up everything and die as apparently the old buffalo had done.

Cooper walked to the tree on which hung forage for his horse and mule, keeping it out of the way so they could not eat it all at once. He lowered the "basket" he had made of beaver hide, grabbed a few pieces of sweet cottonwood bark, hauled the forage back up, and walked unafraid toward the bull.

The buffalo watched him warily, snuffled a few times, then pawed the snow with his front hooves. He turned his great head defiantly toward the mountain man and pawed the ground a few more times as if preparing to charge.

"You don't want to do that, ol' boy," Cooper said calmly as he got within a few feet of the animal. "Couple ol' fellers like us ought to be able to live our last days in as much comfort as we can find. Ain't no call for you and me to have us a disagreement."

The bull grunted a few times.

One look told Cooper that the old bull could barely see and that his hide had some fresh wounds, strong evidence that a younger, tougher bull had forced the older companion from the herd.

The mountain man held out a piece of the bark. "Here you go, ol' feller. A tasty little snack to take your mind off your worries for a short spell."

The bull sniffed at it, then took a small bite and chewed slowly. Then again.

"You're welcome to spend the night here with me and my animals if you'd like, maybe eat a little more, keep you goin' a while."

As he continued to feed the big beast, he began to feel ridiculous. "Ain't bad enough I been talkin' to the mule like it was a person, one with sense and talkin' back, now I'm chattin' with a buffler bull as I'm hand feedin' him," he muttered, shaking his head. Then he grinned. "Well, reckon it ain't as dumb as some of the things I've done in my life. And this ol' boy looks mighty peaceful right now." He raised a hand and patted the matter fur on the bull's massive forehead. "'Sides, couple ol' fellers like us all alone need some company now and again, eh? And you've been hard used, boy, worse'n me by a long shot, I'd say. Best take what comfort you can."

Cooper turned back to the lean-to, tossing out pieces of bark as he went. He worried a little about turning his back on the large beast, then laughed at himself. "That ol' boy ain't got the wherewithal to do you any harm, Hawley. Stop your frettin'."

When he got back to his shelter, he turned and looked. The bull was following along slowly, stopping to eat each piece of bark as he came to it. He stood watching for a little. The animal looked to be in even worse shape than Cooper had thought. He considered shooting the beast and ending its misery. Then he shook his head. It was selfish on one hand and foolish on the other, but in the few minutes since the bull had shown up, Cooper had developed a feeling for the bull, a kinship, really, between two old veterans of the savage mountains and savage land in which they lived. No, he could not kill the old fellow; not yet at least.

"Well, it's robe time for this oil' chil', boy. Bed down wherever you want long as it ain't in my robes." He smiled, though it was a bit sad.

COOPER WOKE, rose, and looked around. The bull was not in sight. For the past three days, the buffalo had slept—or not—close to the lean-to. Cooper sighed, figuring the creature had wandered off somewhere. But then, in the dim light of the foggy dawn, he saw ravens and a vulture or two circling not far off. "Damn," he muttered. He grabbed his rifle and stepped off.

The birds scattered noisily as he neared. As he had figured, the bull was down, but to his surprise, the animal was still breathing, though barely. He stood looking down at the bull for some moments, a sense of sadness and loss growing within him again.

Suddenly he scooped up a few handfuls of snow and flung them at the birds. "Get away from here, you devilish goddamn critters," he bellowed. They left, but not very far, and remained circling lazily in the air.

"Reckon your time here on this earth is about over, ol' boy," Cooper said, a slim modicum of happiness rising in him. "But even as stringy and as poor-tastin' as your meat's gonna be, it'll fill my meatbag and keep me from meetin' up with you in the Happy Huntin' Ground. I know the Blackfeet and Shoshonis and others will still hunt you there, but the Great Spirit Willin', all their arrows, and lead balls, and lances will miss their mark so you can roam free and proud, once again the mighty critter you were."

Cooper sighed again and shook his head, shaking off the sentimentality. He placed the muzzle of his Dickert rifle against the side of the bull's head between the eye and ear and pulled the trigger.

The buffalo jerked once and let loose a short grunt. Its legs jerked weakly a few times, then quieted. Cooper reloaded his rifle and leaned it against the dead bull's neck. Then he pulled his knife, knelt, and made his first slice into the tough hide.

He spent much of the morning butchering out all the meat he could, wrapping it in pieces of hide, occasionally he tossed a handful of pebbled snow at the birds that had landed and were strutting around. He was not afraid that they would really try to get some meat while he was working, but they annoyed him anyway, so he irritated them. For his amusement, he now and again tossed a piece of meat—a small one— at the birds and watched as they fought over the scrap of food.

He finally finished, carried the heavy parcels close to his lean-to, and used the last of his rope to haul all of them but one up into a tree. He was certain he could leave them on the ground, at least for a few days as the bull's carcass would attract the scavengers, if any other than the birds were around, first. But he could see no reason to tempt some ravenous wolves or coyotes.

He washed the blood off his hands in a very small snowdrift and then eagerly set a hunk of the meat on the fire. Before long, he was digging his teeth into the flesh. As he had known it would be, the meat was chewy and tough, but it was buffalo and sent a wave of pleasure through him even though he had to gnaw a little more than usual on the sinewy flesh.

SEVENTEEN

WHILE HE WAS SITTING THERE CHEWING on the fibrous meat, he kept a watch out to where the carcass lay. He was not sentimental about animals—except the mare, which had been an exceptional animal. But something about the old bull's last days was sitting inside of him, trying to carve a hole in his...what? he wondered. His heart? His mind?

He finally shook his head. He had become too maudlin, something that had been growing in him since...

He sat up straighter, food forgotten. It all came to him, thoughts and unknown feelings that had been riding heavily on his shoulder for months began to coalesce.

Trouble and death had been his constant companions since he had met the dreadful Josiah Weeks in St. Louis a decade or so ago. Since then, he had ridden out those troubles either by overcoming them or ignoring them in his drive to survive in such a harsh land as the Rocky Mountains. Or in his desire for revenge over the losses of loved ones or against those who had done him wrong, and there were many of them, both red and white.

Since that fateful day in St. Louis, misfortune had been a regular visitor—a too-frequent regular visitor—in his life.

Over the years he had been in the mountains he had met with much good fortune, it was true: The love of two good women, friendship with good men, an almost bigger-than-life status as both a trapper and an Indian fighter, and the respect of other mountaineers.

But he realized now that the bad had come to outweigh the good. It had taken this long, these many years, to see that mainly, he knew now, the misfortune had been interspersed with the fortunate. The good followed the bad regularly it seemed from the beginning when he met the deplorable Weeks. And it had followed over the years, from being left unconscious with nothing to use for survival in the dead of winter, to the violation of Goes Far by Malachi Webster. From the death of Weeks's Pawnee woman, Tall Grass, to the death of Black Moon Woman at the hands of the Crows. From his being saved by Cheyenne Killer to...the loss of that family.

As he stared across the dark meadow, from which

he could still hear the scavengers feeding on the bull's carcass, he realized that that loss had hurt him more than he had wanted to admit. He had, he knew, a new family with Goes Far, Strong Bow, and others in the Nez Percé village, but it was not the same. He could not say why; he just knew it was true. It was the culmination of a life filled with loss—of friends like Zeke Potts, the Flatheads who had saved his life, and Duncan MacTavish. And worse, the death of Elson Brooks at his hands.

And it was a life that had been filled with blood— that of savage Crows, dozens of even more savage Blackfeet, and foul, evil, White men like Weeks, Webster, and almost too many more to count.

In just the past few years, he had lost Black Moon Woman, one of his best friends in Zeke Potts, another friend in Brooks. And then his family—because of a decision on his part made in the heat of a fraught few moments that could have cost the lives of many men, both his fellow trappers, or the Shoshonis they were visiting.

Nothing had cut him so deep, he now realized, than his rejection by his Shoshoni family. And he could see no way to restore that relationship.

The winter before Black Moon was taken, the two of them had spent an awful time in the mountains, snowed in for weeks, short on food, down to one weakening horse, plews gone, and he with just three lead balls and enough powder to send them on their way. One day, during the worst of it Cooper had told Black Moon that he feared only one thing—not savage Indians nor wild animals—Mother Nature. He could fight Blackfeet, hold his own against grizzlies or wolves, but against a sometimes-malevolent Nature, he had no defense other than an indefatigable will to survive.

Now, he realized, he had another fearsome, infernal enemy, one he was not sure he could defeat —his own future. And in that, he would be fighting himself. His decisions might not be fatal but they could leave him with nothing.

Cooper had thought frequently over the past year or so about what the future would hold for him. He had become more and more convinced that the beaver trade was dying and its death was coming increasingly fast. Suppliers coming from St. Louis had been telling the men at the past couple of rendezvous that beaver was being replaced with silk as the material of choice for top hats. Many of the men did not want to believe it, thinking that it was a plot by the traders to build their profits by paying too little for the furs and asking too much for supplies. Cooper wasn't sure, but he was certain the trade could not last much longer, silk or no silk. He had found the take over the past year was greatly diminished, and by listening to some of the other trappers at rendezvous, others had seen it too, though many did not want to consider that beaver would ever be trapped out. But Cooper did believe it. And with the demise of the beaver trade, he faced an uncertain future at best.

He had thought more than once over the past year what he would do if he had to give up trapping for his living, and the answer was...well, he had decided there was no answer, at least not yet. The trouble was, he was not sure he would ever find an answer.

First off, he had no trade other than trapping. Well, and fighting Indians. There was little call for either in the Settlements. He had been born and raised on a farm, but he had no liking for it when he was young, and even less interest in it now. He could not see himself as a store clerk, though he supposed he could apprentice to a gunmaker or some such. Hunting to supply towns or trading posts might work, though that seemed an unreliable way to provide for himself and his family, if he even decided to take Goes Far and Strong Bow to some town.

And that brought with it a whole new set of problems. What would he do with them? Some of the frontier towns would still accept an Indian wife and half-breed child. But as civilization—if one could call it that, Cooper thought—grew, which was inevitable, that might change. He wasn't sure either that his Nez Percé woman would want to leave her tribe to live in a city. She would be without family, except for Cooper and their child, or friends or foods, and customs that were her people's way. The boy, Cooper supposed, could be educated and perhaps learn a trade. Cooper had heard that some of the mountain men, like Jim Bridger and Kit Carson, had sent children back to family or trusted friends in Missouri to be taken care of and receive an education.

Leaving her behind did not enter his mind. He loved her and was unwilling, maybe even unable, to let go of her. It was agony for him to have left her now while he figured things out. On the other hand, if he couldn't solve the demons that were rummaging around inside him, it would be best for Goes Far and the boy to be left with her people.

He could, he knew, stay with the Nez Percé. They would welcome him, and he would be accorded the respect due to a mighty warrior and hunter. He would have a wife, a child, a surrogate father in Pale Thunder, and even a brother in Sits Down. But he doubted that he would be happy there at least as a permanent home. He enjoyed the Nez Percé, their way of life mostly, and the comforts of a village. But he was not a Nez Percé and as close as he was to the People, he would never be one and likely would be uncomfortable there before long. Besides, he didn't know what he would do there either.

It would be different if he were able to live with Cheyenne Killer's band. The Shoshonis had, in a way, raised him, made a man of him. He spoke their language, knew their ways and customs, and was comfortable among them. Living with them might also become uncomfortable for him, but he suspected it would not for a time. He would be at least content until he decided what to do with his life.

"Well, put that idea out of your head, Hawley," he muttered. "That notion is deader'n that ol' bull out yonder. Deader'n ol' Zeke and ol' Elson, and ol' Duncan and..." He drew in and blew out a gust of breath. "Well, ain't no decision to be made now." He stretched out and pulled his robe over him, but sleep was long in coming.

———

COOPER WAS cranky in the morning as he fed the horse and mule and set to a breakfast of tough buffalo meat. Despite all his realizations the night before, he still had no answers, and he was beginning to think he might never have any.

"Bah," he growled about his gloomy thoughts as he saddled the horse. The animal seemed to be getting more used to him so caused less of a fuss most of the time. This wasn't one of those times.

"Hold still, dammit," Cooper snapped. "I get this damn saddle on you, we'll go for a ride, let you stretch your legs some. So quit givin' me trouble."

The horse settled some and Cooper finally mounted and rode off. When he reached the bull's carcass, having scared off the few remaining scavenger birds, he stopped and looked down. There was little left—the skull with a few small bits of flesh, and bones scattered around as wolves and coyotes had fought over the meat. He dismounted, took out his tomahawk, and kneeled. He grabbed one horn in his left hand and lifted the tomahawk, ready to chop the horn off.

With a shake of his head, he rose and slipped the weapon away. "No, ol' feller," he said quietly. "You've had enough of your dignity taken already. No need for me to add to it. You'll need those when you get to the Great Spirit's world. 'Sides," he added with a small grin, "it might be selfish of me, but maybe Mother Nature will smile a bit fondly at me. 'Least I hope so. Farewell."

Cooper mounted his horse again and was about to ride off when he looked down once more, melancholy settling over him anew. "Maybe my time on this here earth has been used up too, old friend." Which is how he had come to think of the worn old bull. Maybe I should quit fightin' so much to stay alive and let the angels—or the devil—take me into their embrace." As he rode off, though, he knew he would not do so. His survival instinct was too strong and would not let him give in to anything—savage Indians, savage beasts, savage weather, savage land, or savage times.

Thinking himself a fool for his sentimentality over a dead animal the likes of which he had frequently hunted for meat without a thought, he kicked the horse into a gallop, giving the animal its head. He enjoyed the freezing wind against his face, at least for a time, and the horse seemed energized by the run.

A few miles down the canyon, he pulled the horse to a stop and turned back. He had hoped to find some elk but there were no animals to be found other than two rabbits caught in his primitive traps. He thought of leaving them but decided to take them, for a little change in his diet if nothing else.

EIGHTEEN

MALICIOUS MOTHER NATURE finally began to loosen her grip on the little canyon, and Cooper decided it was time to plan to get back on the trail. Unlike other places he had traveled in the cold months or wintered up, the canyon had been reasonably comfortable. There had been less snow, and the wind was not as vicious and life-sapping. But there was no game. The sinewy meat from the old bull had lasted a few weeks, and there had been the occasional rabbit caught in one of the traps. But the food was never enough, and Cooper began to grow gaunt. The animals did, too, as forage for them lessened as the weeks passed.

Cooper rode out one day, letting the horse pick its way slowly through the canyon. Cooper had found another large grove of cottonwoods. He peeled off a hundred pounds or so and tied it across his saddle, then walked the horse back to his camp. The gelding and the mule were mighty pleased to have some new food, though it only lasted two days before Cooper had to make another trek. And another. And another.

But one day he stood outside his lean-to, which had become rather disheveled as it had been battered by snow, wind, rain, and sleet, surveying his canyon, as he now thought of it. Some sprigs of green were popping out in places on the ground, the bushes and trees. It was a welcome sigh. The temperature, which had edged several degrees above freezing, was also a welcome change, though he knew it would not last for any length of time. "This'd make a grand place to live someday," he said aloud. He could see a fine cabin, maybe even a real house under the trees to the east near the creek. He could envision a couple dozen —maybe even a hundred—horses and mules or cattle lazily grazing on the rich grass he expected would be covering the meadow before long.

He sighed. It made for a wonderful picture, but it would not be for him. It would be many years before such a thing could take place here. There would have to be towns and farms whose people would need to buy the animals, and this was far too secluded an area to expect anything like that to arrive here for many years.

Besides, there were the Indians to consider, maybe. He was surprised that he had seen few Blackfeet about. Of course, there could be a thousand of

them within a mile of this place and he wouldn't
know it unless they attacked or he stumbled on them.
Still, it seemed odd. He had never gone so long
without finding some Blackfoot warriors roaming the
land looking to raise hair or steal horses. Well, it
might be odd, but he was thankful for it whatever the
reason.

———————

THREE DAYS later he decided it was time to leave.
The day before a few deer had wandered into the
canyon, and he made short work of a doe who, after
the long winter, was not nearly as plump as he would
have liked. But she would provide meat, which would
be tastier than anything he had had in a while.

He tied the meat, his plews, and buffalo robe, and
few cooking utensils to the mule's back. As he did, he
said, feeling foolish again but at least with a little
chuckle, "Nothing to say, Big Ears?"

His chuckles increased a little as he imagined the
mule responding, "Didn't want you to slow down. I
want to get on the move."

"Me too, Big Ears. Me too."

———————

THEY RODE out under a bright but cold sun,
moving slowly. Cooper did not want to tax the
animals, and he was in no hurry. He figured he could

use the time on the trail to decide what to do and how to defeat the demons that were threatening his existence—or at least the existence he had known for more than a decade. He vowed to himself that he would not let that happen without a fight. He had faced hordes of Blackfeet, stunningly vicious winters, and more. This would not defeat him.

With the earliest beginnings of spring, grass and other greenery were blooming, and the two animals ate their fill whenever they could. And within two days—two hungry days—meat on the hoof was found. Not a lot, perhaps, but enough to keep Cooper's belly full for the most part. He had to be careful with his ammunition; however, running out of powder and ball when he had such a long way to go to rendezvous, much if not most of it through hostile Indian country, would be foolish—and possibly fatal.

The days stayed sunny and almost warm for this time of year, though the nights still had temperatures below freezing. There were a few snow flurries and some cold rain, but they didn't last long, and Cooper thought that the worst was over. Until late one morning when thick, black clouds rumbled across the sky and began leaving a legacy of snow behind. The wind picked up and the temperature dropped. There was no place of refuge before the wooded hillside he could vaguely see a couple miles away, and he was not happy about it.

"Goddammit I hate snow and cold and wind. Damn you Mother Nature. I don't know what I ever did to you to curse me like this so often, but I goddamn resent it. You must be the meanest critter God or the Great Spirit ever created. Goddamn witch, you're colder than the damn temperatures you keep sendin' my way. Leave me alone, goddammit, you saggy-teated old hag. You ain't put me under yet with all your curses and poor dealin's, you invisible shit pot, and I'll be good and damned if I'll let you do so now either."

His anger grew as the horse and mule began to fidget, not liking the weather any more than Cooper did. He fought the reins and the mule's rope for a while, but what little patience he had vanished quickly. He suddenly stopped and turned in the saddle, glaring at the mule.

"I told you before, more than once, you thick-headed son of a bitch, that if you kept actin' up, I'd be eatin' mule steaks and rump meat. It'd like as not make me sick, but I'd do it. This is your last warnin', you fractious, flap-eared walkin' sack of wolf bait. Ain't you, me, or the horse likes bein' out in this weather, but you fussin' ain't makin' the goin' any easier. Now behave yourself and you might make it through the night."

He turned forward again and moved on, picking up speed just a little.

Three hours later, he stopped at the bottom of a small, sloped, tree-sprinkled hill. The hill stopped most of the wind, which was coming from the north. It was a great relief. The place offered little respite from the snow and cold, though. Hungry, tired, and growing angrier by the hour, Cooper set about caring for the animals. When he was done, he patted each animal on the neck a few times. "You fellers have been a lot better of late as we ride," he said. "I'm obliged," Despite his anger, he was somewhat sorry he had chastised the mule. The two critters were as hungry and tired as he was and had gone through everything he had. "You two'll have to find your own feed though."

He set about putting together a fire under a spruce's thick, heavy branches. It wasn't perfect but it was the best he could do at building a fire and keeping it going. He pulled out a several-pound hunk of buffalo hump that he had picked up the day before when he chased a small pack of wolves and lesser scavengers away from the buffalo carcass they had been gnawing at. He ate about half of it, saving the last for the morning. All the while he cursed anything and anyone he could think of, but mostly the vindictive Mother Nature.

Finished eating, he checked his supply of coffee and realized he was down to enough beans for maybe one pot, if that. He debated whether to have it now or save it for morning. He finally settled on the morrow. Pulling his blanket and robe around him, he leaned back against a tree and drifted off to sleep.

He enjoyed the coffee in the morning but it did little to improve his temperament, especially with the day starting the way the previous one had ended—

with lightly falling snow, a swirling mist, and freezing temperatures.

As he was loading the mule, he found himself in another one way "conversation" with the animal.

"Don't look at me that way, dammit," Cooper snapped. "I didn't ask for this weather."

"You sure? It's been this way since I joined you," was the imagined response.

"It's gonna be that way 'til you leave me, too—and that's when you go under. Now mind your manners."

Riding around the hill to get back on their trail, the wind slapped hard at them again. "Damn," Cooper muttered. The two animals seemed to agree.

The weather improved as they rode throughout the day. By the time they found a place to make another camp, the temperature, Cooper estimated, was in the forties, the snow had stopped in the late morning, and the wind was down to a light breeze.

The next week and a half were more of the same weather, and life grew better for man and beast. Grass was popping up all over and trees and bushes were proudly showing off their newfound life. The animals were greatly pleased, and the mule stopped arguing with Cooper, even if it was just in the mountain man's mind. As they rode, Cooper muttered to himself for what seemed to be the hundredth time, "You really must be losin' your reason, ol' hoss. Any chil' hears you conversin' with a mule who ain't—who can't—say anything will for sure tie you down 'til you regained it. Or until you chewed off an arm and a leg to run off screamin' into the wilderness." He even laughed, an unusual case for him these days. It was so rare, that the animals were spooked for a few moments.

That raised Cooper's humor a little. Doing so even more was the fact that game was beginning to appear regularly—deer, elk, the occasional small herd of buffalo. The only drawback to it was that the more game that showed up, the more predators did too. An increasing number of bears hungry after a winter's worth of hibernation, a few mountain lions, and plenty of wolves. Cooper was glad that there were enough herbivores and small game that the predators were kept busy and did not bother Cooper.

A week and a half after weathering the last storm, another started edging up on them. Cooper kept an eye out behind him as dark, heavy clods rolled across the valley. The wind edged up, then began hurtling toward them at increasing speed, pushing the best possible spot for at least a minimal amount of protection from the storm miles away yet as best he could tell.

While he knew they couldn't outrun the storm, they could make it chase them a little harder, he figured. "Let's go fellers," he yelled as he kicked the horse into a run.

They were about halfway to the possible shelter when the storm swept over them. Cooper tried to get a little more speed out of the animals, and they raced along, pushed by the wind and the snow swirling around them.

Cooper spotted something that didn't seem right just a short distance ahead of them. "Holy hell!" he bellowed as he yanked on the reins with all his strength.

NINETEEN

IT WAS NOT ENOUGH.

Man, horse, and mule went over the edge of the small canyon's lip, bouncing and tumbling down the rocky, dirt-, ice- and sage-covered slope, crashing to the bottom and landed. The horse slammed against a large boulder, the mule bounced off a tree, then several small boulders before coming to a halt tangled in several bushes clinging to the side of the hill. Cooper flipped and flopped like a rag doll as he bounced down the hill. He finally managed to grab a sapling and bring himself to a dusty, painful stop. He lay there for some minutes, listening to the frantic braying of the mule and frightened whinnying of the horse. "Can't help you right now, fellers," he mumbled.

He finally tried to pick himself up, but failed, falling back, breathing heavily as pain rippled through him.

He groaned. He decided to lay there, not moving as his mind probed his body trying to assess the damage while trying to ignore the snow. His head was pounding, making him close his eyes every few seconds, trying to will the pain away. His back hurt and his midsection ached, the latter from bruised muscles, not damaged ribs, or so he hoped. One knee had been twisted and a shoulder throbbed. He ached all over. He felt worse than he had a couple of years ago when he, Zeke Potts, and Sits Down had faced the horde of Blackfeet who had raided Cooper and his fellow mountain men in the valley where they had been wintering.

The animals' shrieks of agony and fear were lessening, but Cooper knew he should put them out of their misery. He took a deep breath and let it out slowly. Then he grabbed the small boulder on which he had come to rest and started to push himself up. He hissed as agony roared through him from his head to his knees. He slumped, then fell, the side of his head brushing the boulder. The fight deserted him as did his consciousness.

COOPER DID NOT KNOW how long he had been out, though the snow had stopped. It could've been a minute or a week, though he was sure it was much closer to the former, but not too close. The struggles and pain of the two animals had dwindled almost to nothing, so he figured they were close to dead. Pain still stretched throughout most of his body, but his head was the worst, throbbing and pounding with each heartbeat.

"Damn," he muttered. He knew he should get up and start taking care of business, but his body refused to cooperate. He sighed and let himself drift back into the comforting arms of unconsciousness.

ONCE AGAIN COOPER had no idea of how long he had been out. The aches in his body had diminished but his head was still thumping. After a few minutes, he decided it was time for him to try getting up again. But still, he hesitated. Finally, he sucked in a deep breath and let it ease out. Then he pushed himself up.

His head roared in pain as if the worst thunderstorm he had ever encountered was tripled and banging around in his skull. He stood a few moments, weaving, then plopped heavily down again. His breathing was ragged and heavy, and he felt that his nose was broken. Somewhere in the back of his mind, his brain was telling him not to do it, but he stretched out, rested his head on a bent forearm and let the relief of darkness slip gratefully over him once more.

He awoke, he knew not when, but it was getting to be late in the day he could tell by the falling sun and the sliding temperature. Cold was seeping into his body, and he knew he needed to do something about it, but he was mighty reluctant. It was easier just to sit here and watch the world drift past him. But after a few minutes, he forced himself to stand. He spotted sunlight glinting off his rifle barrel several feet away. He walked to it, knelt, and picked it up. It was battered and covered with dirt but seemed unbroken and serviceable.

Cooper shuffled carefully to the horse, which was closer than the mule. He leaned the rifle against the horse's withers. The animal looked up with pain-filled eyes. There was life in him yet but it was very faint. Cooper knelt and with no emotion, slit the horse's throat.

He went to the mule, which had a little more life in it than the horse. Not much, but enough to where its eyes pleaded, "Fix me."

Cooper almost smiled. One more "conversation" with the beast would not be such a bad thing and this time would not make him think he was losing his mind. "Nothin' I can do, ol' hoss," he said sadly.

"I ain't a horse, I'm a mule."

"You been with me and the other boys long enough that you qualify as a mountaineer, so you're ol' hoss, just like the rest of us."

"Nothin' you can do?"

"No. You're all stove up inside. Hell, you ain't far from crossin' over now.'

"Then do it."

Cooper nodded, patted the animal on the head a few times, and then cut its throat too.

He pushed himself wearily to his feet. He stumbled around, gathering firewood, trying to ignore the roaring pain in his head and the shifting, grinding ache in his knee. He got a blaze going, then cut out a hunk of horse meat and hung it over the fire to cook. Before long he was chowing down. The food, while not all that tasty, gave him a little strength and energy.

Finished, he stumbled back to the mule and ignored the crushing agony that coursed through him as he tugged his blanket and buffalo robe free. Then he gave in to the pains, rolled himself in the robe, and fell asleep.

He woke and slept for three days—he thought it was three days but he was not sure—before he really felt like getting up to do something other than to relieve himself. He rebuilt the fire and cooked up some horse meat—which had stayed fresh in the still-cold temperatures.

As he ate, he cast his eyes around. "You're in some poor doin's, hoss, and there ain't no use denyin' it," he told himself.

He was hundreds of miles, he figured, from where rendezvous would be held or where there might be a trading post, though he had no idea of where one was. He was still in territory roamed by Blackfeet and Crow, neither of whom he wanted to deal with. He was afoot with a minimum of supplies, though they were important ones—rifle, pistol, a fair amount of powder, ball, and caps, a knife, tomahawk, blanket, buffalo robe, possibles bag with fire-making equipment and other small tools, and capote. "Ain't much," he muttered with a wry smile, "but it's a heap more than you had when Josiah Weeks left you."

Still, he sat there considering just giving up the ghost, leaving himself to the clutches of the vindictive Mother Nature or one of her savage minions, either animal or man.

Then he spit in anger. "Like hell you will, Hawley Cooper. That bitch ain't got you yet after all these years, I'll be damned if I'll let her get me now."

He laughed almost bitterly. "Well, now that that is settled, just how are you gonna do that?"

He was in a bad position. He was not sure how far it was to rendezvous, only that he had a long way to go, several weeks at least, he figured. The village where Goes Far and Strong Bow were was as far as rendezvous he figured. Spring was almost here despite the late winter season storms, and then there was summer. That meant there would be game in most places. It also meant traveling in sizzling heat, often without water for a couple of days. And it meant mosquitoes and other annoyances. And it meant the savages would be on the warpath for real, not just some small winter forays—the battle with the horde of Blackfeet two years ago notwithstanding— looking to steal horses or attack some lonely mountain men to raise hair.

Well, he decided, he would decide when he decided.

He spent another week where he was, allowing himself some time to recover. The head cleared up fairly quickly. The abdomen muscles were a different story, though, even after he bound them in a broad strip of beaver plew. Every task he tried to do renewed the pain in them. The wrenched knee was more of a problem. He felt as if the pieces were grinding together with every step. But after a week, he decided he could sit here no longer, stove up knee or not.

He woke two mornings later and somehow knew it was the day to leave. He ate more horse-meat, then set about getting ready. There was almost nothing to do. He rolled his blanket in the buffalo robe and tied it into a long, heavy bundle that he would hang over his shoulder. He wrapped an estimated thirty pounds of meat in a hunk of the horse's hide. He emptied his large possibles sack—the one he carried on his horse—of anything he didn't think he would need anytime soon. He considered adding the coffeepot to the sack then decided against it. He had no beans to make coffee and the possibility of getting some was next to noth-ing, if that.

He pulled on his capote, hung the buffalo robe-blanket bundle over a shoulder, and the meat and possibles bag over the other shoulder, grunting with each maneuver. Gritting his teeth against the renewed pain, and with rifle in hand, he strode out of the camp, not looking back.

———————

THE HORSEMEAT KEPT him going relatively strong for the first five days, but when it ran out, he slowed down, and by the end of a week, he was struggling, even though he had now been relieved of the weight of the meat. Still, he pushed on, footsteps becoming slower and more plodding with every mile he went. Across meadows, up and down hills where no path existed and he had to hack his weary way through underbrush, climb over boulders and fallen trees, wade freezing creeks, skirt severe drop-offs of the kind that had left him in this situation.

More than two weeks after he had left, he pulled to a stop in a grove of trees alongside a small rolling ridge of land and dropped the deer he had been dragging along for the past two or three miles and slumped against a tree trunk, not bothering to take off his bundles. He was too tired. As he rested his head against the tree, he breathed a sigh of relief at having found the place. He was exhausted, more used up than he had ever been. He wanted not just to sleep, but to fade into oblivion, be done with all the pain and tiredness. But he gritted his teeth.

"Nope," he said aloud. "All along I figured it was Mother Nature aimin' to put me under, but I realize now I was wrong, Lord, whoever you might be. She's just your minion. I reckon. Now, while I'm obliged you're lookin' forward to meetin' me in person, Lord, I ain't ready to make a visit—especially a permanent visit—to you just yet. You want me sittin' up there by your side, you best do it yourself or have someone down here do it for you. Mother Nature ain't capable of puttin' me under, and I ain't goin' under just for your enjoyment."

He smiled a little despite his exhaustion. "'Course, it's likely it ain't really you. Maybe you're just lookin' down enjoyin' me bein' tormented for all the sins I may have committed. And I got to admit, there's been a heap of 'em. No, it's more likely your dark counterpart down below that's itchin' to make my acquaintance personally. You can tell him what I just told you when you see him. And tell him I'd be pleased to meet him here on my ground and discuss it with him or have him come agin me, see which one of us can best the other. He might win, but damn, he'll have a fight on his hands. "Waugh!"

A moment later he was asleep.

TWENTY

HAWLEY COOPER LEANED AGAINST A TREE, exhausted, his emaciated body weakened by his long trek. But the end was near, he figured. If he had had any energy, he might have smiled. It would be a different end than he had expected for the past week or so. At least he hoped so.

He didn't know how he knew, but he was certain the camp he sensed a hundred yards or more ahead was that of Two-Faces Beaubien and his compatriots. He pushed himself off the tree and stumbled forward. A few minutes later, a voice drifted out of the growing dusk. "Stop where y'all are, mister, lest y'all catch a lead ball in your lights."

"I'll stop when I'm damned good and ready, hoss," Cooper said, almost managing a shout.

"Hawley?" Bill White asked in surprise. "That you?"

"One and the very same," Cooper said as he shuffled forward.

"Well, come on in, hoss."

"I'm gettin' there."

White thought that strange. He moved out from behind the larch he had been using for protection and hurried forward. He stopped when he spotted Cooper and gasped in shock. "Lord A'mighty, what happened to y'all?" White asked as he hurried forward.

"Had a speck of trouble here and there on my travels," Cooper said as he gratefully settled an arm across White's shoulders as his fellow mountain man shoved the shoulder into Cooper's armpit, supporting him.

"Well, let's get you to camp where y'all can rest a bit."

"Obliged, but I hate to be a burden."

"What booshwa." He started helping Cooper along. As he did, he bellowed, "Two-Faces! Two-Faces!"

"What you want wit' me, eh? I am busy."

"Have your women put a heap of meat on the fire."

"You 'ave your own fire, *m'sieur*." The half-breed sounded a bit annoyed.

"Ain't for me."

"*Alors pour qui?* Then for who?"

"For Hawley. He's in a bad way."

"Hawley?"

"It's me, Two-Faces, yep."

"*Bien.* Paddy, go 'elp our *ami.*" He turned and spoke to two women in French, Nez Percé and Flathead. He turned and waited.

It was mere moments when Cooper, supported by Bill White and Paddy Murphy, shuffled into the camp.

"*Mon dieu!*" Two-Faces Beaubien said as his old friend arrived, his poor appearance made worse by the gloom of the fading day. "Come, *mon ami*, sit at ze fire."

White and Murphy eased Cooper down alongside the fire just outside the lean-to Beaubien and his family used.

Cooper breathed a sigh of relief as he let himself slump.

The other men—some old friends, some he had never met before—gathered around, the former, shocked at their friend's appearance. Cooper was little more than a shell of the healthy, rugged man he had been when the men last saw him. He was gaunt, skin stretched tight across his face, eyes seemingly dim in the firelight. There was little life in him.

"What in the name of the good Lord happened to you, Hawl?" Alistair Wentworth asked.

"Not now," Beaubien snapped. "Our friend must rest, fill his meatbag, 'ave coffee. He will tell of it later."

Seeing that Cooper didn't seem able to serve himself, Dancing Water, one of Beaubien's two wives, handed him a tin plate with a small pile of sliced smoking buffalo meat. She also set a mug of coffee down on the ground next to him.

Cooper nodded thanks and with shaking fingers, picked up a piece of meat and bit off a chunk. He chewed slowly, then swallowed. He closed his eyes and a satisfied smile creased his lips. His eyes opened,. "That shines," he said and dug into the food with gusto.

"Best slow down, *mon ami*," Beaubien said with a chuckle a few minutes later. "You become sick maybe if you eat too fast, eh."

Cooper glared at him for a moment, then nodded and slowed down.

The other men sat, gnawing on pieces of buffalo or smoking their small clay pipes. So intent was he on eating, that Cooper did not see the interest and desire to know what happened to him on the other men's faces.

Cooper soon finished the second plate and Dancing Water handed him another plateful. The meat kept disappearing until Cooper finally shook his head. He picked up the cup of coffee, which he had ignored all along. Before he could take a sip, though, the Nez Percé woman snatched it out of his hands, shaking her head.

"Is cold," she said firmly. "Not good." She dumped out the cold liquid and refilled the tin mug, then asked, "Make sweet?"

"Yes, ma'am."

Dancing Water added a heaping dose of sugar. A moment later she handed him the steaming tin mug.

With a nod, he picked it up, blew on it a few times, then gingerly sipped it. "Waugh! That shines, too," he muttered. "Damn near as much as the buffler."

"Well, what happened, hoss?" Murphy asked eagerly.

"Faced me a heap of hard doin's, I got to tell you. I..." A small smile crossed his face and he fell on his side, asleep before his head hit the ground.

"*Mon dieu*, now we 'ave to wait 'til morning to 'ear what 'e 'as to say," Beaubien commented with a laugh.

The others joined in the laughter, even Dancing Water, who carefully covered Cooper with a blanket.

————

THE MEN GATHERED around the fire again in the morning. All sat waiting—impatiently but trying not to show it—while Cooper polished off another couple servings of buffalo meat.

Then, as Cooper relaxed with a sugary cup of coffee, Murphy said, "Well...?"

"Well what?" Cooper asked innocently.

"Dammit, Hawley, tell us..."

"*Mam'selle!*" Beaubien suddenly interjected, cutting off Murphy. "Where is *mam'selle*? She is all right?"

"Far as I know, she's all right. I left her with her people a few months ago. Went to do some trappin' and some thinkin'."

"Too much thinkin' ain't good for a man," White said.

"Reckon that's about the most intelligent thing any Black man, as unintelligent as they are, has ever said, Bill."

"You callin' me ignorant?"

"Well, you're smarter than a rock, I reckon, but not by much, I'm thinkin'."

There were twitters all around.

"Well, that might be, but at least I don't stink like you. Hell, you're worse than any other cracker I ever met. Lord a'mighty, Hawl, you stink something awful. Like you been humpin' skunks."

"Well, now, I reckon I have in my day. But both were better than your woman though."

"Well, the skunks might be better in the robes than my woman, but at least she don't stink so high."

"I don't know, hoss. With that wide, spacious darkie nose of yours, you ought to be able to tell that ain't true."

"Now you hol' on a minute, mistah," a young Black man said. "You cain't talk to Mistah White like dat."

"That so, boy?"

"You gonna let him call you a darkie and talk to you like some massah from back on de plantation, Mistah White?" the young man said, looking at the seasoned, dark-skinned mountain man. He started to rise, reaching for his knife.

"Sit down, boy," White commanded.

The younger man looked at White in shock. "You ain't gonna stand up for yo'self? Maybe you is afraid of this yellow-bellied cracker, but I ain't. I be ashamed of you, Mistah White. I never thought I'd see you for such a coward, but if you don't stand up for yo'self, I'll have to do it fo' you."

"I said sit down, boy," White said more harshly. Then in a more sensible tone, he said, "This White son of a bitch can call me whatever the hell he likes." He grinned. "I might have to take him on though about speakin' of my woman that way. She don't really smell worse'n skunks. Maybe wet muskrat. And I reckon he don't hump skunks either."

"That's a fact," Cooper offered. "Ain't nearly big enough for a feller as well-endowed as me. Had me a go at a buffler cow once, and a moose another, but, well, they weren't big enough either so I left 'em both for Two-Faces there."

The young man, who had sat, looked wide-eyed from Cooper to White, mouth agape.

The other men could hold back no longer. White burst out in laughter; Cooper did so a moment later, followed by all the others.

"Hawley Cooper, meet Lemrich Bell, late of the Bramblepatch plantation outside Vicksburg, Mississippi. Lem, this here is Hawley Cooper, ugliest White man here outside of all the others."

"Bell? Sounds Irish. He one of your people, Paddy?" Cooper asked, still chuckling.

"Nah. Thought so at first because of the name, same as you. Folks like them are called Black Irish. Don't know why. They ain't got the colorin', of course, or the intelligence of a real Irishman. Finally figured he's one of Duncan's people, one of those funny-soundin' Scotsmen."

That brought out more laughter all around, except from Cooper, who paused a moment, touched by the reference to his old friend Duncan MacTavish, who had been killed by the Blackfeet not so long ago, and Bell, who remained confused, head spinning from one man to the other wondering just what was going on.

"Hell, Lem, we're all just joshin' here," White said. "I know you're still new to the mountains, but it's been my experience, especially with these disreputable sons a bitches, that a man's color don't mean spit out here. Long as a man does his share of the chores, pulls in prime plews regular, don't bellyache too much when starvin' times come on the men, and he stands up tall and proud to face the stinkin' goddamn Blackfeet, he's accorded as much respect as any other man in the mountains, even half-breed reprobates like Two-Faces and damned tater-eaters and Britishers like Paddy and Al."

"Glad to meet you, hoss. Reckon you're a decent feller or else Two-Faces and Bill wouldn't have taken you on."

"Thank you, massah."

Cooper's eyes clouded. "Don't you ever..." he started.

He stopped when Bell grinned. "You and Mistah White ain't the onliest ones who can josh with peoples."

"You been listenin' that ol' duck fart for too long, boy," Cooper said, laughing again. He looked at White. "Where'd you pick this chil' up, Bill?"

"I knew his pa well back on the plantation before I took my leave of that vile place. Ol' Benjamin was thinkin' of makin' a break of it with me but decided he'd stay behind with his family, which included Lem here, who was only a boy then."

"Daddy died not so long ago," Bell said, taking up the story. "I'd knowed Mistah White since I was a boy like he say. I don't know how Daddy found out, but he learned his ol' friend had become a trapper out here in these mountains and was happy things was a heap different than back on the plantation. Daddy always wanted to get me out here somehow to be with Mistah White, who's maybe like an uncle to me. Never got a chance to, but as he was lyin' on his death bed, he told me to make a run fer it soon's I could. So I did nearly a year ago, I reckon now. Took me a time but I made my way toward the mountains. Nearly froze to death sometimes or starved to death at others, but I kept on movin'. Finally, some ol' trappers come on me and took me with 'em." Bell smiled a little. "Worked me near to death too, along the way."

"Wouldn't've been real mountaineers if they hadn't," Alistair Wentworth said with a chuckle.

"I tol' 'em who I was lookin' fer. They knew Mistah White and packed me off with some other trappers we met who said they thought they knew where he'd be."

"We come across 'em up north of the Yellowstone," White said. "Those other boys weren't happy when we charged 'em three packs of plews to take this young snot off their hands, but they finally agreed."

Bell's head snapped around. "You never said..." He stopped when everyone else started laughing again.

"You ol' men sure try a young man's soul," Bell grumbled but then joined the laughter.

The laughter died down and things were mostly silent for a spell as the men chewed on meat or drank coffee.

"And, as you can see, 'Awley," Beaubien said into the silence, we 'ave some other newcomers among us. M'sieurs, meet M'sieur 'Awley Cooper. 'Awley, meet Charley Rice, Ricardo Gonzalez, and Will Perloe."

"All three nodded of gave a little wave of acknowledgment, which Cooper returned.

"They joined us on ze trail not long after you departed with Goes Far." Beaubien paused for a few moments, then said softly, "It's time, 'Awley, *mon ami*, for you to tell us what 'as 'appened to you."

TWENTY-ONE

COOPER SIGHED. This was something he did not look forward to, partly because it brought back unpleasant memories, but more so because it would, he figured, make himself seem weak and incompetent. Losing face in such a way would be humiliating. Still, these men, at least a few of whom he had ridden with for some years now, deserved to hear it. He hoped they would not think too lightly of him after it was told. He sighed again. Despite his concerns, it was time. He shook off the tiredness that wrapped him as close as his skin did and the aches and pains of his recent travails and began.

"I was in Red Leggin's village waiting for Goes Far to hatch our young'un. It seemed to be takin' a lot longer than I thought it would..."

"Always does, *mon ami*," Beaubien said.

White and the others who had children nodded in agreement.

"Winter was comin' on fast, and I was itchy to get back to trappin'. Finally I took a few days and went off huntin' for beaver by myself. When I got back, she still hadn't birthed. As cranky as I've been the past few months, this didn't set well with me. I decided it would be best for me to be off by myself, do some trappin', some thinkin', so I left her at the village and rode off. Hadn't gone far when I spotted a large war party of Blackfeet. I raced back to the village just in time enough for the People to prepare."

"Raised hair on the red devils, I expect," Murphy said.

"That we did, hoss. Raised hair on a heap of those rat-humpin' savages. Then I rode out again, leavin' Goes Far there again—with our newborn child. Strong Bow she calls him."

"Mam'selle was not pleased you left without her, eh?" Beaubien said.

"No, she was not. Thought I was gonna have a bigger fight on my hands with her than I'd had with the Blackfeet."

There were a few soft chuckles from some of the men.

Cooper hung his head for a moment. "Tell true, Two-Faces, I have my doubts she'll take me back. Anyway, so off I went. Trappin' was fair at best— seems a lot of places that used to be teemin' with beaver are near empty."

"We've found the same, Hawley," White said. "Our take has been good, but not like earlier years.

Ito has some of us shaken and worried about the future."

The others concurred.

"I've had the same thoughts. Another thing I had to do some thinkin' on. Seems like the trade is dyin' and I ain't so sure what the future holds for a feller like me."

"Same with the rest of us, Hawl," White said. "Ain't much any of us fellers can do outside of trappin' and tradin'..."

"And fightin' Injuns," Paddy Murphy said.

White smiled a little. "That's a fact." He grew somber again. "Hate to say it, but some of us boys'll have it harder than some others, fellers like me and Two-Faces and Lem. We ain't got the privileges of White men down in the flats." He smiled again, this time weakly.

All the others nodded, knowing the truth of it, and also knowing the truth that what White had said was not an indictment with the longtime friends here.

"Reckon that's mighty true, Bill," Cooper said. "Nothin' can be done about it, I reckon, but I will say this, ol' hoss, you'll be welcome in my home wherever it is at any time. You, too, Two-Faces, you crusty ol' half-breed stinkpot."

"So maybe I stay away forever, eh?" Beaubien said. He looked thoughtful for a moment, then grinned. "But maybe I come with my women and children just to annoy you and mam'selle, eh?" He laughed.

"You would do somethin' like that, you ugly-faced ol' critter," Cooper said as everyone started to laugh. "Never could trust a redskin. A half one is even worse than a full-blooded one."

It took a few moments for the laughter to die down.

"Anyways," Cooper continued, "off I went, wanderin' here and there, tryin' to figure out what was plaguin' me, fearin' I was goin' down the same dark trail as Elson. I didn't know where to go. I thought of tryin' to find you fellers, but then I remembered the stench of such a winterin' place with the likes of all you fellers."

"Hell, y'all, us boys missed your rankness, which had always given our camps a special aroma," White said.

"Hell, Bill," Murphy threw in, "You've been in other winter camps. You know what they smell like."

"That's true, my foreign friend," the Black man responded to the Irishman. "But that's because they were tryin' to match our fragrance, which was set apart by Hawley's presence." He laughed. "And Two-Faces'. Between the smell of them two, no critters dared near our camp, except the Blackfeet, but we all know they got no sense of smell—or any sense at all."

More laughter rippled around the group.

"Well, I always knew I was better at most things

than the rest of you. I'm obliged to have it recognized." The laughter had settled him a little, made him more comfortable. More like the old days. He had always been comfortable with these men. They were often cantankerous and knobheaded, but they were tried and true, and would go to just about any length to help one another.

"So I decided against joinin' you boys as I wasn't ready to be around people just yet. I sort of headed toward rendezvous, moseyin' along, trappin' when I could. I was in no hurry. Had me a few small run-ins with some Indians but nothin' to really talk about." He drew in a deep breath and let it out slowly. "Then I was caught by the Blackfeet."

A gasp circled the men.

"You don' look much worse for it, *mon ami*," Beaubien said. "They didn't torture you, just let you go?" He sounded half skeptical and half amazed. "I nevair 'eard of such a t'ing."

Cooper smiled a little. "They was afraid of me."

"Probably from humpin' a few skunks like y'all are known to do," White threw in, eliciting some laughter.

"Could be. Might've brought back memories of the times you lent your woman to them buggers." Cooper sombered. "They took my capote and tied me to a tree along about dusk. Left me out there for the night givin' me time to think of my fate and freezin' my stones off. They was plannin' on startin' their devilish treatment in the mornin'. But an ol' mountain boy named Tom Douglas, who had been caught by Bug's Boys a few years ago and was reduced to bein' a slave to 'em, come along in the night and set me free. He was gonna stay behind because they partly crippled him, but I wasn't havin' it. He helped me, and by God I was gonna help him. We stole a couple Blackfoot ponies and..."

"We rode like hell. A few days later, we found a spot we thought would be a good place to stay a while. Rest up. But a few of Bug's Boys found us. I was off huntin' when I heard the attack. I raced back to the camp and managed to send those devils to the Spirit World, where they'll be restless forever."

"You took their hair, eh?"

"Of course. And I got there before they could do any cuttin' on Tom, but he was a gone beaver. I buried him, then spent a couple of days resting. Then I took the Blackfoot ponies and rode back to the village."

"You are crazy, *mon ami*," Beaubien said.

"Ain't the first time I've been told that. Likely won't be the last, at least 'til I'm gone from this world into the next, which might not be long, either, like as not. But I couldn't let a man who had saved me from the Blackfoot's tender mercies go unavenged. Besides, the devils had all my plunder. I paid the village a visit a few nights later. I was lucky in that most of the warriors were off on a hunt, or lookin' for us, so there were few men about. I managed to find just about everything of mine—Tom had told me before we fled which lodges housed the men who had my possibles. Even found the mare and the mule."

"Nobody molested you? No old men or boys not quite ready for the hunt or warpath were watchin' over the place?" Charley Rice, one of the new men, asked.

"There were at first. There weren't after I left." He sighed. "Winter was movin' in fast, and I figured I ought to start lookin' for a place to winter. But travelin' across a small meadow, a lone Blackfoot attacked. Killed the mare. Me and the mule come through unscathed. The Blackfoot didn't. Damn, I liked that ol' horse. She was a fine animal." He shook his head. "I tossed my saddle atop the furs on the mule's back and headed off on foot. Couple weeks later, I run across another group of free trappers winterin' near the Big Spring River. I'd met the leader of the band several years ago when Zeke and I..." He paused for a moment to gather himself. "Me and Zeke were lookin' for a place to settle in that winter just before I joined you boys."

"What's his name?" one of the new men asked.

"Jim Thorne."

"Know him a little. Good man, I hear."

"Seems to be. He offered me the chance to stay with him and his boys for the winter. Same deal as El, really: Help with the camp work, help keep up meat supplies, do your own trappin' and such. I told him I'd think about it."

"And..." White asked. "Since you're here, y'all didn't stay with him."

"I went out huntin' the next mornin', lookin' to set off on the right foot with those fellers. One of Thorne's men—feller by the name of George Lynch..."

"Blocky feller with big ears?" one of the other new men asked. When Cooper nodded, Will Perloe went on. "Had a run-in with the son of a bitch one time down to rendezvous. Thought at first it was just the Lightnin' takin' hold of him for a spell like it does the rest of us from time to time. But I heard later that he was a nasty feller at the best of times. Can't understand why Thorne would ever take him on."

Cooper shrugged. "No tellin' in such things," he said, remembering his own troubles with Malachi Webster. "He followed me and confronted me with the intention of raisin' my hair. I did not allow him that opportunity."

"He say why?" White asked.

"Somethin' about his cousin's unfortunate death at my hands. I told him I never heard of the other feller and I've never been where this killin' was supposed to have taken place, so it couldn't've been me. I asked him where he got such a fool notion. . ." he paused, letting the suspense build for a moment, "and he said it was Dan Anderson who told him."

"*Mon dieu!*" Beaubien spit out.

"But he wouldn't listen. So I made wolf bait out of him. Hauled his carcass back to Thorne's camp and told him what happened. He didn't seem too perturbed. A few of his men didn't seem to be of the same frame of mind. Thorne told me he'd be glad to have me stay on, but I figured it'd do nothin' but cause trouble. So I rode out a lot better than I walked in. I got the horse I had been ridin' and my mule, and enough supplies to make it a week or so. To help keep the peace, Thorne gave me half of Lynch's plews and split the other half among the other men."

"So what happened to y'all?" White asked. "You come in here lookin' like the Great Spirit was makin' plans for your arrival. You said you had a horse, a mule, a rifle, and some possibles, all of which I saw you didn't have when you got here. Seems like somethin' else must've happened to y'all."

"Well, yep, my luck had tumbled again," Cooper said with a sour look.

"What happened?"

"Well, I was still moseyin' along tryin' to figure out where to go. Spring was on me, but I'd get some snow or sleet or freezin' rain, like you fellers know comes at this time of year. It was rainin' and the rain was pickin' up as was the wind. I spotted a grove of trees not too far off that looked like it might give me and the animals some shelter. So I kicked that ol' horse into an easy run. Little did I know there was a deep crevasse a couple dozen yards ahead. By the time I realized it, it was too late. I tried to get that horse to stop, but it couldn't because of the rain-slick ground, though he tried. All three of us went sailin' over the edge and tumbled down the slope, which was cut through with boulders, rocks, stunted trees, and small cactus."

"Ain't ze first time someone's missed a crack in the earth like zat, *mon ami*."

"Reckon not. But I'm still cursin' myself for rushin' headlong through territory I didn't know just to get out of the rain." He felt a rush of embarrassment cross his face.

"Hell, any of us'd do the same like as not," White said. "Ain't a one of us'd not try to get to a shelter when it was rainin' or snowin'. Get under cover, care for the animals, make a fire to get warm and maybe use for fillin' our meatbag. Nothin' to be shamed over, Hawl."

"*C'est vrai, mon ami*. It is true, my friend," Beaubien said.

"Maybe, but I felt like a damn fool, me, a man who's been roamin' these mountains for a decade."

"Can't know every foot of all the country, Hawl," White said. "Even Bridger, who keeps more of a map of this whole land in his head than all the rest of us mountaineers together likely wouldn't have known about that place."

Cooper nodded. "Reckon you're right. Still..." He drew in a deep breath and let it out. "My head ended up hittin' a boulder, and I was out. Didn't know how long it was before I woke, but I had the most godawful headache a man's ever known. I tried to get up but gave up that effort right off and plunged back into the darkness. Again I didn't know how long I was out when I came to again, but the rain had stopped. Both the horse and mule were still screechin' out their wretchedness. Painful as it was gettin' to my feet, I managed and sent the animals over the Divide. Then I lay down again."

"Just like Hawley—always restin' or sleepin' when there's work to be done," Alistair Wentworth said. He winked when Cooper cast a baleful eye at him, letting his fellow mountain man was just joshing.

Cooper nodded just a bit. "I took a day or two to recruit myself, feastin' on horsemeat—it wasn't great, but I don't cotton at all to mule meat. The next day, I wrapped up my blanket and capote and slung 'em over my shoulder. Over the other I hung my possibles bag, as empty as it was, shootin' bag, and a hunk of hide with horsemeat. Ready to step off, I looked down at the plews I was leavin' behind. I spent some time wrackin' my still throbbin' head trying to figure out a way I could get them free in my state, find a good place for a cache, then use just a 'hawk to dig a hole and bury 'em."

"Ain't surprised," Wentworth said quietly. "Nothin' any of us chaps could've done."

"I expect so, but it sure as hell hurt me to leave 'em behind the way I did. I might go back and check someday, but if some mountaineer ain't come by and took 'em, wolves and other such critters will have laid waste to 'em." He sighed once more, unhappiness overcoming him at the loss.

Cooper shook his head. "Took me most of the day to find a way out of that damned crevasse. Must've walked six, seven miles 'til I came to a place shallow enough I could manage to climb out. It was another couple of miles 'til I got to the copse I'd seen that brought about all these troubles. I was glad to, though, as the rain was startin' up again. Not hard but steady. Figured I'd rest up a bit there, let the rain die out."

"See, told you boys he was a slackard."

Cooper managed a grin. "Hell, Al, I ain't ever seen you do a lick of work. All the other boys know that."

"True words," Paddy Murphy said about Alistair, his trapping partner and longtime friend.

"In a couple, three days, I was feelin' almost human, I reckon. Head still hurt like hell and I was still achin' all over from my joyful bounce along the rocks and scrub down the slope. It was not near as bad as the beatin' I took from the Blackfeet back in that valley a few years ago, but it wasn't much fun. I couldn't see any reason to stay where I was though, so I moved on. Better to say I limped along. I tell you, boys, a mountaineer—especially one who's taken a real beatin'—ain't much of a feller without a horse."

The other men nodded solemnly. Most of them had been in a similar situation at one time or another, though maybe not for as long a time.

"So, on I wandered, day after day, not sure after a while where I was, even less certain of where I was goin'. I just stumbled on. Some days were better than others, but none of 'em shined. Had starvin' times more often than not. Water was mighty scarce in many parts. Got snow once or twice, same with sleet, but it seemed to rain every other damned day. My mocs are about worn through."

"You 'ad no rifle, *mon ami*? With one you could hunt, eh?"

"Did have at first, well for a spell. It was banged up some from the fall, but all right. I got enough game at times when I had it. Wasn't that often, though, that game was easy to find."

"What 'appened?"

"I was crossin' another interminable meadow. For once it was warm and the sun was out. Saw a critter comin' toward me, and my mouth began to water. It'd been three, four days—they all run together after a spell—and here was some game on the hoof comin' straight at me. Figured it was a small elk or maybe deer. But as it got closer I realized that it was a wolf. That give me pause as that critter didn't seem right to me ever at some distance."

"Wolf madness?" White asked.

"The closer it got, the more certain I was that it was so afflicted. I stopped and waited a bit, hopin' the damn thing would wander off up into the hills and the forest. But it kept comin'. I let it get to within about fifty yards. About the same time it started chargin' toward me. I dropped to a knee and put a lead ball in his direction. I hit him, certain I did, but it didn't slow him much if at all. I started hurryin' to reload, but I was weak enough at that point that I was havin' trouble doin' so especially because I was in a rush."

Cooper paused for a sip of coffee, which had gone cold, then continued. "He was comin' on fast and I realized I wasn't gonna be able to reload before the damn critter was on me—I'd got powder and ball in, but wasn't able to manage a cap. I stood, takin' the rifle in my hands by the barrel. At five feet or so, he leaped for my throat. I swung that ol' rifle with what little strength I had. Caught that son of a bitch full across the muzzle with the stock. The stock broke, but the wolf was layin' there whimperin' in pain from its shattered face."

"It didn't come at you again?" White asked.

"Looked like he might be plannin' on it, but he was in bad shape. I got a cap on the Dickert, walked up from behind him, and managed to hold the stock together enough that I could pull the trigger and put a ball in the devilish critter's brainpan. I knew then for sure that it was sick and was mighty damn glad that beast didn't get his fangs into me."

"And ze rifle, it was gone, eh?" Beaubien asked.

Cooper nodded. "I carried it with me for a week, hopin' I could find a way to patch it up but there was nothin' I could do. Might've wrapped rawhide around it and let it bind together enough to use, but I didn't have some and no way to get any. I took some wolf meat—a meal I'd never eat if I weren't starvin'; lordy is that foul—and some of the hide and tried usin' that to secure the stock, but it wouldn't work. Finally I just left it behind at one of the places I spent the night. I'm gonna miss that ol' rife, even more than I miss the mare. I've had that piece since not long after gettin' to the mountains."

"Any man'd be lost without his favorite gun," White said. "I'd not know what to do without this ol' Hawken of mine."

Cooper nodded. "I gotta say, though, that for a spell, I wasn't sure it mattered. I figured I was gettin' close to goin' under. Without enough meat or water, I was gauntin' down and runnin' out of strength. There was many a time over the weeks that I considered just lyin' down and lettin' the Great Spirit—or more like Beelzebub himself—come to fetch me."

"You weren't scared were ye?" Murphy asked, no condescension in his voice. He couldn't believe Hawley Cooper to be afraid of anything.

"Of dyin'? Nope. Can't say I was pleased with the thought, but death is something you, me, and all the others here face every day we're in these Stony Mountains. But thoughts of Goes Far and Strong Bow—and even you ugly cusses—kept me goin'. Wouldn't let me succumb to such a death. I ain't gonna ever give in to such a thing. I aim to go out with a Blackfoot arrow in me, or bein' run over by a buffler, or now that I've almost experienced it, fallin' down a mountainside."

"If you'd rather," Wentworth said with a laugh, breaking the tension a bit, "us boys can help ye on your way if you so desire. Even let ye keep your hair."

Cooper shook his head as a smile grew. "I'm obliged for your concern, Al, but I reckon I'll wait for the good Lord's or the Great Spirit's call to me directly rather than lettin' you boys speed up that time."

The others chuckled.

"I was still headin' in the general direction of rendezvous, wonderin' whether I had enough strength to make it there and in time for the festivities. It was seemin' more and more doubtful that such a thing would happen. Then one day as I was travelin', my mind cleared up for a spell, and I realized it was about the time you boys would be headin' there. From where I figured you had wintered and hunted, I thought I'd know how you were gettin' there. So I veered off and headed this way. Sure enough, day before yesterday I sensed you were nearby. And yesterday I was sure when I smelled this camp and saw some dead game. I figured the stench had killed 'em. Almost did me too. I began to think it might've been better for me to have just given up and gone under out there somewhere than turn up here and abide by the foulness of the place."

The men laughed, and Beaubien said, "You lie, *mon ami*. You 'ave missed the comforting aroma of our homey camps. It's 'ow you found us. Your nose brought you 'ere from many miles away."

"You could be right, Two-Faces," Cooper said with a chuckle. I got to admit it does feel right that I'm back with you boys, even though you're all troublesome."

"So what now, Hawl?" White asked. "You plannin' on stayin' with us now that you're back?"

"I ain't so sure, Bill. I'll have to do some thinkin' on it. Partly depends on how I'm feelin'."

TWENTY-TWO

"WELL, y'all best make up your mind soon, Hawl," White said. "I ain't waitin' forever to decide. Us boys got business to tend to at rendezvous. Of course, you bein' so old and feeble as you've become, the rest of us might just give you an old nag of a horse and find y'all an old nag of woman to accompany y'all for the six, seven months it takes you to get there."

"Damn Bill, I always knew you were a carin' feller deep down in your innards." Cooper chuckled, as did the others, though his was somewhat forced. He finally rose. "Hate to say it, boys, but Bill might be right about me bein' old and feeble," he said sourly. " Reckon I need some rest." He wandered off into the thick stands of trees and found a good Douglas fir away from the sounds and smells of the camp. He sat and rested back against the trunk.

When he woke, he was no more rested than he had been. He rubbed his still-tired eyes and then opened them. Two-Faces Beaubien was sitting, back against a tree, puffing silently on his pipe.

"*Bon jour, mon ami.* Or should I say *bon après-midi?*"

"I been out long?"

"Two, t'ree 'ours maybe."

"You been here all that time watchin' me sleep?" Cooper asked. He was irritated at the very notion.

Beaubien shook his head. "*Non.* Just a little time."

"Why?" His irritation was not dimmed.

"We need to talk, *mon ami.*"

"About what?"

"About you. You need to figure out what to do about your miseries, and I try to 'elp."

"Ain't nothin' you can do, Two-Faces. It's something I got to figure out by myself."

"'Elping a friend is what friends are for. You 'ave 'elped me and many others many times, 'Awley. Now I 'elp you. I 'ave said this to you before."

"Like I said, nothin' you can do. I'm obliged for your offer though."

"So, what will you do, eh? You 'ave no money, no 'orse, nothing except ze 'skins you wear, and they ain't worth using to cover the 'horses 'ooves when we cross harsh land."

"I'll figure out something," Cooper said bitterly. He rose. "I reckon I need more rest."

"Sit down, *mon ami!*" It was said quietly but there was no mistaking the command.

Cooper glared at him. "If I wasn't so worn down by my struggles of recent, I'd cut your heart out for that, you son of a bitch."

"If you were 'ale and 'earty, *mon ami*, you would not even t'ink such a t'ing. Now, sit, *s'il te plaît*, and we will talk. For real this time."

Still steaming, Cooper retook his seat on the pine-needle-covered ground under the tree.

"What makes you so troubled, 'Awley?"

"If I knew that for certain either I'd fix it or, I don't know, maybe go off by myself."

"Like now, eh?"

"Reckon so."

"When did these bad spirits come to you?"

"Ain't sure. I was fine, then I realized some darkness and melancholy were overcomin' me. I was afraid I was becomin' like El."

"You are 'appy with Goes Far—and ze boy?"

"Yep. Though I ain't so sure she'll have me after bein' gone so long."

"You plan to meet 'er at rendezvous?"

"I was plannin' to, but of late I ain't so sure. Not when I still ain't right."

"So you miss 'er?"

"Yep."

"Are there others you miss?"

"Sure. Black Moon Woman and Zeke the most, of course. And El almost as much. But that's a different case 'cause I had to put him under. I miss Duncan too, and Tall Grass."

"Ze one who was killed by zat *fils de pute* Weeks?"

Cooper nodded.

"Others?"

"Reckon so. Seems like people all around me go under regular, except you, you crusty ol' fart, and that damned black-faced slackard back there in camp."

"Like who? Ze Blackfeet?"

"Yep, the Blackfeet," Cooper said sarcastically. "Hate seein' my blood brothers get made wolf bait of." He sighed, trying to let the anger in him subside. "No, folks like those Flatheads who helped and wound up gettin' butchered because of it. And Tom Douglas, who helped me escape from the Blackfeet. And Sam, who had gone from a real greenhorn to a young man who deserved respect. Hell, even ol' Jacque, despite his bein' an ill-tempered reprobate."

"Some of zese people—and more you did not know—'ave gone under around me, but I don' blame myself. You shouldn't either. It's the way of the mountains. You know zat. Life 'ere in ze mountains is 'ard. Men go under all ze time from ze Indians and wolves and bears, even buffalo. From bad weather and bad water. From crossing wild rivers. From starvin' tines. Accidents like shootin' selves or 'avin' a friend do so by mistake. Sickness of many kinds. Life is 'ard, 'Awley. *Dur, très dur*—Hard, very hard. You learned that early in your days out here, from that *fil de pute*."

"Hell, I know that, Two-Faces, but..."

"Then you cannot place ze blame on your shoulders. Many others—including me—would 'ave been sent to the Spirit World if you 'ad not pulled our nuts out of ze fire. And more zan once."

"But..."

"You 'ave strong medicine, *mon ami*. Good medicine."

"Wasn't good enough to save Black Moon or Zeke." Cooper's voice had gone cold and distant.

Beaubien knocked the dead ash from the bowl of his pipe and shoved the pipe into the heart-shaped buckskin holder hanging around his neck on his chest. "The Great Spirit—or God—calls everyone home, some too soon."

"Then why wasn't it me, dammit, instead of Zeke or Black Moon or the Flatheads. God could've sent the Flatheads on their way leavin' me to die, but no, dammit, he let those folks save me, then get slaughtered by the goddamn Blackfeet."

"As Elson 'as told us more than once that we 'ommes can't know the workings of ze mind of Great Spirit, either white or red. Ze black robes tell us God 'as reasons for all zese t'ings." Beaubien shrugged. "I don't know if I believe those 'oly men, but I can't say zat they are wrong. It is somet'ing we men must live with as best we can."

The half-breed pulled off his hat and ran a hand through his long, greasy, black hair. "So put such t'ings from your mind, *mon ami*. If ze black robes are to be believed, then the Great Spirit 'as somet'ing in mind for you, which is why you are still 'ere."

"What is that, huh? You got an answer for that?"

"*Mais non.* As I say, we men cannot know zese t'ings. But maybe is to 'ave you and Goes Far 'ave many babies, build up ze Nez Percé, make ze tribe stronger." He grinned a little. "Or maybe you are 'ere to keep this ill-natured old 'alf-breed alive so 'e can repopulate both ze Nez Percé and Flathead tribes!" He chuckled.

Cooper couldn't help but join in. "I always knew you were crazy, Two-Faces. I just didn't know you were this crazy."

"Ah, *oui. Je suis fou. Très, très fou*—I am crazy. Very, very crazy."

The small laughter faded, and Beaubien said quietly, "But there is more, *mon ami, n'est-ce pas*—isn't that right?"

"And what would that be?" Cooper responded flatly.

"You tell me, eh?"

"Got no idea of what you mean, old man." He wondered why he had suddenly called Beaubien "old man." The half-breed was no more than half a dozen years older than Cooper. Then he recognized that it was not a matter of age but of wisdom. He was surprised for a moment, then realized he shouldn't have been. Beaubien had shown that for a long time; Cooper had just failed to grasp it.

"*Merde de buffle*—buffalo shit."

"All right, I'm wonderin' what to do when the trade dies. Nothin' can be done about that."

"Zat is not what I meant, *mon ami*. You know zat. We 'ave talked about zat. You will do what is best for you and for Goes Far and Strong Bow."

"I ain't so sure of that."

"You 'ave me worried, 'Awley," Beaubien said solemnly. "Zere is more eating at your insides. And in ze years I 'ave known you, *mon ami*, you 'ave nevair seemed so uncertain of yourself. You 'ave more courage and strength of will zan any man I know, yet 'ere you are worrying about ze future when no one knows what will 'appen. Maybe ze trade dies tomorrow, maybe not for ten years. Maybe something men like us can do will come along to replace it if it does go under. Maybe we will be like motherless buffalo calves, eh. If not'ing comes along, we can always go stay with our wives' people. Such a life wouldn't be so bad, eh? Hunt ze buffalo. Cover our women. Play with our children. Fight ze Blackfeet. A good life, *non*?"

"Might be," Cooper admitted. "Ain't sure it'd work for a one-breed."

"*Mon dieu*, 'Awley, you more red now zan white."

"Reckon you're right on that. Don't know how long I'd last, though was I to try becomin' a full-blood, or maybe just a full-time, Nez Percé. Especially if I was mostly forced into it."

"Well, per'aps you could try it for a spell, see 'ow you take to it."

"Might do that," Cooper said, not sounding sincere.

"But what of Goes Far and Strong Bow?"

"What about 'em?"

"You 'ave mentioned the trouble taking zem to a pale-face town. You may 'ave to make a choice—you become Nez Percé or leave zem and go back to being a White man because you are afraid to take zem with you to White man's land."

"You're a half-breed," Cooper spit. "You should know it ain't easy livin' in a White man's town."

"Zat is why I stay out 'ere in ze mountains, *mon ami*."

Cooper just grunted.

"But there is more I t'ink. There is a great 'ole inside you, *mon ami*. Zere is somet'ing missing. Family maybe?"

"I already told you I miss Goes Far and Strong Bow."

"You 'ave—or 'ad—other families."

"Like who?" Cooper started, voice angry and bitter.

"You 'ad a family back in ze States, eh?"

"The main word there is 'had.' I ain't goin' back there even if I leave the mountains, that's certain. They didn't want me back then, and I don't want any part of 'em now."

"And you 'ave us 'ere. We are like family, eh?

Live together, work together, fight together, both against Indians and ourselves. Just like all families."

"Reckon that's a fact. Might be why I left off to be by myself for a spell. Get away from you boys and your fart-stinkin' camps." Despite his gloom, he managed a slight—very slight—smile.

"But such a camp is 'ome to men such as us, eh?"

"Well, I got to admit that beyond the smell and the arguin' and the carin' for animals and such, it is comfortable among us ol' fellers."

"And you 'ave a Nez Percé family."

"Not a whole one, just me, Goes Far, and the baby."

"What about Sits Down and Pale Thunder? Ain't they your brother and father?"

Cooper shrugged.

"Maybe not, eh. Maybe because you 'ave another family who..."

"Don't say it, Two-Faces. Just don't." His voice was divided between anger and sorrow.

"I t'ink that is where ze problem lies for you, *mon ami*. You 'ave lost your family—your 'real' family as you had come to t'ink of the Shoshonis—because you made a decision zat you thought was right at ze time. I t'ink it was right too. 'Ad you not done so, Malachi Webster would 'ave gone under. Zat would not 'ave mattered, and it would 'ave saved you much grief. But zere was no assurance zat those warriors, with their blood up, would 'ave stopped at killing Webster. If zey did not, zere would 'ave been much blood spilled.

Some of our men would 'ave gone under, but so would 'ave some Shoshonis. T'ings would 'ave been bad, very bad."

"Reckon that's so, but it doesn't change things."

"Maybe you should put your Shoshoni family behind you, *mon ami*. Replace them in your heart with your Nez Percé family." He smiled a little. "And with your family 'ere, with us wild and savage mountaineers. You do zat and ze other t'ings maybe won't be so troublesome. Ze blood and loss of friends will ease in your mind but not heart. And ze future will stay in future."

"I ain't so sure about any of that, Two-Faces."

"T'ink on it, *mon ami*. Do much t'inking. You can defeat these black spirits, 'Awley. Like you 'ave defeated many Blackfeet." Beaubien rose. "*Oui*. T'ink 'ard." He strolled off.

Cooper watched him leave, his melancholy returning at the prospect of trying to work things out, something he had been trying to do for months and had made no progress. He did not think he would resolve it now either. The near future looked no brighter than the far-off future.

TWENTY-THREE

"WE'LL BE PULLING out tomorrow, 'Awley," Two-Faces Beaubien said.

Cooper nodded. "I'll be ready. But I ain't headin' your way."

"*Non?*" Beaubien asked, surprised. "Where will you go, *mon ami?*"

"It may be plumb foolish, but I figure to head back to where I went over that cliff, see if any of my plews are left. Ain't likely, but I've got to see. If there's enough to trade for some supplies, I can kick up dust down to rendezvous."

"And you call me *très fou*. You are crazier than me."

"Reckon I am." Cooper's face turned down.

"What is it?"

"Well, you were kind enough to let me use one of your horses heading to rendezvous." He hesitated.

After a moment, the half-breed nodded. "And

you t'ink I will take it back now because you aren't going with us?"

"I was thinkin' you might. I owe you a heap already."

"I tell you before, friends 'elp friends. You can keep ze 'orse. You can pay me back someday. It will cost you only a t'ousand plews, and t'ree gallons of Lightnin'; ze saddle and rifle only cost you five pounds of tobacco."

Cooper stared at him goggle-eyed, unable to speak, wondering where his friend had gotten so greedy.

But seconds later, Beaubien could not contain himself. "I make a joke, *mon ami!*" He burst out laughing, slapping his knee as tears spring from his eyes.

Some of the men who had drawn close enough to hear the exchange started laughing too. Even the women were giggling.

Realization hit Cooper after a moment then his face contorted as he tried to contain his laughter but quickly failed. "You had me goin' there, you half-breed son of a bitch," he said between guffaws. "Damn, now I know the truth—your ma was a Blackfoot and your pa was ol' Beelzebub himself." For the moment, he realized, he felt better than he had in ages.

As the laughter dwindled, Beaubien said, "Of course you will keep ze 'orse, *mon ami*. You know I would nevair leave my *très bein ami* afoot out 'ere.

No, you will keep ze 'orse. And I'll give you a mule too. If t'ings go well for you, you can give zem back when we meet again. If not..." He shrugged. "*C'est la vie*, eh?"

"It's about time you opened your purse strings to help a friend, you miserly hearted bastard. I ain't ever seen you give a starvin' man so much as a thimble full of meat." He grew somber, walked up and shook Beaubien's hand. "Thank you, Two-Faces. I don't know if..."

"Say no more, 'Awley. We are friends, and you would do ze same for me or any of the others if our situations were reversed."

"I don't know as if he would," Bill White said, though a grand smile cracked his dark face. "Can't trust any of these white devils." He chuckled. "Me and the others are slim on supplies, Hawl, but I'll hand over what I can."

A chorus of "me, too" ran through the crowd.

"Obliged, boys. I don't know what to say. I'll try to pay you all back one day."

"Come now, ol' chap," Alistair Wentworth said. "You don't owe us anything. You've done more for us lads than any of us. Now shut that pair of flappin' lips of yours."

Cooper glanced from one man to the other, then nodded. "Thanks, boys."

The men drifted back to their work, and Beaubien clapped Cooper on the shoulder and nodded. "They are right, *mon ami*. Remember zat." He walked off.

LEMRICH BELL, Bill White's young companion, whom the latter thought of as an uncle stopped a few feet from where Cooper was saddling his horse. "Mistah Cooper?" he said shyly.

Cooper's face crinkled in wonder, and then he wiped the look off his face and turned. "No need to call me Mr. Cooper. Hawley or just Hawl will do."

"Yes, sir."

Cooper was about to correct him on the use of "sir," too, but decided such references to White men had been ingrained in him since birth and must be hard to overcome. "So what can I do for you, Lem? Is it all right if I call you Lem?" It had been a little more than a week since Cooper had returned to the camp but he had not really had a chance to talk to the young man, had seen no reason to as he wrestled with his troubles and his recovery.

"I be thinkin' maybe you'd let me ride alongside y'all, sir, on yo' trip."

"Why in hell do you want to ride with a nasty old curmudgeon like me?"

"Well, I hear you be goin' for some plews that might be there, but maybe not. If they be there, you maybe need he'p loadin' 'em and such. I be a strong boy."

"You're a man, Lem, not a boy."

"Yes, sir."

"And I think there's more to this request or offer than helpin' me load some plews that might not even be there."

Bell shuffled his feet a little, looking down in embarrassment. He finally raised his head, gathering his nerve. "I treated you bad when I first saw y'all. Treated you with disrespect. It ain't right for a Black boy to be so disrespectful to a White man. I..."

"Whoa there, hoss. You've been in the mountains a year, long enough to know that you're one of us as long as you pull your weight. This ain't no plantation. You've seen the way Bill has been treated by the others. I reckon you've gotten the same treatment— which is no different than the others receive, White, Black or half-breed."

"Reckon that's true, suh. Ever'body's treated me well. Like you said. But when y'all come into camp, I didn't know y'all, and you treated Uncle Bill mighty poorly, least at fust. It sounded to me like you was really insultin' Uncle Bill, and I figured I'd make y'all stop, that maybe it'd raise my standin' among the men, what with me bein' the youngest and least experienced of y'all."

"Don't matter. That's an admirable thing that you did. Or what you were plannin' to do. And I reckon it's a good thing Bill stopped you before you got to me."

Bell looked a little surprised. Then he nodded

and a rueful smile crossed his face. "Reckon you would've stomped my young Black ass into the dirt. And did it without much effort."

Cooper grunted. "Condition I was in, likely not. And nothin' come of it. But that still don't explain why you're fixin' to go with me now."

"To make up for what I done."

"You didn't do anything except maybe think of raisin' my hair 'cause of the way I treated ol' Bill. You should know that he and I and all the others josh like that all the time."

"I know, I seen it with the others. But you was diff'rent." He shrugged. "I don't know why, but even in yo' poor state, I felt somethin' different 'bout y'all."

"Then you learned different right away."

"Yes, suh. But I should've had enough sense to wait and see what kind of fellah you were befo' makin' a fool of myself. And since I showed y'all so much disrespect, I'd like to make my name good with you, to..." He stumbled to a stop.

Cooper's face and body froze as flashes of the past roared into his brain—a time when it was almost spring, a winter camp along the Yellowstone, the wreckage of Cooper's small camp, a young man named Zeke Potts who was responsible, a chase after a stolen horse, and...

"What's wrong, Mistuh Cooper?" Bell asked nervously.

But Cooper was still far away, sunken in his memory—Cooper's rage, Potts's abject apology, then the young man asking to ride with Cooper to atone for his serious misdeeds, a growing friendship, Potts with a Blackfoot arrow in his throat, a litter bearing a young mountain man's body nestled in a tree in a hidden valley.

"'Awley!" Two-Faces Beaubien said, shaking Cooper. "*Mon ami*! Come back to us!"

The light started returning to Cooper's eyes. He blinked several times, then shook his head.

"*Content de te revoir*—Welcome back, *mon ami*."

Cooper nodded, still a little foggy.

"Where 'ave you been?"

Fully recovered from his sad journey through his memories, he said, "Many places. Back to when Zeke..." He stopped and took a deep breath.

Beaubien turned his glance from Cooper to Lemrich Bell, then back again. "A rash young man, new to ze mountains, 'e acts a fool, zen wants to earn your respect. Just like Zeke. Zat it, mon ami?"

Cooper nodded. "Yes," he said quietly.

Beaubien grinned. "Zen you will take this young pup with you and teach 'im 'ow to be a great mountaineer, like ze great 'Awley Cooper, not like ze rest of 'ommes 'ere."

"I don't cotton to the idea, Two-Faces. I..."

"Sure you do, *mon ami*," Beaubien said almost joyfully.

"If it be troublesome for y'all, Mistuh Cooper, I'll start with the others. It be all right."

"Hush, boy," Bill White said, standing nearby, leaning on his rifle.

"I don't know if I can do that, Two-Faces. You know what happened to the last young buck I took under my wing."

"*Oui*. But zat is not your fault. Zat is on ze heads of ze Blackfeet bastards. You taught Zeke well. 'E became a man under your tutelage, brave, a master trapper, a grand Indian fighter. 'E was just called 'ome too soon by ze Great Spirit."

Cooper stood in thought for a bit, his face a mask of indecision and sadness. Then he straightened and his face returned to its regular almost handsomeness. He looked at Bell. "You got a horse, boy? Rifle, powder, lead? Supplies?"

"Yes, suh."

"Then gather your things and saddle up. I'll be pullin' out in maybe half an hour. You ain't ready, I'll leave by myself."

"Yes, suh!" The young man dashed off.

Cooper finished saddling and bridling his horse. Then the other men brought over what supplies they were able to give and Beaubien helped Cooper load the mule.

"You sure you want to do zis, *mon ami?*" the former asked the latter. "I know I said you should but..."

Cooper nodded.

"And you are sure you want to take ze pup?"

"Well, as long as he behaves himself we'll be fine.

First time he shows himself to be a troublesome feller, I reckon I'll take raise his hair and dump his carcass in a ravine somewhere." He grinned when he saw the look of horror on Bell's face. The young man was nearby, holding the reins to his horse.

"Relax, boy," White said. "You been with us long enough to know when we're just joshin'. Hell, if he wanted to raise your hair, he'd do so here and now, then raise hair on anyone who tried to stop him. This man is about the toughest hellion I evah met. He might be quiet and moody at times, often for days, but he won't let any harm come to y'all if he can help it. Wish we could give y'all more supplies, Hawl, but we're all short on things."

"We got enough. Plenty of powder and ball. We'll make out. Wish you fellers weren't so greedy drinkin' coffee all the time. Would've been nice to have some to take along."

"Hell, you don' need coffee, *mon ami*," Beaubien said. "We gave you a bladderful of Lightnin' to tide you over."

"Reckon it will, Two-Faces," he said with a grin.

"Just don't drink it all tonight," White said.

"You fellers take all the joy out of man's life," Cooper said, still grinning. Then he grew serious. "Again, I thank you boys—all of you—for puttin' yourselves a mite short by givin' us some of your supplies."

"Not to worry, old chap," Alistair Wentworth said. "We'll be at rendezvous soon and will refill our possible sacks then."

Cooper nodded. "I'd also like to thank you boys for takin' me in and nursin' me back to health and vigor."

"Hell, boy-o, we did it just to get rid of you," Paddy Murphy said. "We don't want the likes of you foulin' our camp."

All the men laughed a little, except Bell and Cooper, who still wore a serious expression. He looked over at the young Black man. "Ready, hoss?"

TWENTY-FOUR

COOPER KEPT his quiet as he and Bell rode, the latter towing the pack mule. He could see by his random glances that the young man was full of questions. But Cooper was in no mood to answer any. He was still caught up in the painful remembrance of Zeke Potts.

After three days on the trail, though, he was able to tuck the memory away in a corner of his brain and he felt his mood improve ever so slightly.

It was drawing close to dusk on the third night and the two made an early camp after a hard day of traveling. They were relaxing, sipping coffee, the last they had brought from Beaubien's camp.

"Lem, go fetch me four trade knives. I reckon they're dull and I want to sharpen 'em up in case we get a chance to trade." He did not see the stricken look on his companion's face.

He glanced over at the young man, wondering what was taking so long for such a simple task. Before he could snap at the young man, he thought he knew the problem. "You don't know numbers, do you?" he asked.

Bell turned to face him. His face was strained and he was close to tears, "No, suh. They don't teach us nigras anything. They say we get education, we might run off."

"No letters either?"

"No, suh. I be plumb ashamed."

"Nothin' to be ashamed about, hoss. You can't know something unless someone teaches it to you. So I reckon it's time for you to learn. I ain't much of a teacher, mind you, not about such things as numbers and letters, but I should be able to get you the basics. It might not be easy, especially with me as your teacher. And we might's well start now. Come on back over here to the fire."

Bell sat, face bright with anticipation.

"Hold up one hand with the fingers spread a little." When the young man did so, Cooper touched each one and counted, "One, two, three, four, five. Now hold up the other. Six, seven, eight, nine, ten." He grinned. "You want to count higher than that, you'll have to take off your mocs and count on your toes."

Bell looked at his hands as if magic had suddenly turned them into something far better than digits.

"You do it."

The Black man counted slowly, then looked up at Cooper with an expression torn by worry that he had not gotten it right and joy that he had gotten it right.

"You did just fine."

"More, Mistuh Cooper," Bell pleaded.

Cooper started to wonder at what he had gotten himself into. But he sighed. "All right. You know that numbers are used to count things like money or plews or bales of cotton, right?" When Bell nodded, Cooper said, "Hold up two fingers on one hand, now two fingers on the other."

The young man did so, looking timorously at Cooper, who nodded.

"What you just did is called addition. If somebody gives you two plews and someone else gives you two, how many plews do you have?"

Bell's face wrinkled up as he worked through the puzzle. Then he looked at his hand. His head jerked up, eyes wide. "Four?"

"Yep, you shine boy, you really do. I ain't seen a feller come to learnin' numbers as fast as you."

Bell beamed.

"Now, there's the opposite. It's called subtraction. It's when you have a certain number of things and you have fewer left. Like if you gave somebody some, or if you lost 'em or if you just used 'em up. Now show me all your fingers. How many is that?"

"Ten." It was said confidently.

"All right, so you have ten plews and you sell six to someone. How many do you have left?"

Bell puzzled that over too for a bit, then shook his head. He closed the proper number of digits and with a great smile, said, "Four!"

"Yep. I think you're already better at mathematics—numbers—than I am."

"Teach me more, Mistuh Cooper," Bell said eagerly.

"Not tonight, lad. It's robe time for this ol' chil'."

AS THEY RODE along the next few days, Cooper would call out things like twenty-seven minus thirteen or six times eleven. There were some stumbles on the young man's part for a day or two, but he quickly picked up on it and answered only seconds after the question was posed.

Five days out from Beaubien's camp Cooper stopped early for the evening. Bell was surprised but said nothing. After camp was made, and the men had eaten, the younger man said, "Give me more numbers, Mistuh Cooper."

"Nope." Cooper grinned at Bell's suddenly sad face. "It's time we moved onto something else—letters."

"Really?"

"Yep. Really." He got a piece of dry bark and a

piece of charcoal. He wrote for a few moments, then showed it to Bell. "That's called the alphabet. Those are the letters we use to make words. Follow along as I say them. A...B..."

"There be a lot of 'em," Bell said when they had finished.

"Not that many. And you can make any word you want with 'em."

"I don' think I be able to do that."

"Sure you can. It'll take a heap of time. Just stick with it, hoss, and you'll do all right." Cooper grabbed another piece of bark. "C'mere." When Bell had done so, Cooper started writing, pronouncing each letter as he did—L-E-M-R-I-C-H."

"What's that?"

"Your name, Lemrich." He handed the makeshift writing tablet to his companion.

The young man looked at it in awe, then ran a forefinger over each letter, trying to pronounce it. Then he looked at Cooper.

"You didn't do bad for the first time."

Bell handed the bark back to Cooper. "Write your name, please," he asked solemnly.

Cooper did so, mouthing each letter as he did. "Read them."

With some hesitation, he did, looking expectantly at Cooper when he finished.

"Not as good, hoss, but my name uses some letters that ain't very common."

———

THE LESSONS CONTINUED. Cooper was pleased with Bell's progress but he was worried about his teaching. He was not all that well-versed in writing as math. He could read most anything, though it often took him a while as he strived to understand the often unfamiliar words. Worse, he had little opportunity for reading, though there were usually some books around winter camps and such, brought in by some mountain men, some of whom would read to the men, many if not most, who could not read.

He was surprised when Bell picked up letters far faster than he had expected, which worried him even more. He did as best he could, though and managed to stay ahead of his young student.

A week and a half later, they were riding across a meadow semi-circled with sharp jagged peaks when Bell said nervously, "I see Injuns ahead, Mistuh Cooper."

"I was wonderin' when you were gonna tell me you saw 'em."

"You saw 'em? When?"

"Oh, maybe a half mile back or so. Couldn't tell what they were then, though."

"They Blackfoot?"

"That what you think?"

Bell hesitated a moment, then said, "Yes, suh."

"Well, then, you're right. Seems you're smarter than your ol' Uncle Bill said you were."

"Well, he also told me you ain't half as smart as yo' think you are." He glanced over only a little anxiously.

"That so?" Cooper grinned. "Well, I reckon he's right."

Both men laughed. Bell was relieved. He and his companion had been slowly becoming more at ease with each other. And Bell was appreciative, especially when he was nervous about encountering the Blackfeet. He had fought them before, but not out in the wide open like this. He glanced at Cooper again. The mountain man looked tense with anticipation but not worry. The young man breathed a sigh of relief.

When they were still about three hundred yards from the Blackfeet, Cooper and Bell stopped. Cooper dismounted and handed his reins to his companion. "Give me your Hawken. After I fire, I'll toss you my rifle. Reload as fast as you can while I use yours to take down another of those demons."

Bell nodded and handed his weapon to Cooper.

The latter knelt and waited a few seconds until the now charging Blackfeet were within two hundred yards. He fired. He did not wait to see if the Indian went down, just stood, handed his rifle to Bell, then knelt, picked up his partner's rifle, and fired again. He stood and exchanged rifles with Bell, glad to have his own again.

"You only got two of 'em, Mistuh Cooper."

"I only shot twice."

I know, but from what all the fellers in camp said, I thought you could get four of 'em with two shots." A bright grin showed sparkling teeth.

"Well, there's another feller might be the third to go under right here," he said with a chuckle. He knelt and fired once more. Another Blackfoot went down.

"My turn. Mistuh Cooper."

"Sure you can hit him at this distance?"

"Ain't certain. Maybe I'll just wait till he's close enough to shake hands."

They grinned at each other. "Take him down, boy."

Bell happily did so.

The fifth Beckfoot seemed to almost break his pony's neck as he jerked the rein and raced off the way he had come.

"Waugh! That's makin' those devils come!"

They reloaded and rode forward, stopping to take the scalps.

"I was mighty sick fust time I did this," Bell said as he peeled the scalp off.

"Most of us boys were, I expect. I was. Well, not really. By the time I did, I was used to seein' worse."

Then they were on the move again. They rode in silence for a while before Bell asked, "How'd you come to be out here, Mistuh Cooper?"

The older man glanced at the younger and saw that Bell seemed truly interested. He hesitated but could think of no reason not to tell the story. "I run away from my farm and ended up in St. Louis with nothin'. No money, no job, no food, nothin' but the clothes I was wearin' and they weren't in very good shape."

"Sounds like my life," Bell said bitterly.

"That was different."

Bell cast now angry eyes on Cooper.

"Calm down, Lem. My case was different than yours. I didn't say as bad or worse. You were forced into bein' like that by some son of a bitch who said he owned you and could treat you anyway he desired."

"Damn right, the cracker son of a bitch."

"I, on the other hand, brought my troubles on myself."

"You're right. Diff'rent."

Cooper nodded. "I met a crusty ol' son of a bitch named Josiah Weeks. He hired me, or at least he called it hirin' me, but it almost like bein' his slave." He glanced over and saw the anger on Bell's face again. "Ah, hell, Lem, I ain't sayin' it was slavery, but I reckon it come fairly close in some ways anyway. Like you, I had nothin' to call my own. Weeks had supplied me with everything, sayin' I could pay him back when we returned next spring."

"Did you?"

"Ain't got that far in the story. The big difference between me and you was that I could leave whenever I wanted, which I couldn't really. Leavin' wasn't a good idea, though I considered it often. But I was in the middle of the plains somewhere. Didn't know where exactly. Hundreds of miles from civilization if that's what you could call St. Louis. And there were all kinds of redskins between me and the States. So, I did have a choice, which you didn't. Big difference, though my choice wasn't very good."

"You be a strange fellah, Mistuh Cooper."

"Why's that?"

"Your feelin's to'ard folks like me."

Cooper shrugged. "I don't hold no hatred for any man—'cept Blackfeet or any other son of a bitch tries to harm me or those close to me. A man who proves his mettle to me is my friend. Don't matter what color his skin is."

"That's what makes you strange."

Cooper shrugged again. "Nah, most of the other boys out here are the same, at least somewhat. Might be different if they went back to the States I reckon. You and Bill've always been treated well by the others, I figure."

"I was."

"I wasn't always this way though. I was raised in cotton country. Family didn't own any slaves, so I never thought much of it. Didn't go out of my way to be friendly to any I met but didn't go out of my way to degrade 'em either. But when I run into some of the Black trappers, men like Ed Rose and Jim Beckwourth—master trappers, brave men, tough men—I began to change my thinkin' a little. But when I began ridin' with Bill, my thinkin' changed entirely.

I'd stand back-to-back with him against a horde of goddamn Blackfeet before I would with most any other White man. I'd say the same about Two-Faces, one of the best men I've ever known."

They rode along in silence again for a short while before Bell said, "You never did finish tellin' me about your early days in the mountains."

TWENTY-FIVE

"WELL, we headed west. When we got to the mountains, Weeks started trappin'. He had said he would train me to do so, but he showed no such inclination. I picked up most of it on my own from watchin' him when I could. All he did was trap, hunt, drink, and fornicate. He had picked himself up a Pawnee woman named Tall Grass. Got my first taste of Injin fightin' soon after." He did not think Bell needed to hear of the "gift" Weeks had given him courtesy of an emasculated Pawnee warrior.

"Things started out bad and kept gettin' worse. He beat Tall Grass regularly and walloped me more than once too. He was a crusty ol' reprobate but he was a strong feller. Wasn't much I could do about him at first. But I grew stronger as time went by, and I began to fight back some. I even protected Tall Grass a few times. She crept into my robes at times to thank me when Weeks was passed out from whiskey.

"He found out about that though, and one night knocked me on my head and stole everything I had except the clothes I was wearin', and a few pieces of jerky and a foldin' knife I had hidden. Middle of winter. So cold I don't think all the fires of hell could warm it up any. I wandered off. I had no idea where I was or where I was goin'. I just stumbled along tryin' to stay alive. Eventually, I was attacked by a pack of hungry wolves, and I was certain I ws gone beaver I felt myself goin' down. Next thing I knew, I woke up in a Shoshoni lodge, bein' cared for by an old squaw and the prettiest woman God ever created named Pony Woman. As I was recoverin', Cheyenne Killer—the war chief who rescued me—adopted me, making me his son. I was half-froze to marry Pony Woman but now she was my sister and that was out of the question."

"So what happened? Ain't you married to a Nez Percé?"

"Am now. Back then though, Pony Woman introduced me to her best friend, Black Moon Woman, an equally beautiful and accomplished woman. I married her. My best friend among the Shoshonis, Cuts Throat, married Pony Woman."

"Did Black Moon throw yo' things out de lodge, like I hear women do when they don't want a man no mo'."

Cooper's face clouded in sadness and anger. "Don't go askin' about such things." He kicked his horse into a slightly faster pace and put some distance between him and his puzzled companion.

———

TWO NIGHTS LATER, as he and Bell, who had hardly spoken during that time, were sitting at the fire after polishing off a large haunch of deer, suddenly said, "Black Moon Woman was carried off by the Crows. They attacked our camp as winter was setting' in. Knocked me down into a gully. By the time I got back up to the camp, the Crows—with Black Moon—were long gone as were all the horses and mules. Though I was a little better off than the last time, I was still afoot so I couldn't carry much in the way of supplies. Couldn't move very fast either. I finally got to the Bighorn. Knowin' I needed help, I headed south. The Bighorn and Wind rivers merge some distance south, and up the Wind is usually where Cheyenne Killer stakes his village. It was deep into winter. Again."

Cooper sat silently for a few minutes puffing on his pipe. Then said, "I was shocked when my father said they couldn't help. The village feared an attack by the Blackfoot. But he did give me a horse and mule and a few supplies, and off I went again, down the Wind and back up the Bighorn. There were some doin's along the way, but nothing of any importance to me. I finally found the village where the Crows were holdin' Black Moon. I was tryin' to get her out of the village, but she took an arrow in the back. She went under a little later. 'Least I was with her." His voice had turned cold with bitterness and melancholy.

"That be a horrible thing, Mistuh Cooper. The Good Lord ought'n't let such things happen. No, suh."

"I got to agree to that, but what should be and what is are usually two different things, I've found."

"So what happened then?"

"Well, it took some time but I found the sons a bitches and with the help of a new friend; made wolf bait out of 'em."

"New friend?"

"Young feller, about your age then."

Bell was shocked by the look of sadness that had overcome Cooper. "I won't be askin' nothin' mo', Mistuh Cooper."

The White man just grunted and headed off to his robes.

───────

TWO DAYS LATER, as Cooper and Bell were sitting to breakfast, Cooper said, unexpectedly, "I met Zeke Potts in a winter camp of Rocky Mountain Fur boys up on the Yellowstone. He was part of the group of free trappers led by Elson Brooks."

"The fellahs have mentioned him."

Cooper nodded. "I wasn't with them at the time,

though El had asked me more than once to join up with him and the others. It was Zeke's first winter in the trade, at the time he had been out here less time than you have now. He helped a feller steal my horse and mule and wreck my small camp. I found out who did it and confronted Zeke. I was half-froze to raise his hair, but El talked me out of it at least for the time being. A couple days of hard ridin' and I caught up with the scum who had planned the raid and goaded Zeke into it."

"I reckon you made that hoss pay fo' it."

"I did. Got my animals back and returned to confront Zeke again. Once more, El talked me out of it by offerin' me compensation—all of Zeke's plews." A smile curled his lips for the first time in a couple of days. "Zeke was some put out by it."

"I'd be too. 'Sides, weren't the men free trappers just trappin' together for safety from Injuns? Didn't they get to keep all the plews they took?"

"All that is true, just like these days. But to El as captain, it was a matter of givin' me those plews or watchin' me put Zeke in the ground. 'Course he and Two-Faces were fixin' to stop me from doin' so if I was still bent on it. But the deal prevented a lot of bloodshed. I wasn't sure I liked the deal but I took it. I decided for some reason to stick with the group, so I moved into Two-Faces's lodge with his family."

"Another reason I think you be a strange man."

"Reckon I am a wee bit crazy sometimes. A few days later, I was goin' huntin' and Zeke asked to come along. He had said he wanted to earn my respect. Another crazy doin' on my part but I relented and took him."

"Like me."

"Yep, though he had a hell of a lot more to pay for than you do. Soon after, as winter camp was breakin' for the spring hunt, I was goin' to head off and look for the Crows who had taken Black Moon. Zeke asked to come along again—for the same reason. I agreed, and we headed out together."

"You raised their hair?"

"That we did, Zeke and me. After that, we went to see if anything was left at the camp where Black Moon had been taken. By then, it was too late to catch up to El and the others, so Zeke and me spent a winter trappin' in the Absarokas, then met up with the group. By then, Zeke had become my best friend."

"What happened to him? I heard he was killed by..." Bell looked alarmed and slammed his mouth shut at the hard, sad face of his companion. "I sorry, Mistuh Cooper," he said hastily. "I didn't mean to..."

Cooper sighed. "It's all right, Lem. It's been a few years, but I still ain't completely got over his goin' under. I know a man ain't supposed to feel such a thing, 'least not for long, but..." He stopped, a spark of realization washing over him. *Grieving*, he thought. *I ain't allowed myself the time to properly grieve for the loss of friends, the loss of others who helped me, the loss of my family. I was always too busy livin', helpin' others, tryin' to stay alive.*

"You all right, Mistuh Cooper?" Bell said urgently.

Cooper shook himself out of the dark place he had been and nodded. "Yeah, Lem. I just remembered something important."

"That be good. But you don't have to say no mo'."

"That's all right. I don't mind talkin' about it now. Yeah, Zeke was killed by Blackfeet."

"Was that the big fight in some valley where thousands of Blackfeet tried to overrun you fellahs that Uncle Bill told me about?"

Cooper nodded. "There was a heap of 'em, but not even close to thousands." He managed to smile a bit. "We mountaineers have been known to stretch the truth a mite. It was poor bull for certain. Bug's Boys kept comin' after us. Finally me, Zeke, and a Nez Percé named Sits Down managed to get behind them and attacked."

"Just the three of you?"

"Yep. Sits Down shined he did. He was like a whole war party by himself. The Blackfeet finally got the three of us surrounded, and it looked like our days were over. Then Zeke took an arrow to the throat." His voice hitched a little, but he continued, "But I got to him and killed the three devils about to raise his hair—and perform other of their evil ways on him. It looked like me and Sits Down were gonna go under right soon, but El, Bill, Two-Faces, and the others come to our aid."

Bell sat wide-eyed. "If you wasn't so trustful as I know you to be, and if Uncle Bill and the others hadn't told me some of that, I'd swear you was tellin' me a big, fat ol' lie."

"Hell, if I hadn't gone through it and just heard it, I'd think the same thing."

"And you wasn't hurt in all dat?"

"Not wounded, no, not really. But I got a real good knock on the head that had me stumblin' around for a spell. And every goddamn Blackfoot in the Rocky Mountains counted coup on me with a coup stick, lance, gun, or anything else they could lay their hands on."

"You was lucky then."

"Reckon I was, but it didn't feel like it. Still don't." He realized this was another reason for his malady these days. Not only had he not had time to grieve properly, but he still couldn't accept that Potts had been killed instead of him.

"That's pretty amazin'. You evah been wounded like by a lead ball or something?"

"More than once. Worse was takin' a Blackfoot arrow to the chest one time. Thought I was a gone beaver for sure that time too. But some Flatheads come along and saved me." Another burst of guilt roared through him.

"And did you and Mr. Potts...?"

"That's enough for now, Lem. We best be on our way soon."

"How far we got to go, Mistuh Cooper?"

"If my figurin' is right, we should be there around midday if we get our asses movin' now."

"You sayin' I'm slow and a slackard?" Bell grinned.

Cooper returned it. "Was I to say you were slow and a slackard would be high praise considerin' how truly slow you are in everything you do. 'Cept feedin', of course. You ain't no shirker when it comes to fillin' your meatbag. Now let's get to it."

"Yes, suh."

TWENTY-SIX

COOPER FOUND the steep slope that he had climbed out of the gulley and decided after a quick look around it was about the best spot to use to get back down. The two men eased their horses down the slope, the animals' legs stiff, knees locked out ahead of them as often as not while their rumps nearly scraped the soil and rocks. But they made it to the bottom.

"I think we be havin' trouble gettin' back up there," Bell said.

"I expect you're right, but I'll worry about that later."

"Like my pappy always said, 'Always put off 'til later what you don' feel like doin' now—or evah'."

"Your pap was a smart feller."

They slowly followed the rocky, scrub-strewn floor of the gully for a mile or more before Cooper stopped and pointed.

"Hope we find somethin'," Bell said.

"Something useful," Cooper added before moving on again. They tied their animals to a twisted little pinyon that seemed to take more of the weather's brunt than the small thicket of pines a few feet behind it.

The bones of the horse and mule were scattered, wiped clean by fangs, claws, beaks, and weather. The bridle of the horse was mostly gone, with just a few strips waving lazily in the light breeze. Cooper had expected as much. It was the plews he was interested in, and his initial glance indicated that it would not be anywhere near what he hoped it would be. Many plews were strewn about and had been chewed on. Others stretched out from where the remains of the pack saddle were, moving off in all directions as scavengers fought over them. They too, were chewed through large swaths across the pelts.

"This be bad, Mistuh Cooper."

"That's a fact, Lem. Ain't much of a surprise though. I was expectin' as much but I had to look to make certain. Tell true, I was expectin' worse. Way it looks, the bigger critters were satisfied with the meat, while the lesser critters had to be satisfied with the plews and smaller bits of leather."

"Think you can save some of dem plews?"

"Ain't sure. I reckon some are salvageable. Whether there's enough to try to gather them, well..." He shrugged. "I'll need to start checkin' 'em."

"You want to start that now? It took longer than

we expected to get here and there ain't much daylight left."

"I'll just wander about a bit, take the measure of things, try to decide if I should make any effort. Let's tend to the animals, and then you can get a fire goin' and meat roastin'.'"

"Yes, suh."

Half an hour later, they were slicing hunks of deer meat from the haunch hanging over the flames and enjoying the savory, dripping meat.

"What's yo' thinkin' on it now, Mistuh Cooper?"

Cooper sighed, irritated. "How many times I got to tell you to stop callin' me 'Mister'?"

"Yes, suh."

"And sir. I've told you a heap of times, it's Hawley or even just Hawl."

"Yes, su...I'll be tryin'." Bell seemed abashed.

"See that you do." He settled himself. "I still ain't sure. One minute it looks as if there's enough for almost a pack, the next it seems there ain't enough altogether to make a single hat. Well, I've got nothin' better to do, I reckon, so I'll gather up what I can and check 'em out. Some have been chewed to pieces, others I can cut large hunks off. They don't need to be whole plews to trade 'em, I figure, as long as they're big enough to be used by a hatmaker."

"You be all right, Mistuh...uh, Hawley."

"Optimistic young cuss, ain't you?"

"Yas, suh."

Cooper almost chuckled. "We best get ourselves

to sleep. I reckon tomorrow we'll be busy. Ain't gonna be hard work, I'm guessin', but it sure won't be excitin'."

COOPER WAS right about it not being hard work. However, it was dull, tedious, and time-consuming. The longtime mountain man grew more morose as the day wore on and the pile of usable plews grew very little. As dusk was approaching, he finally called a halt to their labors. "We've looked at every damn plew here, and," he said, shaking his head in annoyance, "there ain't even half a pack, I figure. If the rates are lower than they were last year, and that's likely, I might be able to buy myself a pint of whiskey, a twist of tobacco, and enough powder and ball for three, maybe even four shots." He spit into the dirt. "Don't see why I should even drag 'em out of here."

"That'd be a waste."

"Reckon so. But I doubt if it'd be worth it to carry 'em all the way to rendezvous. You got another idea?"

A great grin spread across Bell's dark face. "Y'all could give 'em to me."

Cooper's eyes blazed red and he thought his head would explode as anger roared through him. *After all I've had been through this past winter and spring, this greenhorn thinks I'll just hand him over what few plews I got?* he thought. Then, for some reason he could not fathom, the anger shattered. He glanced at

Bell, who looked as if he had seen a ghost—his own—and broke into a belly laugh. "You are some audacious critter, boy, I'll say that for you."

Still unsure of himself, Bell asked, "What that mean?"

"Means you're a darin' critter. It can also mean it shows that you don't respect me."

"No, suh, no, suh, I ain't disrespectin' yuh." Some of the color had drained from Bell's face.

Still laughing, Cooper said, "I know that, boy. And I'll think on it. Tell true, I'd rather do that than leave 'em here for the buzzards and such."

The young man's grin returned.

THEY WERE in no rush to pack things up in the morning, laziness being their main motivator. The weather was nice, the sun bright, the temperature warm down in the ravine. Cooper started putting what plews he thought were usable into a small pile and stood there looking them over. After a few minutes' thought, he decided it would be foolish to waste the time building a small press. Instead, he would just wrap the furs in a canvas tarp, making two pouches of a sort with a flat space in the middle to hang over the mule's back.

As he worked, he cocked his head now and again, trying to discern whether he had heard something or if it was just the wind. Finished, he stood and listened again. The sky was bright blue as far as he could see in the depths of the gulley, but something was still tugging at him.

Bell looked up from where he was packing their small stock of supplies. "You all right, Mistuh...um, Hawley?"

Cooper stood a few more moments, then swung around. "Finish that up right quick, boy, and get your horse saddled."

"But..."

"Now, dammit!"

The young man did not hesitate, he just dove into his work.

Cooper quickly flung the sacks of furs over the mule and tied them down. Then he added the buck-skin sacks of supplies that Bell hurriedly brought him. When he finished, he found that the young man had saddled his own horse and was just beginning to saddle Cooper's.

As Cooper took over, Bell asked, "What be the trouble?"

"Ever been caught in a flash flood?"

"Nope. It bad?"

"Can be very bad."

"But it don't even look like rain. De sun is shinin' bright."

"Don't mean it ain't rainin' somewhere."

"But?"

"Didn't the boys ever explain this to you?"

"No, suh. It never came up."

"Well, a storm could be goin' on miles away, but if it fills a gulch somewhere, that might flow to another and another, and people miles away get caught in a gulley or arroyo suddenly boiling with floodwater."

"That happenin'?"

"Ain't sure but I don't aim to wait and see. I heard thunder, faint but unmistakable. Can't tell you how far it is, but the sound is coming straight from where this gulley heads. If it rains hard five or ten miles from here, this ravine could be a roarin' river in minutes. Like I said, I ain't sure, but I ain't waitin' to learn whether it is or not."

"Well, then, let's get movin'."

"I'm waitin' on you, you dark-skinned slackard."

"All you're gonna see is my Black ass chargin' up that slope there if you don't get a move on."

"Yes, sir, Captain Bell, sir."

Bell looked aghast.

Though he was concerned about the possible flood, he winked at Bell. "You ready?"

"Yep."

They swung into their saddles and galloped off to where they had entered the gulley. As he rode, Cooper cursed himself for not having taken some time to try to find an easier way out. He had planned to do so after the work was done, thinking they had plenty of time and might even spend another day or two here.

They dismounted in a hurry. Cooper tied his

horse and the mule to a warped tree. Cooper now knew why the tree was so gnarled—there had been many a flash flood here over time.

"All right, Lem, up you go."

"Dis horse ain't gonna like it."

"You ain't gonna like it neither, I expect. But you're welcome to stay here and see if my worries are real. Get you a nice bath."

"Well, now, that's changed my mind fo' me. I could face a flood, even a big 'un, but a bath, uh-un, no suh."

"Then move. If I'm right, I reckon we don't have much time."

Bell nodded. "Do I ride 'er?"

"Reckon you should start, but I ain't so sure she'll make it to the top with you on her back. That horse starts flailin' and slippin', you best dismount and walk her up as best you can. We try to push 'em too hard, and any of 'em might just slip back down to the bottom here, dead or so used up they'll be about as useful as if they were."

Bell nodded again and swept into the saddle. "Here goes." He backed off a few dozen yards thinking that giving the horse a running start might be a good thing. He spurred the animal.

In its initial bolt up the hillside, the mare made it more than halfway up, but then began to falter. Bell whipped the beast hard with the long reins, but the horse started slipping back a little.

"Get off her, you damn fool!" Cooper shouted.

Bell slid out of the saddle and, with reins in hand, urged the horse up the slope, tugging occasionally, cursing often. It took more than ten minutes, but they made it.

Below, Cooper saw them go over the top. He untied the mule and said to the horse, "I'll be back for you soon, ol' feller." He towed the mule to the foot of the slope. "Now you listen here, you ornery critter. I am in no mood for cantankerousness. I told my last mule that I didn't favor mule meat and wouldn't usually eat it. But I said I'd make an exception if the critter made too much of a fuss. Now I'm tellin' you the same. Now let's go on up the hill without being irksome."

The climb began peacefully and easily, and Cooper was shocked when the mule kept right on going even as the slope steepened. It was a powerful animal and seemed to know just where to put its hooves for the best purchase. They made it to the top in several fewer minutes than Bell and his horse. Cooper had hardly sweated.

"Damn, Mistuh...un, Hawley, maybe I should've let you bring my gal up here. I didn't think I evah saw a mule so calm in such an instance."

"Me neither. I think he's plannin' some deviltry and is tryin' to get me to put my guard down and think of him as a friendly critter. Son of a bitch ain't foolin' this ol' chil', though." He turned, scanning the sky. Then pointed. "Look."

"The storm," Bell said.

"Yep. It's headin' this way and fast, but the flash flood will get here even faster."

"You certain the flood is comin'?"

Cooper nodded. "We ain't got much time. Keep an eye on these two animals, try to keep 'em calm if the thunder really starts actin' up. I'm headin' downhill to get my horse up here."

TWENTY-SEVEN

COOPER BOLTED DOWN THE SLOPE, stumbling, slipping, and sliding, at times bouncing on his ass, tripping on rocks. But he made it to the bottom intact. He ran to the tree and untied the horse. The animal's eyes were rolling, its nostrils flaring as it shuffled nervously in fright.

"I know you don't like this, ol' feller. It don't shine with this ol' chil' neither. But if you don't cooperate, there's a damn good chance we'll both go under. Now let's move, and don't you go fussin'."

They headed up the slope, moving quickly. But about halfway up, the gelding started to hesitate and resist.

"C'mon, dammit. If I didn't need your flea-bitten ass to get me to rendezvous, I'd let you slip back to the bottom to have a good swim. Now, let's go." He stumbled a few feet ahead and tugged hard on the reins.

The horse moved ahead a foot or so, then balked again.

"Dammit, horse, you're tryin' my patience." He tugged, and the horse moved a step or two. "Don't stop now, dammit. You don't want to move, you wretched critter, I'll give in to your desire, and hogtie you and leave you floppin' 'round on this hill for the wolves to come and partake of a fine meal of horsemeat."

Cooper tugged and made a few more feet of progress before the animal hesitated again. He was coated with sweat now, his arms and legs shaking with the effort. He yanked some more, as hard as he could, hoping the whole thing wouldn't pull off. The only thing preventing it so far was the throat lash, and that wasn't enough to keep it in place for long given Cooper's tugging. He could hear the roar of water coming ever closer.

Suddenly Bell came down the hill, sliding on his rump most of the way. He managed to jam his moccasins in the dirt and stop him some feet past the horse. He scrambled up and waded through the dirt and rocks behind the animal.

"No!" Cooper shouted. "Not behind...!"

"Shut yo' mouth, Hawley, and pull!"

Cooper did so, and Bell slapped the horse's rump as hard as he could. The horse moved a few more feet and stopped as Bell shook his hand, trying to remove the sting from the slap.

The horse didn't move. "Goddamn stupid beast,"

he shouted. The coming river's roar washed over his words.

The horse jumped forward, trying to escape the second sharp sting on his rear, but as it did, a hoof caught Bell a glancing blow on one side. He fell, gasping in pain.

Cooper barely managed to drop the reins and jump out of the way as the horse charged by. He rolled and slid a bit, then looked at Bell. "Damn," he mouthed as he stood. He hurried as best he could to his friend's side. "You hurt bad?"

"Ain't sure. Feels like fire though."

"Such things often do. Can you get up?"

Bell tried but grimaced and hissed in pain. "Ain't so good. You go on, Hawley. I'll try to make do on my own."

"Like hell, boy. I didn't do all this work just to let you set here and take a bath." He offered a pale grin. "Not that you don't need one. Now, come on." He helped Bell up and, with a shoulder under the young man's armpit and an arm around his waist, helped the staggering friend gingerly but urgently up the hill. Cooper dropped Bell, who eased himself up onto his side, a hand on the side of his head, holding it up. Cooper plopped down on his rear.

And they watched as a thirty-foot-tall wall of water thundered through the gulch.

"Looks like we didn't need to hurry so much," Bell said, wincing.

"Now you tell me. If I'd known, I'd have left you

down there to get back up here on your own. Maybe you wouldn't be complainin' so much."

"Weren't fo' me, you'd still be down there fightin' with that horse." Bell glanced around. "Don't see it anywhere."

"Likely havin' himself a good run tryin' to calm down. He'll be back. I hope. If not, we'll have to find him."

"You'll have to find him. I ain't goin' nowhere."

"Plannin' to run off with my plews as soon as I'm outta sight?"

"Could be," Bell said with a grin. "Paltry as the take is."

"Then I'd have to follow you and put you under."

"You do that and you'll have to bury me."

"Who says I'd bother to bury you?"

Both laughed, and Bell groaned as the laughter kicked up the pain in his side.

"I best have a look at that," Cooper said. "Don't know as I'll be able to do much, but..."

"Yes, suh, I understand."

Cooper knelt and pushed Bell's shirt up. "I'd say it was lookin' might colorful already but with your dark skin, I can't tell. It does seem as if there is some yellowish hue comin' through. Brace yourself, I'll need to probe it a little."

Bell did but he still hissed, and his eyes widened as Cooper gently prodded the young man's side.

Cooper rocked back on his heels. "I ain't no doc, you understand, but I don't think any ribs are broken, doesn't feel that way. But I'd say a couple might have been bruised some. I can't tell for sure, of course. If they're broken, it'll take a long spell for you to heal up. If they're just bruised, you should be good in a couple of weeks maybe. Even if they're broke, I don't think they've poked anything vital in your innards. I don't know as if there's anything I can do other than bind you up real good and hope that'll keep your insides from movin' around too much to let things heal. You'll have to be careful in what you do, not movin' too much to keep those bones from healin'. 'Course that won't be hard for you since you don't do anything anyway. I don't know why I keep draggin' you along when I have to do all the work."

"Ah, Hawley, y'all know that ain't true. Wasn't for me you would have gone under a long time ago. Hell, y'all didn't even know how to piss befo' I showed y'all."

"Well, no wonder I feel better these days," Cooper said with a grin. He patted Bell on the shoulder. "Sit tight, Lem, while I go fetch some things."

"Like I said, I ain't goin' nowhere."

Cooper cut off a piece of beaver fur, then stood, trying to figure out what he could use to bind the fur to Bell's body. Finally he sighed. He figured he would have to use a couple of the leather straps that held the pack saddle on the mule. He could use some of the rope they had for the saddle but he didn't think it would be good for his companion.

"You painin'?" he asked as he knelt again at Bell's side.

"Yas, suh."

"Ain't much I can do about it."

"I know. I'll be all right. Y'all might have to do more of the work though." He sounded apologetic.

"Hell, you do so little it won't make me no never mind." He grinned.

Bell returned it weakly.

"Hell, if you'd been doin' your share of the work 'round here, you'd have toughened up those muscles and wouldn't be ailin' now."

"I'll try to 'member dat. Someday."

Cooper knelt and helped his companion into a sitting position, eliciting another hiss of pain, then handed the fur to Bell. "Hold it against the spot. When the young man did, Cooper wrapped one leather strap around Bell's midsection and tied it on the opposite side of the injury. He repeated it with the other. "You all right?"

"It be hard to breathe some, but I'll do fine."

"Well, you take your ease while I try to rustle us up something to fill our meatbags. Don't know if we have anything that'll appeal to your royal majesty."

Bell chuckled, then groaned with the pain. "Hell, Hawley, y'all know I'll eat anything from donkey nuts to gopher innards."

"Glad you ain't doin' the cookin' right now."

Cooper started a fire and then got the chunk of

deer meat that was only two days old and hadn't quite rotted and hung it over the fire.

While he waited for the meat to cook, he wandered to the edge of the chasm and looked down. The flood was still thundering, though it looked like it might be easing a little. It carried rocks and trees, and anything else that was in its roaring path. While he stood there, he wondered about his luck. He seemed to have a heap of it, though it did not seem to rub off on those around him. And his luck had run out with the Shoshonis, which, he had decided, hurt the most. He wasn't sure why. He had many friends and even another family with the Nez Percé. But there was still a stronger bond between him and Cheyenne Killer's band. They had rescued him, nursed him back to health, made a man and a warrior out of him. He had found love with Black Moon Woman, and great pain in her death, and the Shoshonis had shared both with him. He had found a best friend in Cuts Throat, and when he and Zeke Potts had partnered in trapping, he had two best friends, one red, one white. Now one was dead and the other had snubbed him. He loved his sister, Pony Woman, who had married Cuts Throat. And he loved Little Elk, the almost two-year-old child of Pony Woman and Cuts Throat. There had been troublesome times, yes, but still, there was a...

"Hawl, you best check on the meat before it burns," Bell called out.

Cooper shook away the gloomy thoughts as best he could and returned to the fire.

———

BELL WAS in considerable pain the next morning, and as he had yesterday, Cooper helped him sit up a little with his upper back against a fallen log so the young man could eat.

"Get some rest," Cooper said. He stood, sliced off a piece of meat from the fire, and then chewed on it as he strolled over to the edge of the gulley again. The water had stopped flowing but had left large pools and a jumble of debris.

He stood there a long time, the same thoughts rumbling around in his head. Strong and endless, they soon turned his mood from melancholy to anger —at himself, his situation, and his annoying worrying. Growling at himself, he turned and found a piece of bark with a shiny white inside. He picked up a cool piece of charcoal from the fire and wrote 'Gone huntin' on it, then and set it gently on Bell's chest. The young man had been practicing his letters and numbers every night on the trail and had become proficient at reading simple words.

Cooper saddled his horse and affixed the bridle as best he could, then mounted up and rode off. It was several hours before he saw a small herd of antelope. Antelope meat was too goatlike for his taste, but it was far better than horse or mule. He downed one and butchered out enough meat to last a day or two. Anything more would rot quickly at this time of year.

When he got back, Bell was sitting up again leaning against the log. His dark face seemed a little pale, but he was awake, though he looked to be in pain.

"You were able to read my note?"

"Yas, suh."

"You're learnin'. I got us some antelope meat."

"Never had any of dat."

"Well, it's better'n some things, worse'n others. Besides, if you ever see starvin' times, you'll make do with skunk ass."

"Never had de pleasure of dat either and nary want to try it. We ever get in such bad shape, you can have it all to yo'self. I'll eat my mocs." He chuckled, but then groaned.

"But you'd eat donkey nuts or gopher guts like you said?"

"Be a tough choice, but I reckon I'd stick with those two rather than skunk ass," he said with another grin. He grimaced as if he were having some trouble other than his ribs.

Cooper thought it odd. "Something else plaguin' you, Lem?"

"Um, I...well..."

"Out with it, boy."

"I need help standin' so I can make a stop in the bushes. You don't and I'll end up shittin' my britches, and as sure as I am that God's lookin' over us, I ain't happy about the notion."

"I wouldn't be either. Did it once. I was mortified."

"What's dat mean?"

"Shamed to high heaven. All right, let's get you up on your feet."

Cooper gingerly helped him up and watched the young man toddle off.

TWENTY-EIGHT

"IT'S BEEN THREE, four days, Hawley, oughtn't you be on the trail to rendezvous?" Bell said.

"You ain't well enough to travel yet, boy," Cooper grunted. He did want to be on the move. They had a far distance to go and little time to reach the site along the Green River. But some things took precedence.

"But y'all need to get movin'."

"I know that."

"Then why..."

"There might be some mountaineers," Cooper snapped, "that leave an ailin' companion behind, but I ain't one of 'em. We'll stay here 'til I say you're fit to travel, which you ain't now."

"I—"

"I'll hear no more if it, boy. Now clap your trap shut and take some more rest."

"I'm tired of restin'."

"That ain't my concern."

"Should be if you evah want to leave here. I ain't gonna get no bettah settin' here on my rump all day every day."

"You've been up every day."

"For a few minutes at a time so I don't shit myse'f. I need to get movin' some, even a little at a time. Maybe make things heal faster."

Cooper thought it over for a few minutes. "I'll let you up, but you ain't to do anything. No bendin', no reachin', no liftin' things. You do any of those things and make your injury worse and I'll stake you down so you can't move."

"Afraid I'll knock you down and do as I please?"

Cooper burst out laughin', as did Bell.

"That's something I'd like to see."

"Me, too. Now he'p me up."

IN THE FOLLOWING THREE DAYS, the exercise, if that's what it could be called, did not seem to help any in Bell's healing. The young man would move around pretty well for a few minutes, but then his dark face paled and he would begin sweating heavily. Within half an hour, he would be resting again, hating to ask Cooper for help in getting down, but needing it. Maybe an hour later, he would try again, with Cooper's help in the opposite way. He hated that too; hated himself for it, and his mind worked furiously to conceive of ways to make his recovery happen in days instead of perhaps weeks. But nothing came to mind.

———

ON THE SECOND DAY, Cooper grabbed an extra tomahawk, honed it, then approached a short, thick pine that stood just a couple yards from their fire. He started chopping. More than halfway through, he hitched up the mule to the section that was to come down and had the mule pull it. With a few more strokes of the tool, the upper part of the tree tore off loudly and crashed to the ground. Cooper started whittling away at the sharp shards that had been left.

Bell came hustling up, moving as fast as he dared. "What happened?" he called well before he reached Cooper but received no answer.

When he reached the older man, Cooper said, "Sit," and waved the 'hawk at the stump.

Bell looked at him curiously, then shrugged and sat. He smiled. "This here shines, it do."

Cooper bobbed his head. "Stay there." He walked off and returned with a long branch that had a "V" at one end. He pulled Bell to a stand, stuck the "V" under his arm and measured the stick. He cut off half a yard and handed the makeshift crutch to his companion. "Sit," he ordered again. When the young man had done so, Cooper said, "That should help you get up from that seat. Won't do you no good, I expect, when you're lyin' down., but this might be better than nothin'. Now try it."

Bell did, several times, eyes gleaming, mouth wide in a grin. "This be de best, Hawley. 'Dis work real fine."

BELL SAT ON HIS THRONE, as he liked to think of his stump chair, the next night and thought. He was still angry at himself for getting hurt but was angrier because it was keeping Cooper from going forward with his journey. He didn't want his mentor to miss out on rendezvous with his friends because of his injury.

As he sat there the next afternoon a plan began to form. It wasn't a good one but with some luck it might work. And it was the best he could think of. As he stumbled around later, he thought more about it but still could not conceive of anything better, and he wavered. He kept his silence mostly through their late meal, then went to sit on his makeshift chair.

Soon after, Cooper called, "Robe time for this chil'. You need any help?"

"Nah, suh. I'll be along directly." He waited a while to make sure Cooper was asleep. Then he carefully pushed himself up and walked as quietly as he could to where his saddle lay, thankful that the moon was almost full in the cloudless sky. He lay his crutch down, knelt, got a grip on the saddle, and pulled.

"Lord a'mighty," he hissed, hoping the sound did not wake Cooper.

He grabbed his crutch, rose, and stood, thinking. Sweat beaded his brow and trickled down from under his arms. He began to wonder if this was a plan at all. He glanced over at the sleeping Cooper, and his resolve firmed. The longtime mountain man had treated him well, taught him letters and numbers, taught him more than Uncle Bill and the others had done in a season, things not directly related to trapping. In the month or so they had been together, Cooper had become more of a father to him than even his uncle. He could not delay Cooper any longer. No, he would have to do what was necessary, even if that meant he had to leave things like his saddle behind.

He shuffled to the fire, which was down to embers, thankful for the crutch, and grabbed a little of the meat they had and a couple handfuls of chokecherries he had gathered. He also picked up a length of rope and headed back to where his saddle was. He got his possibles bag and his shooting bag, tied them together, and hung them over the horse's neck. He fashioned a rope rein on the animal's mouth. Taking the rope in hand, he walked toward his seat.

"This should be interestin'," he muttered. An owl hooted from a nearby tree, giving Bell a shiver of fear. It was a bad omen, he thought. He got the horse as close as he could to the stump, then one hand on the animal and the other pushing with the crutch, he climbed onto his perch. He almost bit his tongue in half as he tried to keep the pain-filled moan that wanted to burst forth. He stood there, a hand on the horse, letting the agony subside and the shaking stop. *You got this far*, he thought. *Don't stop now*. Sucking in a deep breath, he slid onto the horse's back and sat for a few moments both happy and surprised that he had made it.

He rode out of the camp and followed the rim of the gulch for more than eight miles until it was easy enough to cross. When he did, he turned northwest. Cooper was heading south and a little east, so Bell figured that going in the opposite direction would throw Cooper off. "Dis be de right thing to do, Lem," he told himself firmly.

———————

COOPER KNEW something was amiss as soon as he awoke. He didn't think hostiles were about because his senses would have woken him sooner. At least they always had before. He slowly moved a hand and picked up a pistol and rolled 'til he was up on one knee. He scanned the area, weapon ready. But there were no Indians to be seen in the breaking dawn. Bell's horse was not there either.

"Damn fool," he murmured. He uncocked the pistol and shoved it in his belt as he headed to where the young man had made his bed. Bell's saddle was there but his possibles bag and shooting bag were gone. Cooper blew out a deep breath. "Damn fool," he said again, this time aloud. "Ain't got the brains of a mule's tail."

He took a quick spin around the camp but none of his things had been taken or even disturbed. "At least the idiot's not a thief."

Cooper went to the fire and picked up the last of the meat, noting that his companion had taken the other half. "Well, at least he'll not starve to death before I run him down."

He sat and ate.

Done quickly, he checked the stump Bell had been using as a seat and immediately picked up his companion's tracks. He hurriedly saddled his horse, slung his rifle over his shoulder, and began following the trail. He got about two miles before he checked again, having figured he knew which way Bell was heading.

"You're the damn fool, Hawley," he scolded himself.

He eventually found the trail and followed it at a good pace, slowing now and again to make sure he was still on the right path. He crossed the gulch where it narrowed. He figured it must have been little more than a slit in the earth until the recent flood had torn a savage path through it.

A couple of miles farther on he spotted Bell's horse, standing cropping grass. As he drew closer, he saw his young companion lying on the ground, struggling to get up. Cooper pulled up alongside him and looked down from his horse. "Comfortable?" When Bell said nothing, he said, "This ain't the time or place for a nap, Lem."

Again, he got no response, so he dismounted and knelt beside the young man. "Where were you plannin' to go, boy?"

"Don't know. I just wanted to get away from y'all."

"Get away from me?" Cooper asked, surprised. "What in hell did I ever do to you to make you want to get away from me? I've treated you well."

"I know. Too well, mebbe. But I was tired of holdin' you up. You need to get to rendezvous but wouldn't leave me behind. So I thought I'd get out of yo' way and let you get on with yo' business."

Cooper snapped. "You goddam fool. You think I'm the kind of feller who'd leave behind a companion? I told you I ain't that kind of man. You think I wouldn't come after you? Damn, I swear I ought to pound you good, whip you 'til you was an inch from death. I..." He slammed his mouth shut when Bell tried to curl into a ball.

"Don't hurt me, massuh. I'll do what you say. I don't run no mo. Don't hurt me. Don't whip me. Don't..." He was close to tears.

Cooper realized what he had said and felt the sickness rise in him from the shame. *You stupid, fuckin' bastard, Hawley!* He shouted the words in his mind. Aloud, he said urgently, "Lem! Lem, listen to me. I didn't mean what I said. I didn't know what I was sayin'. It was just fool things—hurtful things, I realize—that poured out of my mouth. I ain't your master, and I never will be. I'll kill any man who tries to be your master. And I ain't gonna hurt you. I promise that. Never. You got to believe me. I won't ever hurt you, Lem. Nope."

Bell turned a fear-filled face to him, but there was a little light of hope in his dark eyes. "You won't?"

"Hell no. I'd sooner kick my own ass—or have you do so—all the way to St. Louis. Maybe I ain't told you or you ain't figured it out, but I'm as dumb as a donkey's pecker. And that's on my best days."

A tentative smile crossed Bell's face as he swiped at his eyes and nose with a sleeve, thankful no tears had spilled out. But it vanished in an instant. "I ain't so sure I can trust you anymo', Mistuh Cooper."

The hurt of his own making that raced through Cooper was like a kick to the testicles and the heart at the same time. In a moment, he pulled a pistol and cocked it. Bell's eyes rose wide in fear. Cooper shook his head, turned the pistol, grabbing it by the barrel and holding the butt toward Bell. "Take it, Lem," he said firmly, shame pounding through his head. "You deserve to do that."

Bell tentatively reached out a hand, then jerked it back. "No, Mistuh Cooper. I ain't gonna do dat."

TWENTY-NINE

COOPER TURNED THE PISTOL AROUND. "Then I reckon I'll have to do it myself." He raised the gun and pointed it at his right temple. His face was set, and he showed no fear. The only thing that passed through his mind was that it was time to end it all. End the pain he had caused so many others. *Yes,* he thought solemnly, *it's time.*

Bell jerked up and slapped Cooper's hand as hard as he could. He didn't knock the pistol loose but did shift it away from his friend's head. "Don't you do no such thing, Mistuh Cooper," he snapped as he fell back, breathing hard as the pain kicked up again.

"That was a fool thing to do, Lem. After all I just did to you—and all the harm and pain I've brought to others, it's about time I—"

"You be right, Mistuh Cooper. You be dumber'n a donkey's dick. But you done m're good dan bad in yo' life."

"You don't know me that well, Lem."

"Mebbe I don't. But you treated me fine since I been ridin' wit' you. I saw de way Uncle Bill and the others treated you and you dem. And I've heard stories about you, Mistuh Cooper. Stories that sometimes sound like the tall tales mountaineers be tellin'. But they ain't. I know they ain't. Those stories are of a great man, one who be of de same caliber of men along with de others dat are kings of de mountains. Men like Jim Bridger, and Jim Beckwourth, and Kit Carson. I ain't been in de mountains long, but all de boys talk about men like those three—and you."

"You said a minute ago you don't..."

"Dat's true. I don't completely trust you after what happened today. But I don't distrust y'all completely either. Now, put dat pistol away and let's talk about what we gonna do."

Cooper stared at him for some moments, then uncocked the pistol and hung it on his belt. "The way I see it, Lem, we're havn' a contest to see who's dumber than the other."

"I think you'd win—you be a lot older and had more practice at it." He gave a wan smile.

Cooper returned it.

"So what do we do now, Mistuh Cooper?"

"Still Mister Cooper?"

"Yas, suh. I ain't ready yet to start callin' you Hawley no more."

Cooper nodded in melancholy understanding.

"YOU EVER RIDE IN A TRAVOIS?"

"Nah, suh. I seen Injuns ridin' in 'em. Looked like mostly old folks and chillun."

Cooper nodded. "Women who are too old or feeble, old men, even wounded warriors at times too."

"Why you ask me this?"

"Think you could ride in one?"

"Never did, so I don't know. You plannin' to set me in one?"

"Thought to. Should've thought of it before. Might be rough on you thinkin' on it now."

"I'll take dat risk if it be gettin' us on de trail again."

Cooper looked around. "We best get back to our camp; there's no likely trees hereabout. Now c'mon." He helped Bell up and they headed to the two animals, which were still quietly grazing. Cooper led Bell to his own horse.

"I can't ride your horse, Mistuh Cooper."

"Yes, you can. It'll be easier for you. Now get up there." He bent and cupped his hands. Bell placed a moccasin in the cup and Cooper jerked his arms up. Bell almost flew over the horse but caught himself and breathed a sigh of relief.

Cooper gathered his companion's few possessions and handed them up to the young mountain man. He flung himself onto the other, bareback, horse and they moved on.

They made it back to the camp in a little more than three hours.

"How'd you do, Lem?" Cooper assed he help his companion down from the horse.

"Pretty well. Pained me some but not so bad as I was thinkin'."

Cooper stood there looking around for a few minutes. Then he nodded. "Might be best if we forget usin' a travois. I ain't sure we got enough makin's for one and you seemed to do right well on a horse."

"Y'all gonna have to lift me on and off regular."

"You givin' me orders now?"

"Yas, suh. I figure I be de master now." He was having trouble keeping laughter bottled up.

"Well, I don't take kindly to be given orders, least of all a snot-nose duck humper like you. So I figure I'll just take off on my own and leave you here to try gettin' up on that horse every day."

"You be a hard man, Hawley. Got a heart as cold as a rock in winter. And I ain't no duck humper. Critter's way too small fo' this chil', if you catch my drift."

Both laughed, then Bell said solemnly, "I be sorry, Hawley, for actin' the way I did. Jus' like a baby who cain't find his mama so she could give him her teat."

"Hell, Lem, we both were fools, though you had a lot more reason than me considerin' your past. I did learn something though. I learned that even a skunk-ass-eatin' critter like you can be an almost decent cuss."

"That don't mean much, old man, you ol'...what's that word you and Two-Faces use all the time?"

"Reprobate?"

"Yas, suh. I don't rightfully know what dat is but you be one."

Cooper laughed. "That's the truth. Now let's get a move on. There's plenty of daylight left and if you can bring yourself to pick up your usual pace we can make some distance."

"You'll be eatin' my dust."

"I HOPE we find some folks still dere," Bell said. "It be the fust rendezvous I'd be to."

"Weren't you at last year's?"

"Yas, suh, but only fo' a short time, and I really weren't able to take part in much. I didn't have no money. Uncle Bill give me ten dollars. Ten dollars! Can you imagine havin' that much dollars at one time! I never had to care about money befo' of course, so I thought I was a rich man." He sighed. "That ten dollars didn't last long though. Two pints of whiskey and it was gone. Are things always so dear out thisaway?"

"With the traders, yep. It ain't so bad back in the States, or at least it wasn't when I left. It's been more'n ten years now, and I ain't been back since, so I don't know for certain. But the traders have always taken us boys for whatever they could. Many if not most of us made good money over the years, but the price we get for beaver the last couple of years has been pretty lean, and I expect it will only get worse. Still, we spent all of it while we were at rendezvous. Money went through our hands like the water of a rushing stream does when we put our fingers in 'em."

"Still, it be somethin' I want to do even if I ain't got much money."

"You will. By my reasonin'—and I ain't so good at such things—by the time we get there, they'll have been spreein' for about a week, maybe a day or two more, maybe a day or two less. Should be plenty of time for you to join the festivities."

"I be lookin' for'ard to them doin's," Bell said, eyes beaming with excitement.

"Then get your ass movin' a little faster. Lord if you ain't slower'n a turtle with two broken legs."

"You the one been slowin' us down, old man."

"That's 'cause I've had to take care of you all the time." He grinned, then more seriously asked, "How are you feelin' these days, Lem?"

"Some sprightly, I reckon."

"Maybe you don't need my help so much anymore."

"I ain't *that* sprightly. But I be feelin' much better. Reckon it'll take a long time fo' it to heal all right."

"Likely. But you'll be fine. We're a hardy bunch of fellers, us mountaineers. We get time someday, maybe I'll tell you stories of boys like Hugh Glass, and Pegleg Tom Smith, and Ol' Jed Smith. Ol' Jed ain't with us no more. Got himself killed by Comanches searchin' for water on the Santa Fe Trail some years ago. Hugh Glass too, has gone under some years ago. Got himself done in by some Blackfeet."

"I've heard Uncle Bill and the others talkin' about you and some of your doin's and how you almost went under."

"That's true, yep, but you don't need to hear those stories. Ain't much to 'em anyways."

"But they..." He shut up when Cooper threw a glance at him telling the young man he had gone far enough.

———

A LITTLE OVER two weeks later, the two sat on their horses looking down at the verdant land along Henry's Fork of the Green River. The camp—or, rather, series of camps—was spread along the river for, at best as Cooper could figure from where he sat, five miles. Clusters of lodges from Shoshonis, Nez Percé, Flatheads, and even some Crows sat in relative orderliness compared with the haphazard array of trappers' tents and lean-tos, and even some buffalo sleeping robes thrown down by a small fire. Hundreds of horses grazed on the other side of the river under the watchful eyes, Cooper figured, of some of the various tribes' young men. Cooper wondered where the horses from Bill Sublette's trading party were, as well as those from the old Rocky Mountain boys, now working for whatever American Fur was officially called now. Between the two groups, as well as some smaller ones, there would be hundreds of their horses and mules too.

"Looks like there be an almighty passel of folks down there. It didn't seem that big when I was here last year."

"From what I can see from here, it looks to be the biggest trade fair for us mountaineers."

"That's good, ain't it?"

"Ain't sure. The way prices have been fallin' the last couple years, I was thinkin' the trade was about over. But lookin' at all the folks here, maybe things have changed for the better. I doubt it though. Beaver are gettin' scarce, and the folks back east are makin' hats of something called silk." He sighed. "Well, I reckon you'll be seein' for yourself right quick."

"*I'll* be seein' it?" Bell questioned, surprised.

"Yep."

"You're not?"

"Nope. Like I said before, I got business to tend to, and it's time it was taken care of."

"You want company?"

"No. I need to do this alone." His eyes grew distant, and he looked like he was in another world. "Whatever *this* is," he finished quietly.

"Anything I can do fo' you, Mistuh Cooper?"

"Mister again?"

"Way of me payin' my respects to you."

Cooper nodded and he seemed to drift off into the unknown for a few moments. He shook his head to clear it said, "Ya know, boy, if you weren't so goddamn lazy, ya cantankerous Black savage, it'd almost being like ridin' with ol' Zeke again."

Bell stared at him, eyes wide with shock, then said, "I ain't ever had such welcomin' words from a man befo', especially a white devil, but you be makin' me about the proudest man ever set foot on God's earth. Thank you, Mistuh Cooper."

"Don't go getting' too high and mighty. It's only just me makin' those compliments, and I ain't much of anybody."

"That ain't true. You've learned me more'n anyone, includin' Two-Faces and Uncle Bill, and in jus' a couple months."

"That may be, but don't tell them anything of what I said. They learn that and you'll never have any peace. They might treat you a little better, but more likely they'll treat you worse, at least by makin' fun of you all the time."

"All right. You said you want me to do somethin' for you?"

"Yep. Go on down there and find Two-Faces's camp. Last time we rendezvoused, we laid our camp maybe a mile, mile and a half, upriver from here. When you find 'em, tell Two-Faces I want to see him. Don't tell anyone else, except maybe your uncle. I'll be at the bottom of one of the hills a couple miles east. There was a strange rock formation there.

When we were still in our cups as we were leavin', me and Two-Faces knocked it over. That's what some fool men do when they get too liquored up. He'll know where I mean."

"I can do dat."

"Good. And tell him to be at least mostly sober when gets here. I'll be there no more than two days before ridin' on. He doesn't want to see me..." Cooper shrugged.

"You want me to take the plews down there with me or wait 'til Two-Faces comes to meet you?"

"They're yours now, Lem."

"I cain't take..."

"Yes you can. I got no use for 'em, boy. There ain't enough for me trade for anything. You add 'em to your plews and you might get an extra ten dollars."

"You sure?"

"I am, now get your butt movin'."

"Yes, suh."

Cooper watched for a while. He didn't know why he had taken to the young man. Bell was not like Zeke Potts at all, though maybe in some ways he was, ways that Cooper could not put a finger on. "Oh, well," he told himself, "it doesn't matter. I ain't likely to see him again." He shook his head at the strangeness of it all, then turned his horse and rode off to the not very distant hill.

THIRTY

TWO-FACES BEAUBIEN NEITHER LOOKED, sounded, or acted as if he were completely sober when he rode into the small camp Cooper had made in the shade of the hill. He dismounted and threw his reins to Lemrich Bell, who shook his head partly in annoyance, partly in amusement. The young man tied Beaubien's horse and his own to the only tree in the area, as did Bill White.

"What in 'ell you want with me, *m'sieur?*" Beaubien asked almost with a snarl.

"Good to see you too, Two-Faces," Cooper said, irritation in his voice.

"Bah. You are more trouble zan ever," the half-breed said when he sat cross-legged across the small fire from Cooper. Neither paid attention as Bell filled a coffeepot with water from a canteen, then tossed in a handful of pounded up beans and set it on the fire. He took a seat next to White.

"So what do you want, 'Awley? Ze young pup tells me to come see you *vite, très vite*."

"I did no such..."

White elbowed Bell in the side shutting him up.

"Why you not come to our camp at rendezvous zere, eh? *Non*, you do not, you send for me like I am your servant, expect me to come running to you at your bidding."

"Oh, hell, Two-Faces, you ain't foolin' me, you crusty old half-breed. That's the lightnin' still runnin' 'round in your blood talkin'."

Beaubien chuckled then grimaced as he burped. "*Mais oui, mon ami.* Sometimes, I t'ink I am getting too old for such doin's, eh." He grinned. "But no, is not true. Even an old *'omme* like me must 'ave zis pleasure once a year with his *amis*. But some of zese friends must not like zis anymore, eh. Like ze one sitting before me?"

"Must seem that way, I reckon, but it ain't true. I like bein' around you boys, though I don't know why since you're a passel of pestiferatin' shit piles with no grace or dignity."

"Ah," Beaubien said around his laughter, "zis is coming from ze paragon of gentlemanliness, eh."

Everyone was laughing now. "That's right, and don't you forget it neither."

As the laughter died down, Bell poured coffee for all, then sat back down.

"So, really, *mon ami*, what is zis about? You've found your answer and will leave us friends now?"

"No. I ain't figured it all out, but I'm followin' its trail and it's gettin' close. I got to track it down to the end."

"And zen?"

Cooper shrugged. "Ain't sure. If it works out, I'll be back with you boys in time for the fall hunt." He shrugged again.

"You could come into our camp and 'ave a small spree wit' your friends, then go, eh? Like old times."

"Old times?" White popped in. "Ain't but, what, a year or two?"

"In ze mountains, a year or two is a long time. You should know zat."

"Well, there's another reason. I'd be thankful if you were to go to Red Leggin's village—if they're here, which I assume they are."

Beaubien nodded.

"I'd like for you to tell Goes Far that I still want her and will come to get her as soon as I can. But there's business I got to finish. If I don't, I won't be a proper husband for her with these doin's hangin' over my head. If she still considers herself mine—" He hesitated to see if Beaubien had any reaction, but he didn't. "I'm grateful and miss her. If she's weary of me and my wanderin's and foolishment, I'll understand and won't come 'round no more botherin' her."

"I can do zis for you, *mon ami*." He paused, then said, "She waits for you, 'Awley." With a slight smile, he added, "Though I don' know why. I can see nothing good in you."

"Damn good thing too," Cooper shot back.

There were a few chuckles around the fire.

"I'd prefer you didn't tell no one but her, but if it's necessary, you can tell Pale Thunder."

"And Sits Down?"

With a sigh, Cooper nodded.

Bell rose and got some meat and hung strips of it over the fire. It soon began to sizzle, sending clouds of delightful aroma around the camp.

The men were quiet, refilling coffee mugs, and waiting for the meat to roast. Then they began gobbling down large baits of the meat, adding more to the fire as needed.

As the feasting slowed a little, Cooper said, "I got a couple other things to ask also, Two-Faces."

"*Mon dieu*," Beaubien exclaimed. "*Et qu'est-ce que c'est, votre majesté*—And what is that, your majesty?" His voice was not entirely pleasant.

Cooper hesitated. "Forgive me, my friend. I have asked too much already. I won't ask no more."

"What do yo' need, Hawl?" Bell asked. "Mebbe I can he'p."

"Me, too, Hawl," White said.

"No, boys, nope," Cooper said with a shake of his head. "Like I told Two-Faces, I've asked more than enough from all you boys." He looked at the half-breed. "Lem brought your mule down there yester-day. I told him he could have what few plews were on it, but if you want them in payment for all the help you've given me, he won't object to you takin' 'em.

Though they're so paltry it might insult you to take them."

Bell started to say something, but his uncle put a hand on his arm, stopping him.

"The horse is yours too, of course. You can take it with you when you leave today, or you can come back tomorrow and take him before I leave. I appreciate you lettin' me have the use of it for a spell."

"*Bon.*"

I ain't got anything else on me that'd be of any value to you." He raised his hands palm upward, as if to say, "There's nothing I can do."

Beaubien swallowed the last of his food and cleaned his greasy hands on greasier buckskin pants. "I will take ze 'orse now, *m'sieur*," he said as he rose.

Cooper nodded and waved a hand toward where his horse was tied to the tree with the others.

Beaubien swiftly bridled the horse, mounted his own, and rode off, towing the animal.

Bell and White both looked at Cooper. "I don't know what's gotten into him, Hawl. He..."

"It don't matter, Bill. Maybe he and I have been in the mountains too long and some kind of mountain sickness has gone to war with our senses. Just makes sure he does what I asked. He don't, maybe you could do it, Bill, unless that'd be too much of a burden on you."

"Won't be. Hope to see y'all agin in the months ahead. Watch your hair."

"You too, Bill. And you, Lem."

Once again, the young man looked as if he wanted to say something, but he did not. He just nodded once and strode off toward his horse.

COOPER ROSE from his spot at the fire and watched a figure materialize from the fog and drizzle of a gray morning. "Come to take what little I got left, Two-Faces?" he asked as the visitor stopped and dismounted.

"*Mais non, mon ami.*" He tied his horse and the one Cooper had been using to the tree.

"Ain't much meat or coffee left, but you're welcome to what there is," Cooper said as he sat again.

"*Merci,*" Beaubien said as he took a seat across the fire from Cooper. Both men ignored the drizzle.

"So what brings you here, Two-Faces?"

The half-breed chewed silently for a few moments, then swallowed. "I come 'ere to make amends wit' an old friend. A man who 'as done many, many t'ings for me, many more zan I 'ave done for 'im, and who I insulted many, many times but not as bad as yesterday."

"You don't owe me no apologies, Two-Faces."

"But I do, *mon ami.*" He paused. "It is strange for men like us to talk about things of the mind *et le coeur*—and the heart. Our women say we are foolish for zis. Sometimes I disagree with zem, but more often I do, though I will never say zat to zem. *Mais non!* But you and I, we 'ave talked about such t'ings when we are away from ze others. I t'ink we should do so again."

"And why is that?" Cooper responded with a touch of incivility.

"What do you plan to do?"

"About what?" Cooper asked blandly.

"We 'ave been friends for many years now, *mon ami*. We 'ave enjoyed good times and weathered bad times together with all ze men and just between us. Do not insult me now with disrespect."

Cooper started to retort but bit back the words and took a few moments to settle down. "You're right Two-Faces. We've sure seen more than out share of doin's, both shinin' and stinkin'." He sighed. "Truth is, my friend, I really don't know what I'm gonna do. I'm mighty ashamed to say that, like maybe I'm too much a fool or maybe, God forbid, too scared to make up my mind as to what to do despite all the times I've had to reflect on it.'"

"There is no'ting to be afraid of. You are a good man, 'Awley. You 'ave more courage than all the men who 'ave ridden with El and me altogether." He held up a hand to stem Cooper's expected protest. "You 'ave no fear that I can see—at least as far as battles go. No other man I know could 'ave done some of the t'ings you 'ave done, including 'aving to put to death a longtime friend whose mind had been taken over by darkness."

"Don't take much courage to do something like that."

"*Merde de buffle, m'sieur*—Buffalo shit. It takes much courage and a strength of 'eart very few men 'ave. But..."

"Enough, Two-Faces!" Cooper snapped. "I'm just a man, like you or Bill or Paddy, or any of the others we've ridden with or know. You're makin' me out to be some supernatural being that the Blackfeet have conjured up out of one of their superstitions. Kind of like that fellow, what's his name, Lone something?"

"*L'on Farouche.*"

"Yeah, that's him. I've heard they damn near revere him even if he is an enemy."

"It is true."

Cooper's eyes widened a moment in disbelief, then shrugged. "So just pack that nonsense away and tell me what you want to tell me or ask me and be done with it, dammit."

Beaubien grinned a bit. "Now you sound like ze giant, vengeful warrior that ze..."

"I said stop it!" Cooper roared. "You keep goin' on with such gibberish and I'll gut you like a fresh-killed elk." His voice was hard and cold.

Beaubien hesitated a few moments, then nodded. He had enough sense to know he could not poke the bear any longer. "All right, *mon ami*. I will get to what I 'ave to say and to ask."

"About goddamn time."

"You say you do not know what you want to do. But you must figure out what you *will* do. Will you ride around ze mountains wondering what to do, when you don't know what you want? Will you ride alone, without friends, without your woman and child, 'oping zat someday ze Great Spirit will tap you on ze shoulder and say, 'Zis is what you must do, 'Awley Cooper. Zis will make your demons go away.' But you may be an old man by zen, your woman long dead, your son a warrior who never knew 'is father."

Cooper fumed, rage banging around in his head. He was furious at what Beaubien had said, not because the half-breed had said it, but because it was true.

Beaubien waited a bit for Cooper's fury to settle into a slowly bubbling anger, then said, "So I t'ink you must figure out what you want. Zen we can..."

"We?"

"Or you. But you 'ave friends to 'elp. So you must figure out what you want so you can try to plan what to do to get it. If zat goal is even reachable."

"Just like that, eh?"

"*Oui*." Beaubien snapped his fingers.

"I might be the first to tell you this, Two-Faces," Cooper said angrily, "but I think your sense is leakin' out through a hole in your brain pan."

"Maybe, but I don't t'ink so. I t'ink..."

But Cooper was not listening. He was in the distance, seeing things he had not seen before, things that brought a rush of realization over him. "Lord a'mighty, Two-Faces, you're right!"

"I am?" The half-breed was taken somewhat aback.

THIRTY-ONE

"MY FAMILY, TWO-FACES," Cooper said, excitement surging through his voice. "I want my family back. It was always there right in front of me, but I couldn't see it because I'm a ravin', utter fool."

"I say before, you 'ave family. Two families."

Cooper calmed down a little. "I know, my friend. And it's true, but there's something different about my relationship to the Shoshonis. Something, I...I don't know." He fell quiet, head hanging, his mind racing, then he looked up at Beaubien. "The Shoshonis are my birth family, Two-Faces," he said slowly, parsing it out as he went.

The half-breed waited patiently. He pulled out his pipe and decided that he would try to get it going despite the rain, which softened from a drizzle to little more than a mist. It took several tries, but he succeeded.

"I was dead, Two-Faces. Or the next thing to it.

Those damn wolves were about to start fillin' their meatbags on me. But I was saved. Not in the way the Lord or the Great Spirit might save you, but by a man, a Shoshoni named Cheyenne Killer. For all I knew, I was dead. I wasn't aware of anything other than blackness. And then I awoke in his lodge, being treated by..."

"An angel?" Beaubien helped.

"Well, yes and no. This is all startin' to sound like the story of Jesus, But I'll be damned if I'll blaspheme enough to say I'm the new messiah. I blaspheme more'n enough already, but I ain't aimin' to take Jesus's place in the mists of history. No, sir. It was nothin' of the sort. Just the welcome and timely arrival of a flesh and blood rescuer. And I awoke to being treated by a woman, a woman with a gentle heart and a healing art, though she was beautiful enough and carin' enough to be an angel. But then we'd have to make her mother and Cheyenne Killer's other wives angels too, and that don't fit the picture."

Beaubien chuckled a little.

"It was like bein' born. Lookin' at it one way, I was birthed into the Shoshoni Nation. With that thinkin', I am a true Shoshoni." He sounded amazed.

"Now, you must convince Cheyenne Killer and Cuts Throat that you were reborn into the tribe, that the Great Spirit sent Cheyenne Killer to rescue you and provide you with a new life."

"But won't they wonder..."

"What? Confusin' it with the story of Jesus? Hell, ze Shoshoni don't know not'ing about Jesus."

Cooper sat for a spell thinking, then shook his head. "No, no this isn't it. It sounds like I'm tryin' to put myself on Jesus's level, and that ain't right. Besides, if God was thinkin' that way, he sure as hell would've picked someone else considerin' all the blood I've spilled."

"Mostly the blood of Beelzebub or his devilish minions, the Blackfeet."

"That may be, but the rest of it is bushwa. No, I think it's more like I was reborn in spirit, not in flesh and bone. Or maybe the opposite. Just that I was born into a new family to replace the one that had cast me out back east when I was not yet a man. This was a new chance to become a man, which I did under the care of Cheyenne Killer."

"And so you feel like you 'ave lost another family, one zat brought you up in ze second phase of your life, eh?"

Cooper nodded. "I suppose the Great Spirit or God could've had a hand in it, but there ain't no way in heaven or hell or on earth that I've been sent to here to be man's savior."

Beaubien suddenly laughed. Pointing his pipe stem at Cooper, he said with glee, "And if it were the Great Spirit instead of our Christian God and ze Shoshonis or Crows or Nez Percé or Flatheads hear about it, then you will be a savior to red mankind *aussi*." His laughter grew at the shock on Cooper's face. "Ze grand messiah to red men across the mountains and plains too, I t'ink."

"Shut up, dammit."

"Of course," Beaubien continued, still laughing, "most of ze savages don't believe in our God and might take exception to 'aving a white-eyed demon preaching to zem. Maybe you become missionary to ze Blackfeet, eh?"

"Shut up, dammit, you incorrigible son of a bitch!" Cooper bellowed.

The half-breed laughed all the more.

"I can 'ear zem now, calling for ze blessings of *Pere* 'Awley!"

"Damn you, Two-Faces, if carving you up into small pieces of wolf bait would shut you up, I'd give it the most serious consideration."

Amid the bubbling laughter, Beaubien said, "Ah, 'Awley, you know even a starving wolf wouldn't eat ol' Two-Faces Beaubien. It would make zem sick, kill zem right away."

Cooper just grunted in annoyance.

The two men were silent for a while, grateful that the drizzle had stopped and welcomed the break in the clouds.

"I don't mean that I was born again in a religious or even real sense," Cooper repeated softly. "It wasn't so much a rebirth but me bein' given a chance at a new and better life. One with a family who cared about me. Something I never had before."

"I figured zat. But 'ave you 'ad a better life? A new one, *certainment*, but better?"

Cooper thought that over, then nodded. "I reckon so. It wasn't all light and good, for certain, but I got to meet and spend time with Zeke and you and El and Duncan and Bill, and the others."

"All gone now, except me and Bill and a couple others. You said before zat you felt guilty about their loss, zat you 'ad some'ow been responsible for their deaths. Still think your new start gave you a better life?"

"Well, I met and had some good years with Black Moon."

"Also gone and in a horrible way."

"And Goes Far."

"Who you 'ave left while you are on some foolish quest for a 'new' family who 'as treated you so poorly these many months."

"It ain't foolish, dammit," Cooper snapped in irritation.

"I disagree. I t'ink it is a fool's errand. But zat is not for me to say. If zis is where your stick floats, I will not try to stop you. But it brings me back to my question—what will you do?"

"Like I said, I don't know. At least now I know what I want, I have to figure out how to get it—if I even can."

"So, what is your first step, *mon ami*?"

Cooper thought for a moment. "Reckon I'll wander over the Wind River Range to the Wind

River, find a place to hole up close to where they're likely to put up their village."

"Then what?"

"Then I try to figure out how to get back in the Shoshonis' good graces."

"Might be 'ard, 'Awley."

"Hell, Two-Faces, it's likely impossible. But I got to try."

"Of course. But what if you can't?"

"I ain't sure, Two-Faces," Cooper said with a sigh of resignation. "If I can't, my mind tells me to cache it in my head, never to be dug up again. But my heart, well that's a different story."

"Ah, *le coeur*, a troublesome t'ing. Most people believe it means love and 'appiness. But more often, it brings 'urt and despair."

"That's a fact, certainly, yep. But I try to live with the goodness in the heart—*my* heart at least."

"I will tell you a secret about ze grand, stone-'earted Two-Faces Beaubien. 'E lets the 'eart take over sometimes. *Oui*. But not always. My 'eart turns black with 'atred when I t'ink abut ze Blackfeet or others who try to treat me or those who are my family or friends poorly. But sometimes..." He smiled. "When I am in ze lodge with my women and children, I am a different man zan you see outside it. I am a loving man. I feel much pleasure with my women, and not just in ze robes. And my children are a joy in my life, and I love 'aving zem around. But when I am outside ze lodge, I am mountaineer, a crusty, disreputable critter as savage as any Indian."

"Hell, you're worse than that, you gopher-humpin' ol' fart."

"*Mais oui!*" Beaubien said with delight. Then he quieted. "What I say to you, *mon grand et véritable ami*—my great and true friend—is zat you should live for ze moment, for today. Life in ze mountains can be short, very short. You know zis well. We should take our pleasure and joy when we can, not go chasing after dreams, *n-c'est pas?* I say again, you 'ave a family 'ere, and a better one maybe, with ze Nez Percé. You 'ave a *femme extraordinaire*—great woman—and a new son. Enjoy zem, don't go chasing after a family zat no longer wants you."

Cooper was quiet for a bit, then said with resignation, "All you say is true, old friend. But for now, my heart is rulin' my head. If I follow this trail, I'll either have my wish granted by the Great Spirit or my mind will take back over and lead me back to those who really matter."

"*Bon.* No one can ask for more." Beaubien pushed himself up, groaning just a little. "My bones don't like such effort anymore," he said with a wry grin. "I fear I am getting old."

"You ain't old. Well, no older than the mountains and rivers."

Both chuckled.

"Maybe you should head out of the mountains before long, Two-Faces."

"We 'ave talked of zis, me and you, about you doing so. I 'ave been in zese mountains longer zan you. And before zat, I was a trapper among my mother's people. I know nothing else. You could likely find somet'ing to do to earn your keep, being a White man, but a half-breed? I would not be so fortunate." He cheered up a little. "But like I say, I live for now. When zat time comes when ze trade is over, zan I will t'ink of what to do."

"You're a lot smarter than most people would think a half-assed, two-color, dog-eatin' son of a bitch would ever be."

"*Mais oui!*" Beaubien shouted, the joy returning.

Cooper accompanied the half-breed as he walked to where his horse was tied. For perhaps the thousandth time, Cooper realized how short Beaubien was. He had always seemed bigger to Cooper. His personality and vigor had always made him far larger in Cooper's eyes than he was in reality.

Beaubien, shoved his rifle though the loop on his saddle, then untied the animal. "The Shoshonis left two, three days ago. You could probably catch 'em, if you hurry."

"I'd rather wait 'til I see if I can figure out how to approach things."

"*Bon.* There are some supplies—not many but enough for a few days—hanging from ze saddle of your horse." He smiled when he saw the questioning look on Cooper's face. "Yes, *mon ami*, your horse. It is my gift to you." He mounted his shaggy, tough mustang. "I will talk with Goes Far tomorrow or ze next day. Zat will give you time to be on ze trail and not have to encounter her or ze other Nez Percé. It is what you want, eh?"

Cooper nodded. "I'm obliged, Two-Faces, for all you've done for me."

"*Ce n'est rien*—it is nothing." He pulled the horse up next to Cooper and placed his hand on his companion's shoulder. "I 'ope you find what you are looking for. Not ze dream, but what is. I 'ope even more zat you will return to us—me and Bill and Lem. That boy has certainly taken a liking to you, *mon ami*." He chuckled. "And to Goes Far and ze Nez Percé. Goes Far and your son need you, *mon ami*. Do not desert zem." He patted Cooper's shoulder, then turned the horse and rode off into the brightening day.

THIRTY-TWO

HAWLEY COOPER STOOD LEANING against a boulder on a flat spot of a rocky hill watching the slow-moving caravan of Shoshonis. His horse was tied to a stunted cedar behind the rock. All Cooper's weapons were with the horse, lest a glint of sunlight from one of them give him away.

Cooper waited until the front of the procession was about two miles away, with the nearer end a mile and a half or so, he estimated, then put his weapons back into their accustomed spots around his body, climbed into the saddle, and carefully descended the hill.

As he reached the bottom, he spotted several riders heading toward him from the other direction. They were not Indians, so he figured they were white trappers. He shrugged and turned to follow the Shoshonis, moving slowly, in no hurry. In about a mile, he saw several Shoshonis keeping watch for enemies. Cooper recognized one of them as High Back, a warrior Cooper knew, though not well.

High Back seemed to recognize him at about the same time. He whirled his pony and took off like a shot. The others followed, pushing the herd before them.

Cooper continued riding slowly knowing there would be a group to welcome him. Whether that welcome was a good one or not was why he was here. When he saw a delegation galloping toward him, he stopped and waited. Moments later, he heard horses behind him and glanced over his shoulder. The group stopped and Cooper turned his horse to face them.

"What're you boys doin' here?" he asked, glancing from Two-Faces Beaubien to Bill White to Lemrich Bell to two new trappers with Beaubien's party named Ricardo Gonzalez and Charley Rice, and then, to Sits Down.

"We missed you, *mon ami*, so we came to find you." Beaubien grinned.

"Well, you found me, now go back where you come from."

"It's not nice to turn away friends when a bunch of angry-looking warriors is about on us."

Cooper turned around and watched.

The nine warriors led by Cheyenne Killer and Cuts Throat stopped a few yards from Cooper and his friends.

"So," the latter said, "you have brought men to kill us." It was not a question.

"Ain't true, Cuts Throat. If I wanted to kill you, I would've come alone. I don't need a bunch of men to do so. 'Sides, if I wanted to do it, I'd have waited somewhere to catch you alone, not ride in here with half a dozen men or so to take on a whole Shoshoni village."

Cuts Throat and Cheyenne Killer said nothing for a few moments, seeming to be listening to the wind blowing softly in the grand valley near the Little Wind River. Then he asked, "Who are these men then?" the latter asked.

Before Cooper could respond, Beaubien moved alongside him and placed a hand on his arm. Then he looked square at the Shoshoni. "We are friends, *m'sieur*. Grand friends. If it wasn't for 'Awley 'ere, most of us would be wandering aimlessly, 'air gone, pieces of bodies gone, unable to reach the Great Spirit. But more, we 'ave become like family to each other. Most of us out 'ere, we 'ave no real families back wherever we came from. Those families don't want much to do with us hard-headed, independent savages. So we make our own friends who sometimes become like family. *Oui*, zat is ze way of it."

Cheyenne Killer started to say something, but Beaubien cut him off. "Do not interrupt, *m'sieur*. 'Awley and me and Bill and a few others 'ave fought side by side with each other, faced dangers, shared our food, shared our shinin' times, and starvin' times. I once t'ought zat you 'ad taken him into your family because of your good feelings for 'im. But maybe zat was not so. Maybe you just wanted a White man around to gain advantage with other whites at rendezvous. And when you tired of 'im, you sent 'im away like a mongrel no longer wanted. I..."

"That's enough, Two-Faces," Cooper interjected.

"Do not interrupt either, 'Awley." He had never taken his eyes off the Shoshonis. "You sent 'im away for treating another Shoshoni poorly when 'e tried to calm a bad situation. Instead of 'elping, though, he lost a family, a child growing in his woman's belly, and almost lost his woman too. Zat is much to lose for a man who was only doing 'is best to keep from more killing." He paused. "Do you know of ze Shoshoni band zat turned him away when he needed 'elp? 'E asked for an 'orse and some small supplies so he could continue following the Crows who had stolen his woman—a Shoshoni woman—one of your band, of course. But they refused and told 'im to go away."

"He had horse when he came to village," Cheyenne Killer said, confused.

"*Oui.* 'E took it from a Blackfoot 'e killed while several of those *salopards*—bastards—were trying to steal the Shoshoni 'orses."

"Is this true?" Cheyenne Killer asked, turning his gaze to Cooper.

The mountain man shrugged.

"*Certainement* it is true," Beaubien said. "'E would not lie about such a thing."

"He would if..." Cuts Throat started.

But Beaubien cut him off. "*Mais non, m'sieur,*"

he said with a firm shake of the head. "You know better than zat."

"But..."

"Enough!" Cheyenne Killer said harshly. The Shoshoni leader sat in thought. The other men on both sides were silent, with the only sounds coming from the wind, and the horses' shuffling.

The other mountain men sat a little behind Beaubien, watching intently. Cuts Throat sat at his leader's side, his face tight with anger.

"I must think, then we will talk."

"No need to talk," Cuts Throat said. "We kill him. Like we had planned at rendezvous. But he didn't come."

Cheyenne Killer's face grew dark.

"You'd kill me?" Cooper asked, shocked at the vehemence. "We are—were—like brothers."

"You're not like brother. No longer. Not when you attack another of the People. Not since then. Not since you killed Flat Nose and Walkin' Bear," Cuts Throat snarled. "Why did you kill them? Long time they were friends."

Cooper was flabbergasted. "What the hell're you sayin', boy?" Cooper demanded, his voice a mixture of shock and rage. "I didn't kill anyone, let alone friends from my own band. Neither did my friends here."

"That's not what warriors from Slow Bull's band said."

"I don't give a duck's ass what they said. It ain't

true. We didn't kill no one. Hell, I ain't seen Flat Nose since last year or the year before when we and you met up on the trail. Why would I want to kill them? Like you said, they were friends. I never had no quarrel with them."

"Maybe they wanted to make you pay for Slow Bull's humiliation, even though he was not their leader."

Once again Cooper was almost speechless. "You've gone and lost all your reason, Cuts Throat," Cooper sputtered. "Such an accusation against me comes from a mind twisted by dark spirits."

Face a mask of uncertainty, Cheyenne Killer glanced from one man to the next and back. Then he shook his head. He had found it difficult to believe Cuts Throat, who was almost like another son, when the younger warrior had first made this accusation. But the young man had been adamant, and when Cheyenne Killer had no opportunity to talk to Cooper about it, he accepted it, thinking his White son was avoiding him because of his banishment and, later, these killings. He suddenly suspected there was more here than Cuts Throat was saying.

In the few moments that everyone sat in shock at the proclamation, Sits Down moved forward to stop between Cooper and Beaubien. "You want to fight, I fight you in his place," the huge Nez Percé said in his rumbling bass. "Hairy Face is weak from many trials over the past few moons."

"So, the great White Wolf has become so weak

that he needs a fat, ugly Nez Percé to do his fighting for him?" Cuts Throats's voice was full of disdain.

Before Sits Down could replay, Cooper rested a hand on one of the warrior's meaty arms. "No," he said quietly. He looked around as the Shoshonis started circling the White men, most of whom were turning to face the gathering warriors. Then he turned his face back to his one-time best friend. "I fought you once before, Cuts Throat, and beat you. I could do it again. Don't you doubt that. But that would only lead to more bloodshed. I don't aim to have any of my friends here get made wolf bait by you and your fellow warriors. And though you and Cheyenne Killer have cast me out, I'd not be keen on you and any of the others here—most of 'em who I know and most of who I had considered friends—go under because of me. Even with this outrageous accusation you've just made against me.

"I came here today, not to make war with you, Cuts Throat or you, fath...ah, Cheyenne Killer, but to seek reconciliation with you. To rejoin my Shoshoni family after a long time away, hoping that you had talked with Slow Bull and knowing that had I had done nothing to do with anythin' that had led to any deaths there. I don't know why you're insistin' that I killed a couple friends when it ain't true.

"You give me your word—you, too, Cheyenne Killer—that these men will be unharmed, I will take my leave of you and never visit the People again. I will be as a dead man to the Shoshonis."

"I never thought you would be too afraid to fight me. You have grown old and weak."

Cooper shrugged. "Don't matter none to me anymore what you think. You ain't worth frettin' over no more."

Cuts Throats's eyes widened in shock and anger, and he let loose a shrill war cry. He kicked his pony which jumped forward, but as it did, Cheyenne Killer swung his bow, which hit the younger Shoshoni across the chest. the pony ran out from under him, and the warrior landed with a hard thump in the dirt.

Cuts Throat came up with eyes blazing. Cheyenne Killer stared, unconcerned, at him. "If you want to fight someone, you fight me."

"You would take his side, not mine?"

"He is my son, *Too-Shah-Itsup-Mah-Washay*— He-Who-Is-the-White-Wolf-Killer," Cheyenne Killer said calmly, watching Cuts Throat's face.

The younger warrior glared, eyes red with rage. Then he flung himself on the pony, which had wandered back almost instantly. "Do not come near me, White man," he bellowed before charging off. He got no more than a few yards, before he stopped, looked back, and bellowed, "Blackfeet!"

THIRTY-THREE

THE SHOSHONIS SNAPPED their heads around and saw two dozen or more Blackfeet rampaging through the long string of Shoshoni horses, men, women, and children. Cuts Throat was already back on the move racing toward the battling.

"We 'elp, eh?" Beaubien asked hastily.

Cheyenne Killer gave a curt nod.

"You trust us?"

As Cheyenne Killer turned his horse, he shouted, "If my son is with us, we are strong. With his friends beside us, we cannot be defeated." He took off, his warriors alongside him.

The whites were only a few paces behind, except for Cooper, who had sat stunned. *He called me his son!* The words rang through his mind, and it took some moments to regain his concentration and he took off after the others.

The Shoshonis and mountain men charged into

the dust rising from hundreds of hooves. Screams and gunfire rose above it.

Cooper spotted Cuts Throat chasing two Blackfeet who were trying to make off with a bunch of the Shoshoni ponies. Cooper dodged a hastily thrust spear, yanked out a pistol, and shot the warrior in the face.

Then he saw Pony Woman, cradleboard in her arms trying to find some way of escape, though there was none. "Come, sister," Cooper said.

She did not hesitate. She swiftly hung the cradleboard on the saddle horn of Cooper's horse and with his strong arm helping, leaped up behind him. As he charged off, he saw Cuts Throat take two arrows in the chest. The warrior wobbled on his horse's back, but he managed to shoot an arrow deep into his attacker's side.

Pony Woman screamed when she saw the action over Cooper's shoulder.

The mountain man raced ahead and managed to get there in time to catch Cuts Throat as he began to tumble off his horse.

Pony Woman jumped down from her seat behind Cooper and shoved between the two horses to help ease her husband down as Cooper dismounted. The two gently laid his friend—his one-time friend, he thought—on the ground.

The battle was just about over already as Cooper kneeled next to the Shoshoni. "Hang in there, hoss, we'll get you some help."

"No," the warrior said, eyes filled with pain and with something else, Cooper thought. "I lie. I killed Flat Nose and Walkin' Bear. Now I die, my br..."

Then he was gone.

"NOW WHAT, *M'SIEUR* CHEYENNE KILLER?" Beaubien asked.

The half-breed stood on one side of the Shoshoni and Cooper on the other, the mountain men behind them, watching the hastily thrown together camp, which had settled down after almost two days.

With the mountain men's help, the Shoshonis had driven off the attacking Blackfeet with little effort. A young boy, an almost teen girl, and two warriors—one well past his prime fighting days—had gone under, and a dozen or so horses taken. The People had finished caring for the few dead and wounded, and the crying children had been soothed over the two next days. The only sounds from the temporary village now were some faint wails from people who had lost loved ones in the raid.

Before Cheyenne Killer could answer, Cooper, hopeful, asked. "You meant what you said?"

"Yes." The Shoshoni leader held his back straight. "If you will have me as your father."

"I will," he said firmly. "You heard of what Cuts Throat said before he went under?"

"Yes," Cheyenne Killer said sadly. "I thought

maybe...I *should* have thought maybe that he was not telling truth, but..."

Cooper clapped him lightly on the shoulder. "I wouldn't have suspected him either. It is well. We have made peace. Or have we? My sister?"

A small smile crept across Cheyenne Killer's face. "She has—as you White men say—pestered me for a long time asking to bring her brother back to spend time with his family."

"Will there be trouble with any of your People? Some of the warriors might believe as he did."

"There will be no trouble. Many of his friends believe he had fallen under the spell of a demon shaman and has not been the Cuts Throat we knew."

Cooper nodded. "He ain't the first one. seems many of the men i've dealt with have recently been so afflicted," he said as a gust of melancholy swept over him but faded within a minute.

Cheyenne Killer turned to face the mountain men. "And you men," he said, "you are now brothers to the People. Welcome anytime in village."

"Even a fat, ugly Nez Percé?" Sits Down asked, a slight grin on his lips.

"I don't see a fat, ugly Nez Percé," Cheyenne Killer said seriously. "What I see is a big man, a brave one I have heard, who is a great friend to my son."

Sits Down laughed. "Is too late maybe to say I don't know this skinny, hairy-faced White man?"

There was a round of laughter from the men, including the Shoshoni.

"We will talk again soon, my son," Cheyenne Killer said.

Cooper nodded, but said, "It must be very soon, Father. Sadly, even though we have just patched up our family as best we can, me and the boys here got to be on the move. We'll be leavin' at first light."

Cheyenne Killer grunted acknowledgment and left.

Cooper watched him, then turned and stared toward the northwest, eyes wistful.

"She is waiting, *mon ami*," Two-Faces Beaubien said. "*Certainement.*"

IF YOU LIKE THIS, YOU MAY ALSO ENJOY:

BUCKSKIN COUNTY WAR

BRODIE PIKE IS ONE AGAINST MANY—THE ODDS ARE NOT IN HIS FAVOR.

Brodie Pike knew he shouldn't get involved. It would somehow turn out bad, as seemed to happen too often to him, but he couldn't watch four gunmen bully a small-time rancher. The next day, the man he had helped is found beaten to death. Though he knows he is responsible for Dunn's death, he refuses to help the group of small ranchers who know that the Buckskin County Cattlemen's Association will be coming for their land soon.

Months later, he reads that the association has started its campaign of terror against the small ranchers. Against the odds, he decides to throw in with them, facing the association's horde of hired guns, risking his life in the bloody, violent Buckskin County war, where death is always just one bullet away.

AVAILABLE NOW

IF YOU LIKE THIS, YOU MAY ALSO
ENJOY
BUCKSKIN COUNTY WAR

BRODIE FIELDS ONE AGAINST MANY—THE
ODDS ARE NOT IN HIS FAVOR

AVAILABLE NOW